RISE OF THE VALIANT

(KINGS AND SORCERERS—BOOK 2)

Morgan Rice

Books by Morgan Rice

KINGS AND SORCERERS
RISE OF THE DRAGONS
RISE OF THE VALIANT

THE SORCERER'S RING
A QUEST OF HEROES
A MARCH OF KINGS
A FATE OF DRAGONS
A CRY OF HONOR
A VOW OF GLORY
A CHARGE OF VALOR
A RITE OF SWORDS
A GRANT OF ARMS
A SKY OF SPELLS
A SEA OF SHIELDS
A REIGN OF STEEL
A LAND OF FIRE
A RULE OF QUEENS
AN OATH OF BROTHERS
A DREAM OF MORTALS

THE SURVIVAL TRILOGY
ARENA ONE (Book #1)
ARENA TWO (Book #2)

the Vampire Journals
turned (book #1)
loved (book #2)
betrayed (book #3)
destined (book #4)
desired (book #5)
betrothed (book #6)
vowed (book #7)
found (book #8)
resurrected (book #9)
craved (book #10)
fated (book #11)

For Laura Bosselaar,

Your power to keep going is a light unto the world. Every moment you are here is precious. In the same way that my books keep you going, readers like you keep me going. Never stop fighting and never give up. You are a true hero and a true warrior.

"Cowards die many times before their deaths;
The valiant never taste of death but once."

--William Shakespeare
Julius Caesar

CHAPTER ONE

Kyra walked slowly through the carnage, snow crunching beneath her boots, taking in the devastation the dragon had left behind. She was speechless. Thousands of the Lord's Men, the most feared men in Escalon, lay dead before her, wiped out in an instant. Charred bodies lay smoking all around her, the snow melted beneath them, their faces contorted in agony. Skeletons, twisted in unnatural positions, still clutched their weapons in bony fingers. A few corpses stood in place, their frames somehow staying vertical, still looking up at the sky as if wondering what had killed them.

Kyra stopped beside one, examining it with wonder. She reached out and touched it, her finger grazing its rib cage, and she watched in amazement as it crumbled and fell, clattering to the ground in a heap of bones, its sword falling harmlessly by its side.

Kyra heard a screech high overhead and she craned her neck to see Theos, circling high above, breathing flame as if still unsatisfied. She could feel what he was feeling, feel the rage burning in his veins, his desire to destroy all of Pandesia—indeed, the entire world—if he could. It was a primal rage, a rage which knew no bounds.

The sound of boots in the snow snapped her out of it, and Kyra looked back to see her father's men, dozens of them, walking through, taking in the destruction, eyes wide in shock. These battle-hardened men had clearly never seen a sight like this; even her father, standing nearby, joined by Anvin, Arthfael and Vidar, seemed frazzled. It was like walking through a dream.

Kyra noticed these brave warriors turn from searching the skies to looking at her, a sense of wonder in their eyes. It was as if *she* were the one who had done all of this, as if she were the dragon herself. After all, only she had been able to summon it. She looked away, feeling uncomfortable; she could not tell if they looked at her as if a warrior or a freak. Perhaps they did not know themselves.

Kyra thought back to her prayer on the Winter Moon, her wish to know if she were special, if her powers were real. After today, after this battle, she could have no doubts. She had *willed* that dragon to come. She had felt it herself. How, she did not know. But she knew now, definitively, that she was different. And she could not help but wonder if that also meant the other prophecies about her were true. Was she then truly destined to become a great warrior? A great ruler? Greater even than her father? Would she truly lead nations into battle? Would the fate of Escalon truly hang upon her shoulders?

Kyra did not see how it could be possible. Maybe Theos had come for his own reasons; maybe his damage here had nothing to do with her. After all, the Pandesians had injured him—hadn't they?

Kyra no longer felt sure of anything. All she knew was that, in this moment, feeling the strength of the dragon burning in her veins, walking this battlefield, seeing their greatest foe dead, she felt that all things were possible. She knew she was no longer a fifteen-year-old girl hoping for approval in other men's eyes; she was no longer a plaything for the Lord Governor—for any man—to do with as he wished; she was no longer the property of other men, to be married off, abused, tortured. She was her own person now. A warrior among men—and one to be feared.

Kyra walked through the sea of bodies until finally the corpses stopped and the landscape morphed to ice and snow again. She paused beside her father, taking in the vista as down below the valley spread out beneath them. There lay the wide open gates of Argos, a city emptied, all its men dead in these hills. It was eerie to see such a great fort sitting vacant, unguarded. Pandesia's most important stronghold was now wide open for anyone to enter. Its daunting high walls, carved of thick stone and spikes, its thousands of men and layers of defenses, had precluded any idea of revolt; its presence here had allowed Pandesia an iron grip on the whole of northeastern Escalon.

They all set off down the slope and onto the winding road that led to the city gates. It was a victorious but solemn walk, the road littered with more dead bodies, stragglers whom the dragon had sought out, markers on the trail to destruction. It was like walking through a graveyard.

As they passed through the awesome gates, Kyra paused at the threshold, her breath taken away: inside, she could see, lay thousands more corpses, charred, smoking. It was what had remained of the Lord's Men, those late to mobilize. Theos had forgotten no one; his fury was visible even on the fort's walls, large swaths of stone stained black with flame.

As they entered, Argos was notable for its silence. Its courtyard empty, it was uncanny for such a city to be so devoid of life. It was as if God had sucked it all up in a single breath.

As her father's men rushed forward, sounds of excitement began to fill the air, and Kyra soon understood why. The ground, she could see, was littered with a treasure trove of weapons unlike any she had ever seen. There, spread out on the courtyard ground, lay the spoils of war: the finest weaponry, the finest steel, the finest armor she had ever seen, all gleaming with Pandesian markings. There were even, scattered amongst them, sacks of gold.

Even better, at the far end of the courtyard there sat a vast stone armory, its doors wide open as the men had left in haste, revealing inside a bounty of treasures. Walls were lined with swords, halberds, pikes, hatchets, spears, bows—all made of the finest steel the world had to offer. There were enough weapons here to arm half of Escalon.

There came the sound of neighing, and Kyra looked to the other side of the courtyard to see a row of stone stables, and inside there stomped an army of the finest horses, all spared the dragon's breath. Enough horses to carry an army.

Kyra saw the look of hope rising in her father's eyes, a look she had not seen in years, and she knew what he was thinking: Escalon could rise again.

There came a screech, and Kyra looked up to see Theos circling lower, talons extended, flapping his great wings as he flew over the city, a victory lap. His glowing yellow eyes locked on hers, even from that great distance. She could not look anywhere else.

Theos dove down and landed outside the city gates. He sat there proudly, facing her, as if summoning her. She felt him calling her.

Kyra felt her skin prickling, the heat rising within her, as she felt an intense connection with this creature. She had no choice but to approach him.

As Kyra turned and crossed the courtyard, heading back toward the city gates, she could feel the eyes of all the men on her, looking from the dragon to her as they stopped to watch. She walked alone

11

toward the gate, her boots crunching in the snow, her heart pounding as she went.

As she went, Kyra suddenly felt a gentle hand on her arm, stopping her. She turned to see her father's concerned face looking back.

"Be careful," he warned.

Kyra continued walking, feeling no fear, despite the fierce look in the dragon's eyes. She felt only an intense bond with him, as if a part of her had reappeared, a part she could not live without. Her mind spun with curiosity. Where had Theos come from? Why had he come to Escalon? Why had he not come back sooner?

As Kyra passed through Argo's gates and neared the dragon, his noises grew louder, somewhere between a purr and a snarl, as he waited for her, his huge wings flapping gently. He opened his mouth as if to release fire, baring his huge teeth, each one as long as she, and sharp as a sword. For a moment she was frightened, his eyes fixed on her with an intensity that made it hard to think.

Kyra finally came to a stop a few feet before him. She studied him in awe. Theos was magnificent. He rose thirty feet high, his scales thick, hard, primordial. The ground trembled as he breathed, his chest rattling, and she felt entirely at his mercy.

They stood there in the silence, the two of them facing off, examining each other, and Kyra's heart slammed in her chest, the tension in the air so thick she could hardly breathe.

Her throat dry, she finally summoned the courage to speak.

"Who are you?" she asked, her voice barely above a whisper. "Why have you come to me? What do you want from me?"

Theos lowered his head, snarling, and leaned forward, so close that his huge snout nearly touched her chest. His eyes, so huge, glowing yellow, seemed to look right through her. She stared into them, each nearly as big as her, and felt lost in another world, another time.

Kyra waited for the answer. She waited for her mind to be filled with his thoughts, as it once was.

But she waited and waited, and was shocked to find her mind was blank. Nothing was coming to her. Had Theos gone silent? Had she lost her connection to him?

Kyra stared back, wondering, this dragon more of a mystery than ever. Suddenly, he lowered his back, as if beckoning her to ride. Her heart quickened as she imagined herself flying through the skies on his back.

Kyra slowly walked to his side, reached up, and grabbed his scales, hard and rough, preparing to grab his neck and climb up.

But no sooner had she touched him when he suddenly writhed away, making her lose her grip. She stumbled and he flapped his wings and in one quick motion, lifted off, so abrupt that her palms scraped against his scales, like sandpaper.

Kyra stood there, stung, baffled—but most of all, heartbroken. She watched helplessly as this tremendous creature lifted into the air, screeching, and flew higher and higher. As quickly as he had arrived, Theos suddenly disappeared into the clouds, nothing but silence following in his wake.

Kyra stood there, hollowed out, more alone than ever. And as the last of his cries faded away, she knew, she just knew, that this time, Theos was gone for good.

CHAPTER TWO

Alec ran through the woods in the black of night, Marco at his side, stumbling over roots submerged in the snow and wondering if he would make it out alive. His heart pounded in his chest as he ran for his life, gasping for breath, wanting to stop but needing to keep pace with Marco. He glanced back over his shoulder for the hundredth time and watched as the glow from The Flames grew fainter the deeper into the woods they went. He passed a patch of thick trees, and soon the glow was entirely gone, the two of them immersed in near blackness.

Alec turned and groped his way as he bumped off trees, trunks whacking his shoulders, branches scratching his arms. He peered into the blackness ahead of him, barely making out a path, trying not to listen to the exotic noises all around him. He had been duly warned about these woods, where no escapee survived, and he had a sinking feeling the deeper they went. He sensed the danger here, vicious creatures lurking everywhere, the wood so dense it was hard to navigate and growing more tangled which each step he took. He was starting to wonder if he might have been better off staying back at The Flames.

"This way!" hissed a voice.

Marco grabbed his shoulder and pulled him as he forked right, between two huge trees, ducking beneath their gnarled branches. Alec followed, slipping in the snow, and soon found himself in a clearing in the midst of the thick forest, the moonlight shining through, lighting their way.

They both stopped, bent over, hands on their hips, gasping for breath. They exchanged a glance, and Alec looked back over his shoulder at the wood. He breathed hard, his lungs aching from the cold, his ribs hurting, and wondered.

"Why aren't they following us?" Alec asked.

Marco shrugged.

"Maybe they know this wood will do their job for them."

Alec listened for the sound of Pandesian soldiers, expecting to be pursued—but there came none. Instead, though, Alec thought he heard a different sound—like a low, angry snarl.

"Do you hear that?" Alec asked, the hair rising on the back of his neck.

Marco shook his head.

Alec stood there, waiting, wondering if his mind were playing tricks on him. Then, slowly, he began to hear it again. It was a distant noise, a faint snarl, menacing, unlike anything Alec had ever heard. As he listened, it began to grow louder, as if coming closer.

Marco now looked at him with alarm.

"That's why they didn't follow," Marco said, his voice dawning with recognition.

Alec was confused.

"What do you mean?" he asked.

"Wilvox," he answered, eyes now filled with fear. "They've unleashed them after us."

The word Wilvox struck terror in Alec; he had heard of them as a child, and he knew they were rumored to inhabit the Wood of Thorns, but he'd always assumed they were the stuff of legend. They were rumored to be the deadliest creatures of the night—the stuff of nightmares.

The snarling intensified, sounding as if there were several of them.

"RUN!" Marco implored.

Marco turned and Alec joined him as the two of them burst across the clearing and back into the wood. Adrenaline pumped in his veins as Alec ran, hearing his own heartbeat in his ears, drowning out the sound of ice and snow crunching beneath his boots. Soon, though, he heard the creatures behind him closing in, and he knew they were being hunted by beasts they could not outrun.

Alec stumbled over a root and slammed into a tree; he cried out in pain, winded, then bounced off it and continued to run. He scanned the woods for any escape, realizing their time was short—but there was nothing.

The snarling grew louder, and as he ran, Alec looked back over his shoulder—and immediately wished he hadn't. Bearing down on

15

them were four of the most savage creatures he'd ever laid eyes upon. Resembling wolves, the Wilvox were twice the size, with small sharp horns sticking out the back of their heads, and one large, single red eye between the horns. Their paws were the size of a bear's, with long, pointed claws, and their coats were slick and as black as night.

Seeing them this close, Alec knew he was a dead man.

Alec burst forward with his last ounce of speed, his palms sweating even in the icy cold, his breath frozen in the air before him. The Wilvox were hardly twenty feet away and he knew from the desperate look in their eyes, from the drool hanging from their mouths, that they would tear him to pieces. He saw no means of escape. He looked to Marco, hoping for some sign of a plan—but Marco carried the same look of despair. He clearly had no idea what to do either.

Alec closed his eyes and did something he had never done before: he prayed. Seeing his life flashing before his eyes, it changed him somehow, made him realize how much he cherished life, and made him more desperate than he'd ever been to keep it.

Please, God, get me out of this. After what I did for my brother, don't let me die here. Not in this place, and not by these creatures. I'll do anything.

Alec opened his eyes, looked up ahead, and as he did, this time he noticed a tree slightly different than the others. Its branches were more gnarled and hung lower to the ground, just high enough where he could grab one with a running jump. He had no idea if Wilvox could climb, but he had no other choice.

"That branch!" Alec yelled to Marco, pointing.

They ran for the tree together, and as the Wilvox closed in, but feet away, without pausing, they each jumped up and grabbed the branch, pulling themselves up.

Alec's hands slipped on the snowy wood, but he managed to hang on, and he pulled himself up until he was grabbing the next branch several feet off the ground. He then immediately jumped up to the next branch, three feet higher, Marco beside him. He had never climbed so fast in his life.

The Wilvox reached them, the pack snarling viciously, jumping and clawing at their feet. Alec felt their hot breath on the back of his heel a moment before he raised his foot, the fangs coming down and missing him by an inch. The two of them kept climbing, propelled by adrenaline, until they were a good fifteen feet off the ground, and safer than they needed to be.

Alec finally stopped, clutching a branch with all his might, catching his breath, sweat stinging his eyes. He looked back down, watching, praying the Wilvox could not climb, too.

To his immense relief, they were still on the ground, snarling and snapping, jumping up for the tree, but clearly unable to climb. They scratched the trunk madly, but to no avail.

The two sat on the branch, and as the reality sank in that they were safe, they each breathed a sigh of relief. Marco burst into laughter, to Alec's surprise. It was a madman's laugh, a laugh of relief, the laugh of a man who had been spared from a sure death in the most unlikely way.

Alec, realizing how close they had come, could not help laughing, too. He knew they were still far from safety; he knew they could never leave this spot, and that they would even likely die in this place. But for now, at least, they were safe.

"Looks like I owe you," Marco said.

Alec shook his head.

"Don't thank me yet," Alec said.

The Wilvox were snarling viciously, raising the hair on the back of his neck, and Alec looked up at the tree, hands trembling, wanting to get even farther away and wondering how high they could climb, wondering if they had any way out of here.

Suddenly, Alec froze. As he looked up, he flinched, struck by a terror unlike he had ever known. There, in the branches above him, looking down, was the most hideous creature he had ever seen. Eight feet long, with the body of a snake but with six sets of feet, all with long claws, and a head shaped like an eel's, it had narrow slits for eyes, dull yellow, and they focused on Alec. Just feet away, it arched its back, hissed, and opened its mouth. Alec, in shock, could not believe how wide it opened—wide enough to swallow him whole. And he knew, from its rattling tail, that it was about to strike—and kill them both.

Its mouth came down right for Alec's throat, and he reacted involuntarily. He shrieked and jumped back as he lost his grip,

Marco beside him, thinking only of getting away from those deadly fangs, that huge mouth, a sure death.

He did not even think about what lay below. As he felt himself flying backwards through the air, flailing, he realized, too late, that he was heading from one set of fangs to another. He glanced back and saw the Wilvox salivating, opening their jaws, nothing he could do but brace himself for the descent.

He had exchanged one death for another.

CHAPTER THREE

Kyra walked slowly back through the gates of Argos, the eyes of all her father's men upon her, and she burned with shame. She had misread her relationship with Theos. She had thought, stupidly, that she could control him—and instead, he had spurned her before all these men. For the eyes of all to see, she was powerless, had no dominion over a dragon. She was just another warrior—not even a warrior, but just a teenage girl who had led her people into a war they, abandoned by a dragon, could no longer win.

Kyra walked back through the gates of Argos, feeling the eyes on her in the awkward silence. What did they think of her now? she wondered. She did not even know what to think of herself. Had Theos not come for her? Had he only fought this battle for his own ends? Did she have any special powers at all?

Kyra was relieved as the men finally looked away, returned to their looting, all busy gathering weaponry, preparing for war. They rushed to and fro, gathering all the bounty left behind by the Lord's Men, filling carts, leading away horses, the clang of steel ever present as shields and armor were tossed into piles by the handful. As more snow fell and the sky began to darken, they all had little time to lose.

"Kyra," came a familiar voice.

She turned and was relieved to see Anvin's smiling face as he approached her. He looked at her with respect, with the reassuring kindness and warmth of the father figure he had always been. He draped one arm affectionately around her shoulder, smiling wide beneath his beard, and he held out before her a gleaming new sword, its blade etched with Pandesian symbols.

"Finest steel I've held in years," he noted with a broad grin. "Thanks to you, we have enough weapons here to start a war. You have made us all more formidable."

Kyra took comfort in his words, as she always did; yet she still could not cast off her feeling of depression, of confusion, of being spurned by the dragon. She shrugged.

"I did not do all this," she replied. "Theos did."

"Yet Theos returned for *you*," he replied.

Kyra glanced up at the gray skies, now empty, and she wondered.

"I'm not so sure."

They both studied the skies in the long silence that followed, broken only by the wind sweeping through.

"Your father awaits you," Anvin finally said, his voice serious.

Kyra joined Anvin as they walked, snow and ice crunching beneath their boots, winding their way through the courtyard amidst all the activity. They passed dozens of her father's men as they trekked through the sprawling fort of Argos, men everywhere, finally relaxed for the first time in ages. She saw them laughing, drinking, jostling each other as they gathered weapons and provisions. They were like children on All Hallow's Day.

Dozens more of her father's men stood in a line and passed sacks of Pandesian grain, handing them to each other as they piled carts high; another cart clambered by, overflowing with shields that clanked as it went. It was stacked so high that a few fell over the side, soldiers scrambling to gather them back in. All around her carts were heading out of the fort, some on the road back to Volis, others forking off on different roads to places her father had directed, all filled to the brim. Kyra took some solace in the sight, feeling less bad for the war she had instigated.

They turned a corner and Kyra spotted her father, surrounded by his men, busy inspecting dozens of swords and spears as they held them out for his approval. He turned at her approach and as he gestured to his men, they dispersed, leaving them alone.

Her father turned and looked at Anvin, and Anvin stood there for a moment, unsure, seemingly surprised at her father's silent look, clearly asking him to leave, too. Finally, Anvin turned and joined the others, leaving Kyra alone with him. She was surprised, too—he never asked Anvin to leave before.

Kyra looked up at him, his expression inscrutable as always, wearing the distant, public face of a leader among men, not the intimate face of the father she knew and loved. He looked down at her, and she felt nervous as so many thoughts raced through her head at once: was he proud of her? Was he upset that she had led them into this war? Was he disappointed that Theos had spurned her and abandoned his army?

Kyra waited, accustomed to his long silence before speaking, and she could not tell anymore; too much had changed between them too fast. She felt as if she had grown up overnight, while he had been changed by recent events; it was as if they no longer knew how to relate to each other. Was he the father she had always known and loved, who would read her stories late into the night? Or was he her commander now?

He stood there, staring, and she realized that he did not know what to say as the silence hung heavy between them, the only sound that of the wind whipping through, the torches flickering behind them as men began to light them to ward off night. Finally, Kyra could stand the silence no longer.

"Will you bring all this back to Volis?" she asked, as a cart rattled by filled with swords.

He turned and examined the cart and seemed to snap out of his reverie. He didn't look back at Kyra, but rather watched the cart as he shook his head.

"Volis holds nothing for us now but death," he said, his voice deep and definitive. "We head south now."

Kyra was surprised.

"South?" she asked.

He nodded.

"Espehus," he stated.

Kyra's heart flooded with excitement as she pictured their journey to Espehus, the ancient stronghold perched on the sea, their biggest neighbor to the south. She became even more excited as she realized—if he was going there it could only mean one thing: he was preparing for war.

He nodded, as if reading her mind.

"There is no turning back now," he said.

Kyra looked back at her father with a sense of pride she had not felt in years. He was no longer the complacent warrior, living his middle years in the security of a small fort—but now the bold commander she once knew, willing to risk it all for freedom.

"When do we leave?" she asked, her heart pounding, anticipating her first battle.

She was surprised to see him shake his head.

"Not we," he corrected. "I and my men. Not you."

Kyra was crestfallen, his words like a dagger in her heart.

"Would you leave me behind?" she asked, stammering. "After all that has happened? What else must I do to prove myself to you?"

He shook his head firmly, and she was devastated to see the hardened look in his eyes, a look which she knew meant he would not bend.

"You shall go to your uncle," he said. It was a command, not a request, and with those words she knew where she stood: she was his soldier now, not his daughter. It hurt her.

Kyra breathed deep—she would not give in so quickly.

"I want to fight alongside you," she insisted. "I can help you."

"You *will* be helping me," he said, "by going where you're needed. I need you with him."

She furrowed her brow, trying to understand.

"But why?" she asked.

He was silent for a long time, until he finally sighed.

"You possess…" he began, "…*skills* I do not understand. Skills that we will need to win this war. Skills that only your uncle will know how to foster."

He reached out and held her shoulder meaningfully.

"If you want to help us," he added, "if you want to help our people, that is where you are needed. I don't need another soldier— I need the unique talents you have to offer. The skills that no one else has."

She saw the earnestness in his eyes, and while she felt awful at the prospect of being unable to join him, she felt some reassurance in his words—along with a heightened sense of curiosity. She wondered what skills he was referring to, and wondered who her uncle might be.

"Go and learn what I cannot teach you," he added. "Come back stronger. And help me win."

Kyra looked into his eyes, and she felt the respect, the warmth returning, and she began to feel restored again.

"Ur is a long journey," he added. "A good three-day ride west and north. You will have to cross Escalon alone. You will have to ride quickly, by stealth, and avoid the roads. Word will soon spread of what has happened here—and Pandesian lords will be wrathful. The roads will be dangerous—you will stick to the woods. Ride north, find the sea, and keep it in view. It shall be your compass. Follow its coastline, and you will find Ur. Stay away from villages, stay away from people. Do not stop. Tell no one where you are going. Speak to no one."

He grabbed her shoulders firmly and his eyes darkened with urgency, scaring her.

"Do you understand me?" he implored. "It is a dangerous journey for any man—much less for a girl alone. I can spare no one to accompany you. I need you to be strong enough to do this alone. Are you?"

She could hear the fear in his voice, the love of a concerned father torn, and she nodded back, feeling pride that he would trust her with such a quest.

"I am, Father," she said proudly.

He studied her, then finally nodded, as if satisfied. Slowly, his eyes welled with tears.

"Of all my men," he said, "of all these warriors, you are the one I need the most. Not your brothers, and not even my trusted soldiers. *You* are the one, the only one, who can win this war."

Kyra felt confused and overwhelmed; she did not fully understand what he meant. She opened her mouth to ask him—when suddenly she sensed motion approaching.

She turned to see Baylor, her father's master of horse, approaching with his usual smile. A short, overweight man with thick eyebrows and stringy hair, he approached them with his customary swagger and smiled at her, then looked to her father, as if awaiting his approval.

Her father nodded to him, and Kyra wondered what was going on, as Baylor turned to her.

"I'm told you'll be taking a journey," Baylor said, his voice nasal. "For that, you'll need a horse."

Kyra frowned, confused.

"I have a horse," she replied, looking over at the fine horse she'd ridden during the battle with the Lord's Men, tied up across the courtyard.

Baylor smiled.

23

"That's not a horse," he said.

Baylor looked to her father and her father nodded, and Kyra tried to understand what was happening.

"Follow me," he said, and without waiting, he suddenly turned and strode off for the stables.

Kyra watched him go, confused, then looked to her dad. He nodded back.

"Follow him," he said. "You won't regret it."

*

Kyra crossed the snowy courtyard with Baylor, joined by Anvin, Arthfael and Vidar, heading eagerly toward the low, stone stables in the distance. As she went, Kyra wondered what Baylor had meant, wondered what horse he had in mind for her. In her mind, one horse was not much different from another.

As they approached the sprawling stone stable, at least a hundred yards long, Baylor turned to her, eyes widening in delight.

"Our Lord's daughter will need a fine horse to take her wherever it is she is going."

Kyra's heart quickened; she had never been given a horse from Baylor before, an honor usually reserved only for distinguished warriors. She'd always dreamed of having one when she was old enough, and when she had earned it. It was an honor that even her older brothers did not enjoy.

Anvin nodded proudly.

"You have earned it," he said.

"If you can handle a dragon," Arthfael added with a smile, "you can most certainly handle a master horse."

As the stables loomed, a small crowd began to gather, joining them as they walked, the men taking a break from their gathering of weapons, clearly curious to see where she was being led. Her two older brothers, Brandon and Braxton, joined them, too, glancing over at Kyra wordlessly, jealousy in their eyes. They looked away quickly, too proud, as usual, to acknowledge her, much less offer her any praise. She, sadly, expected nothing else of them.

Kyra heard footsteps and looked over, pleased to see her friend Dierdre joining her, too.

24

"I hear you're leaving," Dierdre said as she fell in beside her.

Kyra walked beside her new friend, comforted by her presence. She thought back to their time together in the governor's cell, all the suffering they had endured, escaping, and she felt an instant bond with her. Dierdre had gone through an even worse hell than she had, and as she studied her, black rings beneath her eyes, an aura of suffering and sadness still lingering about her, she wondered what would become of her. She could not just leave her alone in this fort, she realized. With the army heading south, Dierdre would be left alone.

"I can use a traveling companion," Kyra said, an idea forming as she uttered the words.

Dierdre looked at her, eyes widening with surprise, and broke into a wide smile, her heavy aura lifting.

"I was hoping you would ask," she replied.

Anvin, overhearing, frowned.

"I don't know if your father would approve," he interjected. "You have serious business ahead of you."

"I won't interfere," Dierdre said. "I must cross Escalon anyway. I am returning to my father. I'd rather not cross it alone."

Anvin rubbed his beard.

"Your father would not like it," he said to Kyra. "She may be a liability."

Kyra laid a reassuring hand on Anvin's wrist, resolved.

"Dierdre is my friend," she said, settling the matter. "I would not abandon her, just as you would not abandon one of your men. What is it you have always told me? *No man left behind.*"

Kyra sighed.

"I may have helped save Dierdre from that cell," Kyra added, "but she also helped save me. I owe her a debt. I am sorry, but what my father thinks matters little. It is *I* crossing Escalon alone, not he. She is coming with me."

Dierdre smiled. She stepped up beside Kyra and linked arms with hers, a new pride in her step. Kyra felt good at the idea of having her on the journey, and she knew she'd made the right decision, whatever should happen.

Kyra noticed her brothers walking nearby and she could not help but feel a sense of disappointment that they were not more

25

protective of her, that they would not think to offer to join her, too; they were too competitive with her. It saddened her that that was the nature of their relationship, yet she could not change other people. She was better off anyway, she realized. They were filled with bravado, and would only do something reckless to get her in trouble.

"I would like to accompany you, too," Anvin said, his voice heavy with guilt. "The idea of your crossing Escalon does not sit well with me." He sighed. "But your father needs me now more than ever. He's asked me to join him in the south."

"And I," Arthfael added. "I would like to join you, too—but I have been assigned to join the men south."

"And I to remain behind and guard Volis in his absence," Vidar added.

Kyra was touched by their support.

"Do not worry," she replied. "I have but a three-day ride before me. I shall be fine."

"You shall," Baylor chimed in, stepping closer. "And your new horse shall make sure of it."

With that, Baylor pushed open wide the door to the stables, and they all followed him into the low stone building, the smell of horses heavy in the air.

Kyra's eyes slowly adjusted to the dim light as she followed him in, the stables damp and cool, filled with the sound of excited horses. She looked up and down the stalls and saw before her rows of the most beautiful horses she'd ever seen—big, strong, beautiful horses, black and brown, each one a champion. It was a treasure chest.

"The Lord's Men reserved the best for themselves," Baylor explained as they walked, heading down the rows with a swagger, in his element. He touched one horse here and patted another and the animals seemed to come alive in his presence.

Kyra walked slowly, taking it all in. Each horse was like a work of art, larger than most horses she'd seen, filled with beauty and power.

"Thanks to you and your dragon, these horses are ours now," Baylor said. "It is only fitting that you take your pick. Your father has instructed me to give you first choice, even over his."

Kyra was overwhelmed. As she studied the stable, she felt a great burden of responsibility, knowing this was a once in a lifetime choice.

She walked slowly, running her hand along their manes, feeling how soft and smooth they were, how powerful, and was at a loss for which to choose.

"How do I pick?" she asked Baylor.

He smiled and shook his head.

"I've trained horses my entire life," he replied, "I've raised them, too. And if there is one thing I know, it is no two horses are the same. Some are bred for speed, others for stamina; some are built for strength, while others are made to carry a load. Some are too proud to carry a thing. And others, well, others are built for battle. Some thrive in solo jousts, others just want to fight, and others still are created for the marathon of war. Some will be your best friend, others will turn on you. Your relationship to a horse is a magical thing. They must call to you, and you to them. Choose well, and your horse shall be forever beside you, in times of battle and times of war. No good warrior is complete without one."

Kyra walked slowly, heart thumping with excitement, passing horse after horse, some looking at her, some looking away, some neighing and stamping impatiently, others standing still. She was waiting for a connection, and yet she felt none. She was frustrated.

Then, suddenly, Kyra felt a chill up her spine, like a lightning bolt shooting through her. It came as a sharp sound echoed through the stables, a sound that told her that *that* was her horse. It did not sound like a typical horse—but emitted a much darker sound, more powerful. It cut through the noise and rose above the sounds of all the others, like a wild lion trying to break free of its cage. It both terrified her—and drew her in.

Kyra turned toward its source, at the end of the stable, and as she did there came a sudden crashing of wood. She saw the stalls shatter, wood flying everywhere, and there ensued a commotion as several men hurried over, trying to close the broken wooded gate. A horse kept smashing it with its hooves.

Kyra hurried toward the commotion.

"Where are you going?" Baylor asked. "The fine horses are here."

27

But Kyra ignored him, gaining speed, her heart beating faster as she went. She knew it was calling her.

Baylor and the others hurried to catch up with her as she neared the end, and as she did, she turned and gasped at the sight before her. There stood what appeared to be a horse, yet twice the size of the others, legs as thick as tree trunks. It had two small, razor-sharp horns, barely visible behind its ears. Its hide was not brown or black like the others, but a deep scarlet—and its eyes, unlike the others, glowed green. They looked right at her, and the intensity struck her in the chest, taking her breath away. She could not move.

The creature, towering over her, made a noise like a snarl, and revealed fangs.

"What horse is this?" she asked Baylor, her voice barely above a whisper.

He shook his head disapprovingly.

"That is no horse," he frowned, "but a savage beast. A freak. Very rare. It is a Solzor. Imported from the far corners of Pandesia. The Lord Governor must have kept it as a trophy to keep on display. He could not ride the creature—no one could. Solzors are savage creatures, not to be tamed. Come—you waste precious time. Back to the horses."

But Kyra stood there, rooted in place, unable to look away. Her heart pounded as she knew this was meant for her.

"I choose this one," she said to Baylor.

Baylor and the others gasped, all staring at her as if she were mad. A stunned silence ensued.

"Kyra," Anvin began, "your father would never allow you—"

"It is my choice, is it not?" she replied.

He frowned and raised his hands to his hips.

"That is no horse!" he insisted. "It is a wild creature."

"It would as soon kill you," Baylor added.

Kyra turned to him.

"Was it not you who told me to trust my instincts?" she asked. "Well, this is where they have led me. This animal and I belong together."

The Solzor suddenly reared its huge legs, smashed another wooden gate, and sent splinters everywhere and men cowering. Kyra was in awe. It was wild and untamed and magnificent, an animal too big for this place, too big for captivity, and far superior to the others.

"Why should she get to have it?" Brandon asked, stepping forward and shoving others out of his way. "I am older, after all. *I* want it."

Before she could reply, Brandon rushed forward as if to claim it. He went to jump on its back and as he did, the Solzor bucked wildly and threw him off. He went flying across the stables, and smashing into the wall.

Braxton then rushed forward, as if to claim it, too, and as he did it swung its head and sliced Brandon's arm with his fangs.

Bleeding, Brandon shrieked and ran from the stables, clutching his arm. Braxton scrambled to his feet and followed on his heels, the Solzor just missing him as it tried to bite him.

Kyra stood, transfixed, yet somehow unafraid. She knew that for her, it would be different. She felt a connection to this beast, the same way she had to Theos.

Kyra suddenly stepped forward, boldly, standing right in front of it, in range of its deadly fangs. She wanted to show the Solzor that she trusted it.

"Kyra!" Anvin shouted, concern in his voice. "Get back!"

But Kyra ignored him. She stood there, staring the beast in the eye

The beast stared back, a low snarl emanating from its throat, as if debating what to do. Kyra trembled from fear, but she would not let the others see it.

She forced herself to show her courage. She raised a hand slowly, stepped forward, and touched its scarlet hide. It snarled more loudly, showing its fangs, and she could feel its anger and frustration.

"Unlock its chains," she commanded the others.

"What!?" one of them called out.

"That is not wise," Baylor called, fear in his voice.

"Do as I say!" she insisted, feeling a strength rise up within her, as if the will of this beast were pouring through her.

Behind her, soldiers rushed forward with keys, unlocking its chains. All the while the beast never took his angry eyes off her, snarling, as if summing her up, as if daring her.

As soon as it was unchained, the beast stomped his legs, as if threatening to attack.

But, strangely, it did not. Instead, it stared at Kyra, fixing its eyes on her, and slowly its look of anger seemed to morph to one of tolerance. Perhaps even gratitude.

Ever so slightly, it seemed to lower its head; it was a subtle gesture, almost unnoticeable, yet one she could decipher.

Kyra stepped forward, held its mane, and in one quick motion mounted it.

A gasp filled the room.

At first the beast shivered and began to buck. But Kyra sensed it was for show. It didn't really want to throw her off—it just wanted to make a point of defiance, of who was in control, to keep her on edge. It wanted to let her know it was a creature of the wild, a creature to be tamed by no one.

I do not wish to tame you, she said to it in her mind's eye. *I wish only to be your partner in battle.*

The Solzor calmed, still prancing, but not as wildly, as if hearing her. Soon, it stopped moving, perfectly still beneath her, snarling out at the others, as if to protect her.

Kyra, sitting atop the Solzor, now calm, looked down at the others. A sea of shocked faces stared back, mouths agape.

Kyra slowly smiled wide, feeling a great sense of triumph.

"This," she said, "is my choice. And his name is Andor."

*

Kyra rode Andor at a walk down the center of the courtyard of Argos, and all her father's men, hardened soldiers, stopped and watched in awe as she went. Clearly, they had never seen anything like it.

Kyra held his mane gently, trying to pacify him as he snarled softly at all the men, glaring them down, as if he held a vendetta for being caged. Kyra adjusted her balance, Baylor having put a fresh leather saddle on him, and tried to get used to riding up so high. She felt more powerful with this beast beneath her than she'd ever had.

Beside her, Dierdre rode a beautiful mare, one Baylor had chosen for her, and the two of them continued through the snow

30

until Kyra spotted her father in the distance, standing there by the gate, awaiting her. He stood with his men, all of them waiting to see her off, and they, too, looked up at her in fear and awe, stunned that she could ride this animal. She saw the admiration in their eyes, and it emboldened her for the journey ahead. If Theos would not return to her, at least she had this magnificent creature beneath her.

Kyra dismounted as she reached her father, guiding Andor by his mane and seeing the concern flicker in her father's eyes. She did not know if it was because of this beast or for the journey ahead. His look of concern reassured her, made her realize she was not the only one who feared what lay ahead, and that he cared for her after all. For the briefest moment he let his guard down and shot her a look that only she could recognize: the love of a father. She could tell that he struggled in sending her on this quest.

She stopped a few feet away, facing him, and all grew silent as the men gathered around to watch the exchange.

She smiled up at him.

"Do not worry, Father," she said. "You raised me to be strong."

He nodded back, pretending to be reassured—yet she could see he was not. He was still, most of all, a father.

He looked up, searching the skies.

"If only your dragon would come for you now," he said. "You could cross Escalon in but a few minutes. Or better—he could join you on your journey and incinerate anyone who came in your path."

Kyra smiled sadly.

"Theos is gone now, Father."

He looked back at her, eyes filled with wonder

"Forever?" he asked, the question of a warlord leading his men into battle, needing to know but afraid to ask.

Kyra closed her eyes and tried to tune in, to get a response. She willed for Theos to answer her.

Yet there came a numbing silence. It made her wonder if her she had ever had a connection to Theos to begin with, or if she had only imagined it.

"I do not know, Father," she answered honestly.

He nodded back, accepting, the look of a man who had learned to accept things as they were and to rely on himself.

"Remember what I—" her father began.

"KYRA!" an excited shout cut through the air.

Kyra turned as the men parted ways, and her heart lifted with delight to see Aidan running through the city gates, Leo at his side, jumping down from a cart driven by her father's men. He ran right for her, stumbling through the snow, Leo even faster, way ahead of him, and already bounding ahead into Kyra's arms.

Kyra laughed as Leo knocked her down, standing on her chest on all fours and licking her face again and again. Behind her, Andor snarled, already protective of her, and Leo jumped up and faced off with it, snarling back. They were two fearless creatures, each equally protective of her, and Kyra felt honored.

She jumped up and stood between them, holding Leo back.

"It's okay, Leo," she said. "Andor is my friend. And Andor," she said, turning, "Leo is mine, too."

Leo backed down reluctantly, while Andor continued to snarl, albeit in a quieter fashion.

"Kyra!"

Kyra turned as Aidan ran into her arms. She reached down and hugged him tight as his little hands clutched her back. It felt so good to embrace her little brother, whom she was certain she would never see again. He was the one bit of normalcy left in the whirlwind her life had become, the one thing that had not changed.

"I heard you were here," he said in a rush, "and I caught a ride to see you. I'm so happy you're back."

She smiled sadly.

"I'm afraid not for long, my brother," she said.

A flash of concern crossed his face.

"You're leaving?" he asked, crestfallen.

Her father interjected.

"She is off to see her uncle," he explained. "Let her go now."

Kyra noted that her father said *her* uncle and not *your* uncle, and she wondered why.

"Then I shall join her!" Aidan insisted proudly.

Her father shook his head.

"You shall not," he replied.

Kyra smiled down at her little brother, so brave, as always.

"Father needs you elsewhere," she said.

"The battlefront?" Aidan asked, turning to their father hopefully. "You are setting out for Esephus," he added in a rush. "I have heard! I want to join you!"

But he shook his head.

"It is Volis for you," he replied. "You will stay there, protected by the men I leave behind. The battlefront is no place for you now. One day."

Aidan flushed red with disappointment.

"But I want to fight, Father!" he protested. "I don't need to stay boarded up in some empty fort with women and children!"

His men snickered, but her father looked serious.

"My decision is made," he answered curtly.

Aidan frowned.

"If I can't join Kyra and I can't join you," he said, refusing to let it go, "then what use is my learning about battles, learning how to use weapons? What has all my training been for?"

"Grow hair on your chest first, little brother," Braxton laughed, stepping forward, Brandon beside him.

Laughter arose amidst the men and Aidan reddened, clearly embarrassed in front of the others.

Kyra, feeling bad, knelt before him and looked at him, placing a hand on his cheek.

"You shall be a finer warrior than all of them," she reassured him softly, so that only he could hear. "Be patient. In the meantime, watch over Volis. It needs you, too. Make me proud. I shall return, I promise, and one day we shall fight great battles together."

Aidan seemed to soften a bit, as he leaned forward and hugged her again.

"I don't want you to go," he said softly. "I had a dream about you. I dreamt…" He looked up at her reluctantly, eyes filled with fear. "…that you would die out there."

Kyra felt a shock at his words, especially as she saw the look in his eyes. It haunted her. She did not know what to say.

Anvin stepped forward and draped over her shoulders thick, heavy furs, warming her; she stood and felt ten pounds heavier, but it shut out all the wind and took away the chill down her back. He smiled back.

"Your nights will be long, and fires shall be far away," he said, and gave her a quick embrace.

Her father stepped forward quickly and embraced her, the strong embrace of a warlord. She hugged him back, lost in his muscles, feeling safe and secure.

"You are my daughter," he said firmly, "don't forget that." He then lowered his voice so the others could not hear, and added: "I love you."

She was overwhelmed with emotions, but before she could reply he quickly turned and hurried away—and at the same moment Leo whined and jumped up on her, nudging his nose into her chest.

"He wants to go with you," Aidan observed. "Take him—you'll need him far more than I, shuttered up in Volis. He's yours anyway."

Kyra hugged Leo, unable to refuse as he would not leave her side. She felt comforted by the idea of his joining her, having missed him dearly. She could use another set of eyes and ears, too, and there was no one more loyal than Leo.

Ready, Kyra mounted Andor as her father's men parted ways. They held up torches of respect for her all along the bridge, warding off the night, lighting a path for her. She looked out beyond them and saw the darkening sky, the wilderness before her. She felt excitement, fear, and most of all, a sense of duty. Of purpose. Before her lay the most important quest of her life, a quest that had at stake not only her identity, but the fate of all of Escalon. The stakes could not be higher.

Her staff strapped over one shoulder, her bow over the other, Leo and Dierdre beside her, Andor beneath her, and all her father's men watching, Kyra began to ride Andor at a walk toward the city gates. She went slowly at first, through the torches, past the men, feeling as if she were walking into a dream, walking into her destiny. She did not look back, not wanting to lose resolve. A low horn was sounded by her father's men, a horn of departure, a sound of respect.

She prepared to give Andor a kick—but he already anticipated her. He began to run, first at a trot, then a gallop.

Within moments Kyra found herself racing through the snow, through the gates of Argos, over the bridge, into the open field, the cold wind in her hair and nothing before her but a long road, savage creatures, and the falling blackness of night.

CHAPTER FOUR

Merk ran through the wood, stumbling down the dirt slope, weaving between trees, the leaves of Whitewood crunching beneath him as he ran for all he had. He looked ahead and kept in his sights the distant plumes of smoke filling the horizon, blocking out the blood-red sunset, and he felt a rising sense of urgency. He knew the girl was down there somewhere, possibly being murdered even at this moment, and he could not make his legs run fast enough.

Killing seemed to find him; it encountered him at every turn, on seemingly every day, the way other men were summoned home for dinner. *He had a date with death*, his mother used to say. Those words rang in his head, had haunted him for most of his life. Were her words self-fulfilling? Or had he been born with a black star over his head?

Killing for Merk was a natural part of his life, like breathing or having lunch, no matter who he was doing it for, or how. The more he pondered it, the more he felt a great sense of disgust, as if he wanted to vomit his entire life. But while everything inside him screamed at him to turn around, to start life anew, to continue on his pilgrimage for the Tower of Ur, he just could not do it. Violence was, once again, summoning him, and now was not the time to ignore its call.

Merk ran, the billowing clouds of smoke getting closer, making it harder to breathe, the smell of smoke stinging his nostrils, and a familiar feeling began to overtake him. It was not fear or even, after all these years, excitement. It was a feeling of familiarity. Of the killing machine he was about to become. It was always what happened when he went into battle—his own, private battle. In his version of battle, he killed his opponent face to face; he didn't have to hide behind a visor or armor or a crowd's applause like those fancy knights. In his view, his was the most courageous battle of all, reserved for true warriors like himself.

And yet as he ran, something felt different to Merk. Usually, Merk did not care who lived or died; it was just a job. That kept him

36

clear to reason, free from being clouded emotionally. Yet this time, it was different. For the first time in as long as he could remember, no one was paying him to do this. He proceeded of his own volition, for no other reason than because he pitied the girl and wanted to set wrongs right. It made him invested, and he did not like the feeling. He regretted now that he had not acted sooner and had turned her away.

Merk ran at a steady clip, not carrying any weapons—and not needing to. He had in his belt only his dagger, and that was enough. Indeed, he might not even use it. He preferred to enter battle weaponless: it threw his opponents off-guard. Besides, he could always strip his enemy's weapons and use them against them. That left him with an instant arsenal everywhere he went.

Merk burst out of Whitewood, the trees giving way to open plains and rolling hills, and was met by the huge, red sun, sitting low on the horizon. The valley spread out before him, the sky above it black, as if angry, filled with smoke, and there, aflame, sat what could only be the remnants of the girl's farm. Merk could hear it from here, the gleeful shouts of men, criminals, their voices filled with delight, bloodlust. With his professional eye he scanned the scene of the crime and immediately spotted them, a dozen men, faces lit by the torches they held as they ran to and fro, setting everything aflame. Some ran from the stables to the house, setting torches to straw roofs, while others slaughtered the innocent cattle, hacking them down with axes. One of them, he saw, dragged a body by the hair across the muddy ground.

A woman.

Merk's heart raced as he wondered if it was the girl—and if she were dead or alive. He was dragging her to what appeared to be the girl's family, all of them tied to the barn by ropes. There were her father and mother, and beside them, likely her siblings, smaller, younger, both girls. As a breeze moved a cloud of black smoke, Merk caught a glimpse of the body's long blonde hair, matted with dirt, and he knew that was her.

Merk felt a rush of adrenaline as he took off at a sprint down the hill. He rushed into the muddy compound, running amidst the flame and the smoke, and he could finally see what was happening: the girl's family, against the wall, were all already dead, their throats cut, their bodies hanging limply against the wall. He felt a wave of relief as he saw the girl being dragged was still alive, resisting as they dragged her to join her family. He saw a thug awaiting her arrival with a dagger, and he knew she would be next. He had arrived too late to save her family—but not too late to save her.

Merk knew he had to catch these men off-guard. He slowed his gait and marched calmly down the center of the compound, as if he had all the time in the world, waiting for them to take notice of him, wanting to confuse them.

Soon enough, one of them did. The thug turned immediately, shocked at the sight of a man walking calmly through all the carnage, and he yelled to his friends.

Merk felt all the confused eyes on him as he proceeded, walking casually toward the girl. The thug dragging her looked over his shoulder, and at the sight of Merk he stopped, too, loosening his grip and letting her fall in the mud. He turned and approached Merk with the others, all closing in on him, ready to fight.

"What do we have here?" called out the man who appeared to be their leader. It was the one who had dropped the girl, and as he set his sights on Merk he drew a sword from his belt and approached, as the others encircled him.

Merk looked only at the girl, checking to make sure she was alive and unharmed. He was relieved to see her squirm in the mud, slowly collecting herself, lifting her head and looking back out at him, dazed and confused. Merk felt relief that he had not, at least, been too late to save her. Perhaps this was the first step on what would be a very long road to redemption. Perhaps, he realized, it did not start in the tower, but right here.

As the girl turned over in the mud, propping herself up on her elbows, their eyes met, and he saw them flood with hope.

"Kill them!" she shrieked.

Merk stayed calm, still walking casually toward her, as if not even noticing the men around him.

"So you know the girl," the leader called out to him.

"Her uncle?" one of them called out mockingly.

"A long-lost brother?" laughed another.

"You coming to protect her, old man?" another mocked.

The others burst into laughter as they closed in.

While he did not show it, Merk was silently taking stock of all his opponents, summing them up out of the corner of his eye, tallying how many they were, how big they were, how fast they moved, the weapons they carried. He analyzed how much muscle they had versus fat, what they were wearing, how flexible they were in those clothes, how fast they could pivot in their boots. He noted the weapons they held—the crude knives, daggers drawn, swords poorly sharpened—and he analyzed how they held them, at their sides or out in front, and in which hands.

Most were amateur, he realized, and none of them truly concerned him. Save one. The one with the crossbow. Merk made a mental note to kill him first.

Merk entered a different zone, a different mode of thinking, of being, the one that always naturally gripped him whenever he was in a confrontation. He became submerged in his own world, a world he had little control over, a world he gave his body up to. It was a world that dictated to him how many men he could kill how quickly, how efficiently. How to inflict the maximum damage with the least possible effort.

He felt bad for these men; they had no idea what they were walking into.

"Hey, I'm *talking* to you!" their leader called out, hardly ten feet away, holding out his sword with a sneer and closing in fast.

Merk stayed the course, though, and kept marching, calm and expressionless. He was staying focused, hardly listening to their leader's words, now muted in his mind. He would not run, or show any signs of aggression, until it suited him, and he could sense how puzzled these men were by his lack of actions.

"Hey, do you know you're about to die?" the leader insisted. "You listening to me?"

Merk continued walking calmly while their leader, infuriated, waited no longer. He shouted in rage, raised his sword, and charged, swinging down for Merk's shoulder.

Merk took his time, not reacting. He walked calmly toward his attacker, waiting until the very last second, making sure not to tense up, to show any signs of resistance.

39

He waited until his opponent's sword reached its highest point, high above the man's head, the pivotal moment of vulnerability for any man, he had learned long ago. And then, faster than his foe could possibly foresee, Merk lunged forward like a snake, using two fingers to strike at a pressure point beneath the man's armpit.

His attacker, eyes bulging in pain and surprise, immediately dropped the sword.

Merk stepped in close, looped one arm around the man's arm and tightened his grip in a lock. In the same motion he grabbed the man by the back of his head and spun him around, using him as a shield. For it wasn't this man that Merk had been worried about, but the attacker behind him with the crossbow. Merk had chosen to attack this oaf first merely to gain himself a shield.

Merk spun and faced the man with the crossbow, who, as he'd anticipated, already had his bow trained on him. A moment later Merk heard the telltale sound of an arrow being released from the crossbow, and he watched it flying through the air right for him. Merk held his writhing human shield tight.

There came a gasp, and Merk felt the oaf flinch in his arms. The leader cried out in pain, and Merk suddenly felt a jolt of pain himself, like a knife entering his own stomach. At first he was confused—and then he realized the arrow had gone through the shield's stomach, and the head of it had just barely entered Merk's stomach, too. It only penetrated perhaps a half inch—not enough to seriously wound him—but enough to hurt like hell.

Calculating the time it would take to reload the crossbow, Merk dropped the leader's limp body, grabbed the sword from his hand, and threw it. It sailed end over end toward the thug with the crossbow and the man shrieked, eyes widening in shock, as the sword pierced his chest. He dropped his bow and fell limply beside it.

Merk turned and looked over at the other thugs, all clearly in shock, two of their best men dead, all now seeming unsure. They faced each other in the awkward silence.

"Who are you?" one finally called out, nervousness in his voice.

Merk smiled wide and cracked his knuckles, relishing the bout to come.

"I," he replied, "am what keeps you up at night."

CHAPTER FIVE

Duncan rode with his army, the sound of hundreds of horses thundering in his ears as he led them south, throughout the night, away from Argos. His trusted commanders rode beside him, Anvin on one side and Arthfael on the other, only Vidar remaining home to guard Volis, while several hundred men lined up beside them, all riding together. Unlike other warlords, Duncan liked to ride side-by-side with his men; he did not consider these men to be his subjects, but rather his brothers-in-arms.

They rode through the night, the cool wind in their hair, the snow beneath their feet, and it felt good to be on the move, to be heading for battle, to no longer be cowering behind the walls of Volis as Duncan had for half his life. Duncan looked over and spotted his sons Brandon and Braxton riding alongside his men, and while he was proud to have them with him, he did not worry for them as he did for his daughter. Despite himself, as hour followed hour, even though he told himself he would not worry, Duncan found his nighttime thoughts turning to Kyra.

He wondered where she was now. He thought of her crossing Escalon alone, with only Dierdre, Andor, and Leo to join her, and his heart tugged at him. He knew the journey he had sent her on was one that could imperil even some hardened warriors. If she survived it, she would return a greater warrior than any of the men who rode with him here today. If she did not, he would never be able to live with himself. But desperate times called for desperate measures, and he needed her to complete her quest more than ever.

They crested a hill and descended another, and as the wind picked up, Duncan looked out at the rolling plains, spread out before him beneath the moonlight, and he thought of their destination: Esephus. The stronghold of the sea, the city built on the harbor, the crossroads of the northeast and the first major port for all shipping. It was a city bordered by the Sea of Tears on one side and a harbor on the other, and it was said whoever controlled Esephus controlled the better half of Escalon. The next closest fort to Argos and a vital stronghold, Esephus had to be his first stop, Duncan knew, if he were to have any chance of rallying a revolution. The once-great city would have to be liberated. Its harbor, once so proudly filled with ships waving the banners of Escalon, was now, Duncan knew, filled with Pandesian ships, a humbled reminder of what it once was.

Duncan and Seavig, the warlord of Esephus, had been close once. They had ridden into battle together as brothers-in-arms countless times, and Duncan had sailed out to sea with him more than once. But since the invasion, they had lost touch. Seavig, a once-proud warlord, was now a humbled soldier, unable to sail the seas, unable to rule his city or visit other strongholds, like all warlords. They might as well have detained him and labeled him what he truly was: a prisoner, like all other warlords of Escalon.

Duncan rode through the night, the hills lit only by the torches of his men, hundreds of sparks of light heading south. As they rode, more snow fell and the wind raged, and the torches struggled to stay alight as the moon fought to break through the clouds. Yet Duncan's army pushed on, gaining ground, these men who would ride anywhere on earth for him. It was unconventional, Duncan knew, to attack at night, much less in the snow—yet Duncan had always been an unconventional warrior. It was what had allowed him to rise through the ranks, to become the old king's commander, was what had led to his having a stronghold of his own. And it was what made him one of the most respected of all dispersed warlords. Duncan never did what other men did. There was a motto he tried to live by: *do what other men expected least.*

The Pandesians would never expect an attack, since word of Duncan's revolt could not have spread this far south so soon—not if Duncan reached them in time. And they would certainly never expect an attack at nighttime, much less in the snow. They would know the risks of riding at night, of horses breaking legs, and of a myriad other problems. Wars, Duncan knew, were often won more by surprise and speed than by force.

Duncan planned to ride all night long until they reached Esephus, to try to conquer the vast Pandesian force and take back this great city with his few hundred men. And if they took Esephus, then maybe, just maybe, he could gain momentum and begin the war to take back all of Escalon.

"Down below!" Anvin called out, pointing into the snow.

Duncan looked down at the valley below and spotted, amidst the snow and fog, several small villages dotting the countryside. Those villages, Duncan knew, were inhabited by brave warriors, loyal to Escalon. Each would have but a handful of men, but it could add up. He could gain momentum and bolster his army's ranks.

Duncan shouted above the wind and horses to be heard.

"Sound the horns!"

His men sounded a series of short horn blasts, the old rallying cry of Escalon, a sound which warmed his heart, a sound which had not been heard in Escalon in years. It was a sound that would be familiar to his fellow countrymen, a sound that would tell them all that they needed to know. If there were any good men in those villages, that sound would stir them.

The horns sounded again and again, and as they neared, slowly torches lit in the villages. Villagers, alerted to their presence, began to fill the streets, their torches flickering against the snow, men hastily getting dressed, grabbing weapons and donning whatever crude armor they had. They all gazed up the hill to see Duncan and his men approaching, gesturing as if filled with wonder. Duncan could only imagine what a sight his men made, galloping in the thick of night, in a snowstorm, down the hill, raising hundreds of torches like a legion of fire fighting the snow.

Duncan and his men rode into the first village and came to a stop, their hundreds of torches lighting the startled faces. Duncan looked down at the hopeful faces of his countrymen, and he put on his fiercest battle face, preparing himself to inspire his fellow men as never before.

"Men of Escalon!" he boomed, slowing his horse to a walk, turning and circling as he tried to address them all as they pressed close around him.

"We have suffered under the oppression of Pandesia for far too long! You can choose to stay here and live your lives in this village and remember the Escalon that once was. Or you can choose to rise up as free men, and help us begin the great war for freedom!"

There arose a cheer of joy from the villagers as they unanimously rushed forward.

"The Pandesians are taking our girls now!" called out one man. "If this is freedom, then I don't know what liberty is!"

The villagers cheered.

"We are with you, Duncan!" shouted another. "We shall ride with you to our deaths!"

There arose another cheer, and the villagers rushed to mount their horses and join his men. Duncan, satisfied at his growing ranks, kicked his horse and continued to ride out from the village, starting to realize how long overdue Escalon was to revolt.

Soon they reached another village, its men already out and waiting, their torches lit, as they heard the horns, the shouts, saw the army growing and clearly knew what was happening. Local villagers called out to each other, recognizing each other's faces, realized what was happening, and needed no more speeches. Duncan swept through this village as he did the last, and it took no convincing for the villagers, too eager for freedom, too eager to have their dignity restored, to mount their horses, grab their weapons, and join Duncan's ranks, wherever he should take them.

Duncan charged through village after village, covering the countryside, all lighting up in the night, despite the wind, despite the snow, despite the black of night. Their desire for freedom was too strong, Duncan realized, to do anything but shine even in the darkest night—and to take up arms to win back their lives.

*

Duncan rode all through the night, leading his growing army south, his hands raw and numb from the cold as he gripped the reins. The further south they went, the more the terrain began to morph, the dry cold of Volis replaced with the wet cold of Esephus, its air heavy, as Duncan remembered it to be, with the damp of the sea and the smell of salt. The trees were shorter here, too, windswept, all seemingly bent from the easterly gale that never ceased.

They crested hill after hill. The clouds parted, despite the snow, and the moon opened up in the sky, shining down on them, lighting their way enough to see by. They rode, warriors against the night, and it was a night Duncan would remember, he knew, for the rest of his life. Assuming he survived. This would be the battle upon which hinged everything. He thought of Kyra, his family, his home, and he did not want to lose them. His life was on the line, and the lives of all he knew and loved, and he would risk it all tonight.

Duncan glanced back over his shoulder and was elated to see he had picked up several hundred more men, all riding together as one, with a single purpose. He knew that, even with their numbers, they would be vastly outnumbered and would be facing a professional army. Thousands of Pandesians were stationed in Esephus. Duncan knew that Seavig still had hundreds of his own disbanded men at his disposal, of course, but there was no knowing if he would risk it all to join Duncan. Duncan had to assume he would not.

They soon crested yet another hill and as they did, they all came to a stop, needing no prodding. For there, far below, sprawled the Sea of Tears, its waves crashing to shore, the great harbor, and the ancient city of Espehus rising up beside it. The city looked as if it had been built into the sea, the waves crashing against its stone walls. The city was built with its back to land, as if facing the sea, its gates and portcullises sinking into the water as if they cared more about accommodating ships than horses.

Duncan studied the harbor, the endless ships packed in it, all, he was chagrined to see, flying the banners of Pandesia, the yellow and blue that flew like an offense to his heart. Flapping in the wind was the emblem of Pandesia—a skull in the mouth of an eagle—making Duncan sick. Seeing such a great city held captive by Pandesia was a source of shame for Duncan, and even in the black night his cheeks blushed red. The ships sat there smugly, anchored safely, none expecting an attack. Of course. Who would dare attack them? Especially in the black of night, and in a snowstorm?

Duncan felt all his men's eyes on him, and he knew his moment of truth had come. They all awaited his fateful command, the one that would change the fate of Escalon, and he sat there on his horse, wind howling, and he felt his destiny welling up within him. He knew this was one of those moments that would define his life—and the lives of all these men.

46

"FORWARD!" he boomed.

His men cheered, and as one they all charged down the hillside, racing for the harbor, several hundred yards away. They raised their torches high, and Duncan felt his heart slamming in his chest as the wind brushed his face. He knew this mission was suicide—yet he also knew it was crazy enough that it just might work.

They tore down the countryside, their horses galloping so fast that the cold air nearly took his breath away, and as they neared the harbor, its stone walls hardly a hundred yards before them, Duncan prepared for battle.

"ARCHERS!" he called out.

His archers, riding in neat rows behind him, set their arrows aflame, torching their tips, awaiting his command. They rode and rode, their horses thundering, the Pandesians below still not aware of the attack to come.

Duncan waited until they got closer—forty yards out, then thirty, then twenty—and finally he knew the time was right.

"FIRE!"

The black night was suddenly lit up with thousands of flaming arrows, sailing in high arcs through the air, cutting through the snow, making their way for the dozens of Pandesian ships anchored in the harbor. One by one, like fireflies, they found their targets, landing on the long, flapping canvas of Pandesian sails.

It took but moments for the ships to be lit up, the sails and then the ships all aflame, as the fire spread rapidly in the windy harbor.

"AGAIN!" Duncan yelled.

Volley followed volley, as fire-tipped arrows fell like raindrops all over the Pandesian fleet.

The fleet was, at first, quiet in the dead of night, the soldiers all fast asleep, all so unsuspecting. The Pandesians had become, Duncan realized, too arrogant, too complacent, never possibly suspecting an attack like this.

Duncan did not give them time to rally; emboldened, he galloped forward, closing in on the harbor. He led the way right up to the stone wall bordering the harbor.

"TORCHES!" he cried.

His men charged right up to the shoreline, raised their torches high, and with a great shout, they followed Duncan's example and hurled their torches onto the ships closest to them. Their heavy torches landed like clubs on the deck, the thumping of wood filling the air, as dozens more ships were set aflame.

The few Pandesian soldiers on duty noticed too late what was happening, finding themselves caught in a wave of flame, and shrieking and jumping overboard.

Duncan knew it was only a matter of time until the rest of the Pandesians woke.

"HORNS!" he shouted.

Horns were sounded up and down the ranks, the old rallying cry of Escalon, the short bursts that he knew Seavig would recognize. He hoped it would rouse him.

Duncan dismounted, drew his sword, and rushed for the harbor wall. Without hesitating, he jumped over the low stone wall and onto the flaming ship, leading the way as he charged forward. He had to finish the Pandesians off before they could rally.

Anvin and Arthfael charged at his side and his men joined in, all letting out a great battle cry as they threw their lives to the wind. After so many years of submission, their day of vengeance had come.

The Pandesians, finally, were roused. Soldiers began to emerge from the decks below, streaming forth like ants, coughing against the smoke, dazed and confused. They caught sight of Duncan and his men, and they drew swords and charged. Duncan found himself being confronted by streams of men—yet he did not flinch; on the contrary, he attacked.

Duncan charged forward and ducked as the first man slashed for his head, then came up and stabbed the man in the gut. A soldier slashed at his back, and Duncan spun and blocked it—then spun the soldier's sword around and stabbed him in the chest.

Duncan fought back heroically as he was attacked from all sides, recalling days of old as he found himself immersed in battle, parrying on all sides. When men got too close to reach with his sword, he leaned back and kicked them, creating space for himself to swing; in other instances, he spun and elbowed, fighting hand to hand in the close quarters when he needed to. Men dropped all around him, and none could get close.

Duncan soon found himself joined by Anvin and Arthfael as dozens of his men rushed forward to help. As Anvin joined him, he blocked the blow of a solider charging Duncan from behind, sparing him a wound—while Arthfael stepped forward, raised his sword, and blocked a hatchet coming down for Duncan's face. As he did, Duncan simultaneously stepped forward and stabbed the solider in the gut, he and Arthfael working together to fell him.

They all fought as one, a well-oiled machine from all their years together, all guarding each other's backs as the clang of swords and armor pierced the night.

All around him, Duncan saw his men boarding ships up and down the harbor, attacking the fleet as one. Pandesian soldiers streamed forth, all fully roused, some of them on fire, and the warriors of Escalon all fought bravely amidst the flames, none backing down even as fires raged all around them. Duncan himself fought until he could lift his arms no more, sweating, smoke stinging his eyes, swords clanging all around him, dropping one soldier after the next that tried to escape to shore.

Finally, the fires grew too hot; Pandesian soldiers, in full armor, trapped by the flames, leapt from their ships into the waters below—and Duncan led his men off the ship and over the stone wall, back to the harbor side. Duncan heard a shout and he turned and noticed hundreds of Pandesian soldiers trying to follow, to pursue them off the ship.

As he stepped down onto dry land, the last of his men to leave, he turned, raised his sword high, and hacked at the great ropes binding the ships to shore.

"THE ROPES!" Duncan yelled.

Up and down the harbor his men followed his lead and severed the ropes anchoring the fleet to shore. As the great rope before him finally snapped, Duncan placed his boot on the deck and with a great kick, shoved the ship away from shore. He groaned from the effort, and Anvin, Arthfael and dozens of others rushed forward, joining him. As one, they all shoved the burning hull away from shore.

The flaming ship, filled with shrieking soldiers, drifted inevitably toward the other ships in the harbor—and as it reached them, it set them aflame, too. Men leapt from ships by the hundreds, shrieking, sinking into the black waters.

Duncan stood there, breathing hard and watching, his eyes aglow, as the whole harbor soon lit in a great conflagration. Thousands of Pandesians, fully roused now, emerged from the lower decks of other ships—but it was too late. They surfaced to a wall of flame, and left with the choice of being burned alive or jumping into a death by drowning in the freezing waters, they all chose the latter. Duncan watched as the harbor soon filled with hundreds of bodies, bobbing in the waters, crying out as they tried to swim for shore.

"ARCHERS!" Duncan yelled.

His archers took aim and fired volley after volley, aiming for the flailing soldiers. One by one they found their marks, and the Pandesians sank.

The waters became slick with blood, and soon there came snapping noises and the sound of shrieking, as the waters were filled with glowing yellow sharks, feasting in the blood-filled harbor.

Duncan looked out and it slowly dawned on him what he had done: the entire Pandesian fleet, but hours ago sitting so defiantly in the harbor, a sign of Pandesian conquest, was no more. Its hundreds of ships were destroyed, all burning together in Duncan's victory. His speed and surprise had worked.

There came a great shout amongst his men, and Duncan turned to see all of his men cheering as they watched the ships burn, their faces black with soot, exhaustion from having ridden through the night—yet all of them drunk with victory. It was a cry of relief. A cry of freedom. A cry they had been waiting years to release.

Yet no sooner had it sounded when another shout filled the air—this one much more ominous—followed by a sound which made the hair rise on Duncan's neck. He turned and his heart dropped to see the great gates to the stone barracks slowly opening. As they did, there appeared a frightening sight: thousands of Pandesian soldiers, fully armed, in perfect ranks; a professional army, outnumbering his men ten to one, was preparing. And as the gates opened, they let out a cry and charged right for them.

The beast had been roused. Now, the real war would begin.

CHAPTER SIX

Kyra, clutching Andor's mane, galloped through the night, Deidre beside her, Leo at her feet, all racing through the snow-filled plains west of Argos like thieves fleeing through the night. As she rode, hour passing hour, the sound of the horses thumping in her ears, Kyra became lost in her own world. She imagined what might lie ahead of her in the Tower of Ur, who her uncle might be, what he would say about her, about her mother, and she could barely contain her excitement. Yet she also had to admit, she felt fear. It would be a long trek to cross Escalon, one she had never done before. And looming ahead of them, she saw, was the Wood of Thorns. The open plains were coming to an end, and they would soon be immersed in a claustrophobic wood filled with savage beasts. She knew all rules were off once they crossed that tree line.

The snow whipped her face as the wind howled across the open plains, and Kyra, her hands numb, dropped the torch from her hand, realizing it had burned dead long ago. She rode through the dark, lost in her own thoughts, the only sound that of the horses, of the snow beneath them, and of Andor's occasional snarl. She could feel his rage, his untamed nature, unlike any beast she had ever ridden. It was as if Andor was not only unafraid of what lay ahead—but openly hoping for a confrontation.

Wrapped in her furs, Kyra felt another wave of hunger pains, and as she heard Leo whine yet again, she knew they could not all ignore their hunger much longer. They had been riding for hours and had already devoured their frozen strips of meat; she realized, too late, that they had not brought enough provisions. No small game surfaced on this snowy night, and it did not bode well. They would have to stop and find food soon.

They slowed as they neared the edge of the Wood, Leo snarling at the dark tree line. Kyra glanced back over her shoulder, at the rolling plains leading back to Argos, at the last open sky she would see for a while. She turned back and stared at the wood, and a part of her was loath to move ahead. She knew the reputation of the

51

Wood of Thorns, and this, she knew, was a moment of no turning back.

"You ready?" she asked Dierdre.

Dierdre appeared to be a different girl now than the one who had left prison. She was stronger, more resolute, as if she had been to the depths of hell and back and was ready to face anything.

"The worst that can happen has already happened to me," Deidre said, her voice cold and hard as the wood before them, a voice too old for her age.

Kyra nodded, understanding—and together, they set off, entering the tree line.

The moment they did, Kyra immediately felt a chill, even in this cold night. It was darker here, more claustrophobic, filled with ancient black trees with gnarled branches resembling thorns, and thick, black leaves. The wood exuded not a sense of peace, but one of evil.

They proceeded at a quick walk, as fast as they could amidst these trees, snow and ice crunching beneath their beasts. There slowly arose the sounds of odd creatures, hidden in the branches. She turned and scanned them searching for the source, but could find none. She felt they were being watched.

They proceeded deeper and deeper into the wood, Kyra trying to head west and north, as her father had told her, until she found the sea. As they went, Leo and Andor snarled at hidden creatures Kyra could not see, while she dodged the branches scratching her. Kyra pondered the long road ahead of her. She was excited at the idea of her quest, yet she longed to be with her people, to be fighting at their side in the war she had started. She already felt an urgency to return.

As hour followed hour, Kyra peered into the wood, wondering how much further until they reached the sea. She knew it was risky to ride in such darkness—yet she knew it was also risky to camp out here alone—especially as she heard another startling noise.

"Where is the sea?" Kyra finally asked Dierdre, mainly to break the silence.

She could tell from Dierdre's expression that she had stirred her from her thoughts; she could only imagine what nightmares she was lost in.

Dierdre shook her head.

"I wish I knew," she replied, her voice parched.

Kyra was confused.

"Didn't you come this way when they took you?" she asked.

Dierdre shrugged.

"I was locked in a cage in the back of the wagon," she replied, "and unconscious most of the trip. They could have taken me any direction. I don't know this wood."

She sighed, peering out into the blackness.

"But as we near Whitewood, I should recognize more."

They continued on, falling into a comfortable silence, and Kyra could not help but wonder about Deidre and her past. She could feel her strength, yet also her profound sadness. Kyra found herself getting consumed by dark thoughts of the journey ahead, of their lack of food, of the biting cold and the savage creatures awaiting them, and she turned to Dierdre, wanting to distract herself.

"Tell me of the Tower of Ur," Kyra said. "What's it like?"

Dierdre looked back, black circles beneath her eyes, and shrugged.

"I've never been to the tower," Dierdre replied. "I am from the city of Ur—and that is a good day's ride south."

"Then tell me of your city," Kyra said, wanting to think of anything but here.

Dierdre's eyes lit up.

"Ur is a beautiful place," she said, longing in her voice. "The city by the sea."

"We have a city south of us that is near the sea," Kyra said. "Esephus. It is a day's ride from Volis. I used to go there, with my father, when I was young."

Dierdre shook her head.

"That is not a sea," she replied.

Kyra was confused.

"What do you mean?"

"That is the Sea of Tears," Dierdre replied. "Ur is on the Sea of Sorrow. Our is a much more expansive sea. On your eastern shore, there are small tides; on our western coast, the Sorrow has waves twenty feet high that crash into our shores, and a tide that can pull out ships in a glance, much less men, when the moon is high. Ours

53

is the only city in all of Escalon where the cliffs lower enough to allow ships to touch to shore. Our has the only beach in all of Escalon. It is why Andros was built but a day's ride east of us."

Kyra pondered her words, glad to be distracted. She recalled all of this from some lesson in her youth, but she had never pondered it all in detail.

"And your people?" Kyra asked. "What are they like?"

Dierdre sighed.

"A proud people," she replied, "like any other in Escalon. But different, too. They say those of Ur have one eye on Escalon and one on the sea. We look to the horizon. We are less provincial than the others—perhaps because so many foreigners touch down on our shores. The men of Ur were once famed warriors, my father foremost amongst them. Now, we are subjects, like everyone else."

She sighed, and fell silent for a long time. Kyra was surprised when she started to speak again.

"Our city is cut with canals," Dierdre continued. "When I was growing up, I would sit atop the ridge and watch the ships come in and out for hours, sometimes days. They would come to us from all over the world, flying all different banners and sails and colors. They would bring in spices and silks and weapons and delicacies of every manner—sometimes even animals. I would look at the people coming and going, and I would wonder about their lives. I wanted desperately to be one of them."

She smiled, an unusual sight, her eyes aglow, clearly remembering.

"I used to have a dream," Dierdre said. "When I came of age, I would board one of those ships and sail away to some foreign land. I would find my prince, and we would live on a great island, in a great castle somewhere. Anywhere but Escalon."

Kyra looked over to see Dierdre smiling.

"And now?" Kyra asked.

Dierdre's face fell as she looked down at the snow, her expression suddenly filled with sadness. She merely shook her head.

"It's too late for me," Dierdre said. "After what they've done to me."

"It's never too late," Kyra said, wanting to reassure her.

But Dierdre merely shook her head.

"Those were the dreams of an innocent girl," she said, her voice heavy with remorse. "That girl is long gone."

Kyra felt sadness for her friend as they continued in silence, deeper and deeper into the wood. She wanted to take away her pain, but did not how. She wondered at the pain that some people lived with. What was it her father had told her once? *Do not be fooled by men's faces. We all lead lives of quiet despair. Some hide it better than others. Feel compassion for all, even if you see no outward reason.*

"The worst day of my life," Dierdre continued, "was when my father conceded to Pandesian law, when he let those ships enter our canals and let his men lower our banners. It was a sadder day, even, than when he allowed them to take me."

Kyra understood all too well. She understood the pain Dierdre had gone through, the sense of betrayal.

"And when you return?" Kyra asked. "Will you see your father?"

Dierdre looked down, pained. Finally, she said: "He is still my father. He made a mistake. I am sure he did not realize what would become of me. I think he shall never be the same when he learns what happened. I want to tell him. Eye to eye. I want him to understand the pain I felt. His betrayal. He needs to understand what happens when men decide the fate of women." She wiped away a tear. "He was my hero once. I do not understand how he could have given me away."

"And now?" Kyra asked.

Dierdre shook her head.

"No more. I am done making men my heroes. I shall find other heroes."

"What about you?" Kyra asked.

Dierdre looked back, confused.

"What do you mean?"

"Why look any further than yourself?" Kyra asked. "Can you not be your own hero?"

Dierdre scoffed.

"And why would I?"

"You are a hero to me," Kyra said. "What you suffered in there—I could not suffer. You survived. More than that—you are back on your feet and thriving even now. That makes you a hero to me."

Dierdre seemed to contemplate her words as they continued on in the silence.

"And you, Kyra?" Dierdre finally asked. "Tell me something about you."

Kyra shrugged, wondering.

"What would you like to know?"

Dierdre cleared her throat.

"Tell me of the dragon. What happened back there? I've never seen anything like it. Why did he come for you?" She hesitated. "Who are you?"

Kyra was surprised to detect fear in her friend's voice. She pondered her words, wanting to answer truthfully, and wished she had the answer.

"I don't know," she finally answered, truthfully. "I suppose that is what I am going to find out."

"You don't know?" Dierdre pressed. "A dragon swoops down from the sky to fight for you, and you don't know why?"

Kyra thought about how crazy that sounded, yet she could only shake her head. She looked up reflexively at the skies, and between the gnarled branches, despite all hope, she hoped for a sign of Theos.

But saw nothing but gloom. She heard no dragon, and her sense of isolation deepened.

"You know that you are different, don't you?" Dierdre pressed.

Kyra shrugged, her cheeks burning, feeling self-conscious. She wondered if her friend looked at her as if she were some kind of freak.

"I used to be so sure of everything," Kyra replied. "But now…I honestly don't know anymore."

They continued riding for hours, falling back into a comfortable silence, sometimes trotting when the wood opened up, at other times the wood so dense they needed to dismount and lead their beasts. Kyra felt on edge the entire time, feeling as if they could be attacked at any moment, never able to relax in this forest.

She did not know what hurt her more: the cold or the hunger pains ripping through her stomach. Her muscles ached, and she couldn't feel her lips. She was miserable. She could hardly conceive their quest had barely begun.

After hours more passed, Leo began to whine. It was a strange noise—not his usual whine, but the one he reserved for times when he smelled food. At the same moment Kyra, too, smelled something—and Dierdre turned in the same direction and stared.

Kyra peered through the wood, but saw nothing. As they stopped and listened, she began to hear the faintest sound of activity somewhere up ahead.

Kyra was both excited by the smell and nervous about what that could mean: others were sharing this wood with them. She recalled her father's warning, and the last thing she wanted was a confrontation. Not here and not now.

Dierdre looked at her.

"I'm famished," Dierdre said.

Kyra, too, felt the hunger pangs.

"Whoever it is, on a night like this," Kyra replied, "I have a feeling they won't be keen to share."

"We have plenty of gold," Dierdre said. "Perhaps they will sell us some."

But Kyra shook her head, having a sinking feeling, while Leo whined and licked his lips, clearly famished, too.

"I don't think it's wise," Kyra said, despite the pains in her stomach. "We should stick to our path."

"And if we find no food?" Dierdre persisted. "We could all die of hunger out here. Our horses, too. It could be days, and this might be our only chance. Besides, we have little to fear. You have your weapons, I have mine, and we have Leo and Andor. If you need to, you could put three arrows in someone before he blinked—and we could be far off by then."

But Kyra hesitated, unconvinced.

"Besides, I doubt a hunter with a spit of meat will cause us all any harm," Dierdre added.

Kyra, sensing everyone else's hunger, their desire to pursue it, could resist no longer.

"I don't like it," she said. "Let us go slowly and see who it is. If we sense trouble, you must agree to leave before we get close."

Dierdre nodded.

"I promise you," she replied.

They all headed off, riding at a fast walk through the woods. As the smell grew stronger, Kyra saw a dim glow up ahead, and as they rode for it, her heart beat faster as she wondered who it could be out here.

They slowed as they approached, riding more cautiously, weaving between the trees. The glow grew brighter, the noise louder, the commotion greater, as Kyra sensed they were on the periphery of a large group of people.

Dierdre, less cautious, letting her hunger get the best of her, rode faster, moving up ahead and gaining a bit of distance.

"Dierdre!" Kyra hissed, urging her back.

But Dierdre kept moving, seemingly overcome by her hunger.

Kyra hurried to keep up with her, and as she did, the glow became brighter as Dierdre stopped at the edge of a clearing. As Kyra stopped beside her, looked past her into a clearing in the wood, she was shocked by what she saw.

There, in the clearing, were dozens of pigs roasting on spits, huge bonfires lighting up the night. The smell was captivating. Also in the clearing were dozens of men, and as Kyra squinted, her heart dropped to see they were Pandesian soldiers. She was shocked to see them here, sitting around fires, laughing, jesting with each other, holding sacks of wine, hands full of chunks of meat.

On the far side of the clearing, Kyra's heart dropped to see a cluster of iron carriages with bars. Dozens of gaunt faces stared out hungrily, the faces of boys and men, all desperate, all captives. Kyra realized at once what this was.

"The Flames," she hissed to Dierdre. "They are bringing them to The Flames."

Dierdre, still a good fifteen feet ahead, did not turn back, her eyes fixed on the roasting pigs.

"Dierdre!" Kyra hissed, feeling a sense of alarm. "We must leave this place at once!"

Dierdre, though, still did not listen, and Kyra, throwing caution to the wind, rushed forward to grab her.

No sooner had she reached her when suddenly, Kyra sensed motion out of the corner of her eyes. At the same moment Leo and Andor snarled—but it was too late. From out of the wood there suddenly emerged a group of Pandesian soldiers, casting a huge net before them.

Kyra turned and instinctively reached back to draw her staff, but there was no time. Before she could even register what was happening, Kyra felt the net falling down on her, binding her arms, and she realized, with a sinking heart, that they were all now slaves to Pandesia.

CHAPTER SEVEN

Alec flailed as he fell backwards, feeling the cold rush of air, his stomach dropping as he plummeted toward the ground and the pack of Wilvox below. He felt his life flash before his eyes. He had escaped the venomous bite of the creature above him only to fall to what would surely be an instant death below. Beside him, Marco flailed, too, the two of them falling together. It was little solace. Alec did not want to see his friend die, either.

Alec felt himself crashing into something, a dull pain on his back, and he expected to feel fangs sink into his flesh. But he was surprised to realize it was the muscular body of a Wilvox writhing beneath him. He had fallen so quickly that the Wilvox had had no time to react and he had landed flat on its back, it cushioning his fall as he knocked it to the ground.

There came a thump beside him, and Alec looked over to see Marco land atop one another Wilvox, flattening it, too, at least long enough to keep its snapping jaws away. That left only two other Wilvox to contend with. One of them leapt into action, lowering its jaws for Alec's exposed stomach.

Alec, still on his back, a Wilvox beneath him, allowed his instincts to take over, and as the beast leapt on top of him, he leaned back, raised his boots and put them up protectively over his head. The beast landed on top of them and as it did, Alec shoved with his feet and sent it flying backwards.

It landed several feet away in the snow, buying Alec precious time—and a second chance.

At the same time, Alec felt the beast beneath him wiggle out. It prepared to lunge and as it did, Alec reacted. He spun around quickly, wrapping one arm tightly around its throat in a chokehold, holding it close enough so that it could not bite, and squeezing as hard as he could. The creature struggled like mad in his grip, trying desperately to snap at him, and it took all of Alec's might to contain it. Somehow, he did. He squeezed tighter and tighter. The beast jerked away, turning and rolling in the snow, and Alec held on and rolled with it.

Out of the corner of his eye Alec spotted another beast charging for his now-exposed back, and he anticipated the feel of fangs sinking into his flesh. He had no time to react, so he did what was counterintuitive: still holding the Wilvox, he rolled onto his back, holding it out in front of him, its back atop his stomach, its legs kicking in the air. The other beast, airborne, landed with his fangs—and instead of finding a target in Alec, the fangs sunk into the exposed belly of the other beast. Alec held on tight, using it as a shield, as it shrieked and squirmed. Finally, he felt it go limp in his arms as its hot blood poured out all over him.

It was a moment both of victory and of profound sadness for him: Alec had never killed a living thing before. He did not hunt, like most of his friends, and he didn't believe in killing anything. Even though he knew the beast would have surely killed him, it still hurt him to see it die.

Alec suddenly felt a searing pain on his leg and he cried out and looked down to see another Wilvox biting him. He kicked his leg away before the fangs could sink any deeper and immediately jumped into action. He shoved the dead beast off of him, and as another Wilvox lunged for him, he scrambled to think. He felt cold steel pressing into his belly, and he remembered: his dagger. It was small—yet it might be just enough to do the trick. In a final act of desperation, Alec grabbed the dagger, stiffened his arm, and held it out in front of him.

The Wilvox came down and as it lowered its jaws for Alec, its throat was impaled on the blade. It let out an awful shriek as Alec held tight and the blade sank all the way in. Its blood poured all over Alec as it finally went limp, its razor-sharp fangs just inches from his face, its dead weight atop him.

Alec lay there, his heart thumping, unsure if he was alive or dead, covered in blackness from the beast's matted fur, which stuck to his face. He felt his leg throbbing where he had been bit, heard himself breathing, and he realized he was, somehow, still alive.

Suddenly a shriek ripped through the night air, and Alec snapped out of it and remembered: Marco.

Alec looked over to find Marco in dire straits: he was wrestling with a Wilvox, rolling in the snow, it snapping at him as he barely held back its jaws. As the beast snapped again, Marco's hands, slick with blood, slipped, and the beast's fangs came down and grazed his shoulder.

Marco cried out again, and Alec could see there wasn't much time. The other Wilvox lunged for Marco, too, who lay there prone, his back exposed, about to be killed.

Alec burst into action, not stopping to think twice about risking his life to save his friend. He ran for Marco with all he had, praying to God he made it before the beast did, each of them about ten feet away. They leapt into the air at the same time, the Wilvox to tear Marco apart and Alec to jump in the beast's way and take the injury in his stead.

Alec made it just in time, and as he did, he suddenly felt the horrific pain of the Wilvox's fangs sinking into his arm instead of Marco's. He had achieved his objective, had spared Marco from a lethal bite, but he had received a horrific bite in his stead, the pain intense.

Alec tumbled with the beast, throwing it off of him, clutching his arm in pain. He reached into his belt for his dagger, but he could not find it—and he remembered, too late, that he had left it lodged in the other beast's throat.

Alec lay on his back, barely holding back the Wilvox, now on all fours on his chest, and he felt himself losing strength. He was exhausted from the wound, from the fighting, and he was too weak to fight off this creature, all muscle, and determined to kill. As it leaned in, ever closer, its saliva dripping onto Alec's face, Alec knew he was out of options.

Alec looked for help from Marco, but he saw his friend still wrestling with a Wilvox himself, and losing strength, too. They would both die here, Alec realized, beside each other in the snow.

The Wilvox on top of him arched its back and prepared to sink its fangs into Alec's chest with one final strike, which Alec knew he was too weak to resist—when suddenly, it froze. He was baffled as it lingered there, let out an awful cry of agony, then collapsed limply on top of him.

Dead.

Alec was stumped. Had it been shot in the back by an arrow? By whom?

As he sat up to figure it out, Alec suddenly felt something awful and cold and slimy slithering up his leg—colder even than the snow. His heart skipped a beat as he looked down and realized it was the snake. It must have slithered down the tree and struck the Wilvox, killing it with its lethal venom. Ironically, it had saved Alec.

The snake-like creature slithered slowly, alternately crawling on its legs, like a millipede, around the dead Wilvox, coiling itself around its body, and Alec felt a terror even greater than he had when the Wilvox was on top of him. He scurried out from under it, eager to get away while the snake was distracted.

Alec scrambled to his hands and knees and rushed forward and charged the Wilvox still pinning down Marco. He kicked it as hard as he could, its ribs cracking as it went rolling off his friend, right before it could bite him. The beast whined and rolled in the snow, clearly caught off guard.

Alec yanked Marco to his feet, and Marco turned and charged the beast, kicking it as it tried to get up, again and again in the ribs. The beast rolled several feet, down a bank of snow, until it was out of sight.

"Let's go!" Alec urged.

Marco needed no prodding. They both took off, racing through the wood, the snake still coiled around the Wilvox, hissing and snapping at them as they went, barely missing them. Alec sprinted, his heart pounding in his chest, wanting to get as far away from here as possible.

They ran for their lives, bumping into trees, and as Alec glanced back over his shoulder, wanting to make sure they were in the clear, he saw something that made his heart drop: the final Wilvox. It just would not stop. It scrambled back up the snow bank, and now hunted them down as they ran. Much faster than they, it bounded through the snow, bearing down on them, its jaws widening, more determined than ever.

Alec looked forward and spotted something up ahead: two boulders, taller than he, a few feet apart, a narrow crevice between them. He suddenly had an idea.

"Follow me!" Alec cried.

Alec ran for the boulders as the Wilvox closed in behind them. He could hear it panting behind him in the snow, and he knew he had only one chance to get this right. He prayed his plan worked.

Alec leapt over the boulders, landing on the other side in the snow, as Marco did the same, right behind him. He stumbled in the snow, then turned and watched the Wilvox follow. It leapt up, too, and as he had hoped, the beast, unable to climb, and slipped on the rock and got lodged in the narrow crevice between the boulders.

It wiggled, trying to break free, but it could not. Finally, it was trapped.

Alec turned and examined the beast, breathing hard, flooded with relief. In pain, scratched up, the small bite on his leg hurting, and the big bite on his arm killing, Alec finally realized the nightmare was over. They were alive. Somehow, they had survived.

Marco looked at Alec, eyes filled with admiration.

"You did it," Marco said. "The kill is yours."

Alec stood there, hardly a foot away from the helpless beast, which was snarling, wanting to tear them apart. He knew he should feel nothing but hatred for it. But despite himself, he pitied it. It was a living thing, after all, and trapped, helpless.

Alec hesitated.

Marco reached down, picked up a jagged rock, and handed it to him. Alec held the rock, sharp and heavy, and knew that one decisive blow could kill this creature. He held the rock, feeling the cold weight of it on his palm, and his hand trembled. He could not bring himself to do it.

Finally, he dropped it in the snow.

"What is it?" Marco asked.

"I can't," Alec said. "I can't kill something helpless. However much it may deserve it. Let us go. It can't harm us now."

Marco stared back, shocked.

"But it will break free!" he exclaimed.

Alec nodded.

"It will. But by then, we shall be far from here."

Marco furrowed his brow.

"I don't understand," he said. "It tried to kill you. It wounded you—and me."

Alec wished he could explain it, but he did not fully understand it himself. Finally, he sighed.

"It was something my brother once said to me," Alec said. "When you kill something, you murder some small part of the world."

Alec turned to Marco.

"Let's go," Alec said.

Alec turned to go, but Marco held out a hand and stepped forward.

"You saved my life," Marco said, reverence in his voice. "That wound on your arm you received because of me. If it wasn't for you, I'd be dead back there. I owe you."

"You owe me nothing," Alec replied.

"You risked your life for me," Marco said.

Alec sighed.

"Who would I be if I did not risk my life for others?" Alec said.

They clasped arms, and Alec knew that no matter what happened, no matter what dangers lay ahead of them, he now had a brother for life.

CHAPTER EIGHT

Merk stood in the mud, opposite the ten remaining thugs, all facing him nervously. They held before them their crude weapons and looked back and forth from their dead leader to Merk, now all seeming less certain of themselves. As flames burned all around him, black smoke stinging his eyes in waves, Merk remained calm, preparing for the confrontation to come.

"Drop your weapons and run," Merk said, "and you will live. I won't offer again."

One of them, a tall brute with wide shoulders and a scar across his chin, grunted back.

"You're a proud one, aren't you?" he said in a thick accent Merk did not understand. "You really think you can take us all?"

"There are still ten of us and one of you," another called back.

Merk laughed, shaking his head.

"You still don't understand," he said. "You're already dead. You just don't know it yet."

He stared back at them with his cold, black eyes, the eyes of a killer, and he could see the fear starting to take hold. It was a look he'd recognized his entire life.

One of the men suddenly let out a shout and charged, raising his sword, filled with more bravado than skill. An amateur mistake.

Merk watched him come out of the corner of his eye but did not let on that he knew. He waited and watched, and at the final moment, as the sword came down for his back, he squatted low and felt the thug rush forward. As he felt his body against his back, his sloppy sword slash whiz over his head, he grabbed the thug and threw him over his shoulder. The man went flying, landing on his back in the mud before him, and Merk stepped forward and with his boot, expertly and precisely crushed his windpipe, killing him.

That left nine.

Another thug charged, swinging his sword down at him, and as he did, Merk calmly took the sword from the man he had just killed, sidestepped, and sliced the man's stomach, sending him keeling over.

Two more broke off and charged together, one swinging a crude flail and the other wielding a mace. The flail was a clumsy swing, all power and no finesse, and Merk merely jumped back and let the spiked ball whiz by his face, then stepped forward and plunged his dagger into the man's waist. In the same motion he spun, as the other attacker swung his mace, and slashed his throat.

Merk grabbed the man's mace, turned, planted his feet, and threw the mace at another charging attacker; it sailed end over end and smashed the man's eye socket, stopping him in his tracks and knocking him out.

The five remaining thugs now looked at Merk, then back to each other, exchanging looks of fear and wonder.

Merk smiled as he wiped blood off his lip with the back of his hand.

"I'm going to enjoy watching you all die here, in the same place you killed this nice family."

One of them scowled.

"The only one who'll be dying here is you," spat one.

"A few lucky blows," said another. "We still outnumber you five to one."

Merk smiled.

"Those odds are starting to look a lot worse for you now, aren't they?" he replied.

"You got anything else to say before we kill you?" another snapped, a big man speaking in an accident Merk did not recognize.

Merk smiled.

"That's what I like," Merk replied. "Courage in the face of death."

The man, bigger than all others, threw down his weapon and charged Merk, as if to tackle him and drive him down to the mud. Clearly, this man wanted to fight on his own terms.

If there was one thing Merk had learned, it was never to fight on another man's terms. As the clumsy oaf charged him, his thick hands stretched out before him to tear him apart, Merk made no effort to get out of the way. Instead, he waited until the man was a foot away, squatted, and brought his dagger straight up as the man lowered his chin. It was an uppercut with a knife.

He impaled the blade in the man's throat in an upward motion, dropping him straight down to the ground. The thug fell face-first, dead, the blood pooling in the mud.

The four remaining looked down at their huge compatriot, lifeless, and this time they held real fear in their eyes.

The thug nearest him raised his hands, shaking.

"Okay," he said. "I'll leave." The boy, hardly older than twenty, threw his sword down to the mud. "Just let us go."

Merk grinned, feeling his veins burning with indignation at the sight of the dead family, at the smell of the smoke burning in his nostrils. He stooped down and casually picked up the boy's sword.

"Sorry, my friend," Merk said. "That time has passed."

Merk charged forward and stabbed the boy in the heart, holding him tight as he pulled his face close.

"Tell me," Merk seethed, "which one of this precious family did you murder?"

The boy gasped, blood trickling from his mouth as he fell dead in Merk's arms.

The three thugs all charged for Merk at once, as if realizing this was their last desperate chance.

Merk took two steps forward, jumped in the air, and kicked one in the chest, knocking him to the ground. As another swung a club for his head, Merk ducked, then rammed his shoulder into the man's stomach and threw him over his shoulder, sending him landing on his back. Merk stepped forward and with his boots crushed one man's windpipe, then stepped on the other's chin and snapped his neck, killing both.

That left one.

The sole survivor rushed forward nervously and swung a sword for his head; Merk ducked, feeling it whiz by, and in the same motion grabbed a club from the ground, swung around, and whacked the man on the back of the head. There came a crack, and the man stumbled forward and landed in the mud, out cold.

Merk saw him lying there and knew he could kill him—but he had another idea: he wanted justice.

Merk dragged the man to his feet, holding him in a chokehold as he dragged him forward. He walked him across the mud, toward the girl, who stood there, aghast, hatred in her eyes.

Merk stopped a foot away from her, holding the writhing man tight.

"Please, let me go!" the man whined. "It wasn't my fault!"

"The decision is the girl's," Merk snarled in the man's ear.

Merk saw the grief, the desire for vengeance, in her eyes. With his free hand he reached into his belt and handed her his dagger, hilt first.

"Please, don't," the man sobbed. "I didn't do anything!"

The girl's expression darkened as she grabbed Merk's dagger and stared back at the man.

"Didn't you?" she asked, her voice cold and hard. "I watched you kill my mother. I watched you kill my family."

Without waiting for a response, the girl lunged forward and stabbed the man in the heart.

Merk felt the thug stiffen in his arms as he gasped, and was surprised and impressed by the girl's perfect strike, her ruthlessness.

The man's body went limp, and Merk let him drop down to the ground, dead.

Merk stood there facing the girl, who held the bloody dagger in her hand, and looked down at the corpse. She was breathing hard, her face still filled with fury, as if her desire were unfulfilled. Merk understood the feeling, all too well.

She slowly looked up at him, and as she did, her expression shifted, and he could see the gratitude in her eyes. And for the first time in as long as he could remember, he felt good about himself. He had saved her life. For a fleeting moment, at least, he had become the person he wanted to be.

With the battlefield still, with all the thugs dead, Merk allowed himself to lower his guard, just for a moment. He stepped forward to embrace the girl, to hold her, to let her know that everything would be okay.

But as he did, he suddenly noticed motion out of the corner of his eye. He turned and was shocked to see the boy with the crossbow, the one he'd thought he'd killed, somehow back unsteadily on his feet, even with the sword through his chest. He held the bow with shaking arms, and aimed it right for Merk. For the first time in his life, Merk was caught off-guard. His caring for this girl had dulled his senses.

69

There came the awful sound of an arrow being fired, and Merk stood there, frozen, no time to react. All he could do was watch helplessly as the arrow flew through the air, right for him.

A split second later, he felt the horrific agony of an arrowhead hitting his back, entering his flesh.

Merk sank to his knees in the mud, spitting up blood, and as he did, what surprised him most was not that he would die, but that he would die *here*, at the hands of a boy, in the mud, in the middle of nowhere, so close, after such a long trek to starting life again.

CHAPTER NINE

Kyra struggled against the heavy net as it fell down upon her, caught by surprise, trying desperately to break free. Cast by several soldiers, the net, made of a steel and rope mesh, must have weighed a hundred pounds, and she found herself pinned down by the thick rope as the men yanked on every side, stretching it tight.

They yanked again, and she found herself flattened, face-down in the snow with the others, all pinned down. Andor and Leo snarled viciously, bucking, writhing, and while Leo turned and sank his fangs into the net, his efforts were useless, the steel too hard to chew through.

As Kyra watched the Pandesian soldiers closing in, wielding swords and halberds, she kicked herself for not being more vigilant. She knew that if she did not find a way out, they would all end up back in bondage, with a brutal imprisonment, and this time, a likely death. She could not let that happen. Most of all, she could not let her father down. Whatever the cost, she had to escape.

Kyra struggled as she groaned and reached for her staff, unable to grab it, her arms pinned to the ground. She tried desperately to break free and she knew their situation was dire.

There came a horrific noise, like a lion bursting from its cage, and slowly, to Kyra's surprise, the net began to rise. Kyra turned and was shocked to see Andor, using his tremendous strength to somehow gain his feet. To her shock, he twisted his neck, reached out with his huge fangs, and tore right through it.

It was the most incredible thing Kyra had ever seen. This miraculous beast, a pure specimen of power, chewed through the steel rope and, in a fit of rage, shook his head and tore it to bits. He stood higher and higher, raising the net for all of them, and a moment later, Kyra found herself unrestrained.

Andor leapt forward in a single bound and sank his fangs into the chest of the closest soldier, a man whose eyes opened three times as wide at the sight of him. The man fell, instantly killed.

71

Andor then swung his head to the side and as another soldier charged him with a sword, he used his fangs to slice his chest in two.

Two more soldiers charged from behind and Andor leaned back and kicked them with his mighty hooves, his kick so powerful that he cracked all their ribs and caved in their chests, knocking them to the ground, unconscious.

Kyra spotted a soldier train his crossbow on Andor and she realized that, in a moment, he would be fatally wounded. She felt a rush of panic, realizing she would not be able to reach him in time.

"LEO!" she cried, knowing instinctively that Leo, closer, would know what to do.

Leo burst into action: he charged across the snow, leapt into the air and landed on all fours on the soldier's chest, sinking his fangs into his throat as the man shrieked. He pinned him to the ground and the arrow went flying harmlessly up into the air, sparing Andor's life.

Two more soldiers stepped forward, each raising their bows and aiming at Andor, and Kyra drew her staff, separated it, and stepped forward and threw each half. They flew through the air like spears, and each sharpened end lodged in one of the soldier's chests. The men cried out as they fell to their backs, their arrows shooting up into the trees, hitting branches with a thwack and bringing down a clump of snow onto the forest floor.

Kyra heard a noise and felt something whizz by her head. She turned to see a spear fly by and just miss her, and saw two more soldiers charging, hardly twenty feet away. Each looked determined to kill her as they drew their swords.

Kyra, in battle mode, forced herself to focus: she reached back, drew her bow, placed an arrow and fired. She did not wait to see if it met its mark before she fired again.

Each shot landed in the chest of an attacker as they charged for her, felling them.

Kyra suddenly heard a noise behind her, wondering how many soldiers were out there, how many would emerge from these blackened woods. She turned, too late, to realize a soldier had snuck up behind her, his sword raised and about to slash her arm. She braced herself, the man too close to deflect the blow.

The soldier, though, cried out and fell, lifeless, in the snow beside her. Kyra stared, baffled, wondering what had happened.

She looked up to see Dierdre standing a few feet away, her bow raised, having just fired. She looked down and saw the arrow piercing through the soldier's back. She felt a rush of gratitude. She saw a fierceness in her friend's eyes she had not seen before, could see that the vengeance her friend was taking on these Pandesians was cathartic for her.

Kyra thought the battle was over—but she suddenly heard a rustling in the wood, and she turned to see a soldier taking off. She recalled what happened last time she'd let someone escape, and without thinking she turned, set him in her sights, raised her bow, and fired.

The arrow landed in his back and the man fell face-first in the snow. Dierdre looked at her as if with surprise, but this time, Kyra felt no remorse. Kyra wondered what was happening to her. Who was she becoming?

Kyra stood there, breathing hard in the silence, surveying the carnage. Several soldiers lay there, their blood seeping into the snow, all dead. She looked over at Andor, Leo, and Dierdre, and slowly realized they had won. The four of them had become one unit.

Kyra kissed Leo's head then walked over to Andor, still snarling at the dead soldiers, and caressed his mane.

"You did it, boy," she said to him gratefully. "You freed us."

Andor let out a sound, like a purr, but harsher, and for the first time, his visage softened a bit.

Dierdre shook her head remorsefully.

"You were right," she said. "It was stupid of me to come here. I'm sorry."

Kyra turned and looked out through the wood line, across the clearing, remembering the food. The pigs were still roasting there, hundreds of Pandesian soldiers close by, still not alerted to their presence. She saw all the carriages, too, the faces of all those boys, and it tormented her.

"We are lucky they didn't spot us," Dierdre said. "This must have been a patrol group. Let us go. We need to get as far away as we can, before they do."

But slowly, Kyra shook her head.

"I'm thinking the opposite," Kyra replied.

Dierdre furrowed her brow.

"What do you mean?"

Kyra looked back over her shoulder, at the trail back to freedom, and she knew the safe thing to do would be to ride off quickly and quietly, to continue on her quest.

Yet she also felt that sometimes, it was the detours on a journey that ended up mattering most. She felt as if she were being tested. How many times had her father told her that the ultimate quest in life was to leave no man behind? No matter how far you went, how high you climbed, how far your renown spread, at the end of the day, all that mattered, he had said, all that man could be judged by, was not how far he had went, but how much he had looked back. How many he had taken with him.

She was beginning to understand. Here was her test: an open road to freedom, to safety. Or a road of peril, behind her, across that clearing, to free boys she did not even know. It was, she felt, the right thing to do. And was justice not what mattered most?

She felt it burning in her veins. She had to risk her life, whatever the danger. If she were to turn her back on them, who would she be?

"You're not thinking what I think you're thinking?" Dierdre asked, sounding incredulous.

Kyra nodded.

"It is a long ride across the clearing," she said, a plan formulating in her mind. "But our horses are fast."

"And then what?" Dierdre asked in disbelief. "That is an army out there. We cannot outrun them. And we cannot defeat them. It will mean our deaths."

Kyra shook her head.

"We will make for the carriages. We will sever the chains, free those boys, and when they are on the loose, the Pandesians will have bigger problems to deal with."

Dierdre smiled wide.

"You are wild and reckless," she said. "I knew there was a reason I liked you."

The two exchanged a smile, and without another word, they mounted their horses and took off, galloping into the clearing, throwing all caution to the wind.

The group burst across the clearing, Kyra's heart slamming in her chest as she crossed the snow in the moonlight, hundreds of Pandesian soldiers gathered at the other end, none seeing her yet. She knew that if they detected her before they got close enough, they would never make it.

As they rode, Kyra clutching the sword she had snatched from a fallen soldier, none took notice. These men, apparently, were too distracted by their fires, their feasting, and their drink to be on the lookout for a small group charging in the middle of the night.

Kyra tore across the clearing, her adrenaline coursing so wildly that she could barely see straight. And as she neared the end of the clearing, the carriages looming closer, she saw the faces of the boys in finer detail, looking out desperately, and she watched as some of them began to spot her, to understand. Their faces, so desperate a moment before, suddenly filled with hope.

"Over here!" one boy yelled out, shattering the night's silence.

"Free us!" yelled another.

A great chorus began to rise up inside the carriages, followed by the clanging of iron as the boys slammed shackles against the bars. Kyra desperately willed for them to quiet, but it was too late— the Pandesians turned and began to take notice.

"You there! Stop!" a Pandesian commanded, yelling through the night.

Soldiers jumped up and began to charge them.

Kyra's heart slammed, realizing her window was narrowing; if she didn't free these boys before the Pandesians arrived, she would be dead. But yards away, she kicked Andor harder, as Dierdre kicked her horse, and they each raised their swords and bore down on the carriages packed with screaming boys.

Kyra did not even slow as she rode up beside a carriage, raised her sword high, and brought it down in a great slash, aiming for the thick, iron chains. Sparks flew as the chain, severed, fell to the ground with a great clank.

The metal gate creaked open and there came a great shout and rush of excitement as dozens of boys rushed out, stepping over each other, stumbling into the snow, some wearing boots, others barefoot. Some of them took off, running for the safety of the woods; but most turned around and charged for the wall of incoming Pandesian soldiers, vengeance in their eyes.

Kyra and Dierdre raced from carriage to carriage, slashing the chains, opening the gates, freeing one after the next. One gate would not give, and Leo bounded forward, bit the bars with his fangs, and pulled it open. Another door was stuck, and Andor leaned back and reared his legs and kicked until it shattered.

Soon hundreds of boys poured into the forest clearing. They did not have weapons, but they had heart, and a clear desire for vengeance against their captors. The Pandesian soldiers must have realized, because even while they charged, their eyes soon began to fill with doubt and hesitation.

The boys let out a great shout, and as one they rushed the soldiers. The Pandesians raised swords and killed some of them—but the boys came on too fast and soon the soldiers had no room to maneuver. The mob of boys tackled them to the ground and soon it was hand to hand. Some boys knocked the soldiers out, then stripped them of their weapons and charged for the others. Soon the army of boys became armed.

The forest clearing quickly became filled with cries and shrieks, the sounds of boys liberated and of Pandesian soldiers dying.

Kyra, satisfied, exchanged a look with Dierdre. Their job here was done. The boys had their freedom—now it was up to them to win it.

Kyra turned and raced back for the wood line, away from the clearing, from the shouts of boys and men. Kyra felt arrows flying by her head, just missing her and she looked back and saw a few Pandesian archers had set their sights on them. She urged Andor harder and ducked low, and with one final burst they left the clearing and returned back into the woods, embraced by the darkness. As she did, one final arrow sailed by, just missing her, embedding itself in a tree with a thwack.

They rode back into the darkness, heading north again, toward the sea, wherever it was, while behind them there slowly faded the sounds of the battle, of hundreds of boys embracing their freedom.

She had no idea what the road ahead might bring, but it mattered little: she had not cowered from a fight, and that meant more than anything.

CHAPTER TEN

Duncan raised his sword high, let out a fierce battle cry, and led his men as he charged forward fearlessly, ready to meet the Pandesian army pouring out of the Esephan barracks. These men had clearly recovered from the initial shock of being attacked in the middle of the night, of their fleet being set aflame in the harbor, and Duncan was surprised himself at how much damage he had managed to inflict. The night sky was ablaze behind him with what remained of their fleet, lighting up the harbor and the night sky.

Yet however great that blow was, there still remained this army before him, this Pandesian garrison stationed on land, vastly outnumbering his men. An endless stream poured out as the stone gates opened wider, all professional soldiers, fully armed with superior weaponry, well-trained and eager for battle. Duncan knew the true battle had not even begun.

Duncan was proud to see none of his men back down, all riding beside him, joining him as he hoped they would. They all re-mounted their horses and galloped bravely, rushing to meet the enemy, swords raised, axes and halberds high, spears aimed, prepared for death or honor.

Duncan always prided himself on being first in battle, out in front of his men, and he was determined that this night be no different. He surged ahead and let out a great cry as he raised his sword high and brought it down on the shield of the lead Pandesian soldier, a man who, by his armor, appeared to be an officer.

As Duncan's sword hit, a great clang rang out and sparks flew, the first sparks of battle. The soldier swung back, and Duncan, anticipating it, parried, then swung around and slashed the man across the chest, knocking him off his horse and onto the ground— the first casualty of the battle.

The night air was filled with the sudden clash of arms, swords meeting each other, shields meeting swords, axes, halberds, men shouting and groaning and shrieking as they fell from horses and hacked each other to death. The battle lines quickly became blurred as the two sides melted into each other, each fighting viciously for survival.

Duncan saw Anvin, beside him, swing a flail and saw its spiked metal ball knock a soldier backwards off his horse. He saw Arthfael hurl his spear and pierce the throat of a soldier before him, a broad man who had raised a sword for Duncan. He watched one of his largest soldiers, swing his halberd sideways, chop a Pandesian in his shoulder, and knock him sideways off his horse. Duncan filled with pride at his men. They were all formidable soldiers, the best Escalon had to offer, and they all fought fiercely for their homeland. For their freedom.

The Pandesians, though, rallied, and fought back just as fiercely. They were a professional army, one that had been on the road in conquest for years, and not a force to be deterred easily. Duncan's heart fell as he saw many good men fall on his side, too, men he had known and fought with his entire life. He watched one man, a boy barely his son's age, fall straight back beside him as a spear pierced his shoulder. He saw another lose a hand as a battle axe came straight down upon it.

Duncan fought back with all he had, cutting a path through the carnage, slashing soldiers left and right, urging his horse on, forcing himself forward at all costs, way deeper than all his men. He knew that to stop meant death. He soon found himself completely immersed in battle, surrounded by the enemy on all sides. That was the way he liked to fight—for his very life.

Duncan spun and slashed from side to side, and he caught the Pandesians off guard; they were clearly surprised to find the enemy so deep in their ranks. When he was not slashing, he raised his shield and used it to block blows from swords, maces, clubs—and to smash men sideways off their horses. A shield, he knew, could sometimes be the best—and most unexpected—weapon.

Duncan spun and head-butted one soldier, then yanked a sword from another's hand, pulled him close and stabbed him in the gut with a dagger. Yet at the same moment Duncan received a sword slash himself, a particularly painful one on his shoulder. A moment later he received one on his thigh. He spun and killed both attackers. The injuries were painful, but they were all surface wounds, he knew, and he had suffered enough wounds in his life to not let them startle him. He had received much worse in his lifetime.

No sooner had he killed his attackers than he received a powerful blow as a Pandesian clubbed him in the ribs—and a moment later he found himself falling sideways off his horse and into the throng of men.

Duncan shook off stars and gained his feet, sword in hand, ready to go, and found himself facing a mix of soldiers, some on foot, others on horseback. He reached up, grabbed a soldier by his leg, and dragged him off his horse; the man fell and immediately Duncan mounted his horse. He snatched his lance in the process and swung it around, knocking three soldiers off their horses and clearing a space.

The battle raged on. A seemingly endless array of Pandesian soldiers poured out of the barracks, and with each company of men that appeared, Duncan knew his odds were worsening. He saw his men beginning to falter: one of his younger warriors took a spear in the ribs, blood gushing from his mouth—and a warrior who had just joined his ranks took a fatal sword slash to the chest.

Duncan, though, would not give up; that was not who he was. There would be no retreat, whatever the odds. He had been through many a battle that had seemed bleak, and never once had he turned and fled, as had many of his compatriots. It was what had earned him his reputation, and the respect of the men of Escalon. He might lead them to death, they knew, but he would never lead them to dishonor.

Duncan redoubled his efforts: he charged forward, let out a great cry, and leapt down from his horse holding his lance sideways before him—and taking down several men. He charged, on foot, deeper into the crowd, using the lance and knocking over soldiers in every direction. It was a suicide charge, but he no longer cared—and in that moment of no longer caring, he felt a great liberation, a greater freedom than he had ever experienced.

When Duncan's lance was chopped in half by a soldier, he used its jagged end to stab a soldier, then dropped it, drew his sword and swung with both hands, foregoing his shield and throwing caution to the wind. He slashed and hacked until his shoulders grew tired and sweat stung his eyes, faster than all the others around him—but quickly losing steam. It was a final death charge, and while he knew he would not make it, he took solace in the fact that at least he would die giving it all he had.

As Duncan's shoulders grew tired and several soldiers charged him, as he knew he was looking death in the face, suddenly, there came a whistling sound, like an arrow, followed by a single thwack. To Duncan's shock, the soldier before him fell on his back, an arrow lodged in his chest.

There came another. Then another. Soon the air was filled with the noise, and as the cries of Pandesians rang out, Duncan looked behind him and was amazed at what he saw: the moonlit sky was filled with arrows, a sea of them flying high overhead and landing on the Pandesian side. Pandesians, pierced by the sea of arrows, dropped like flies, falling one by one from their horses. Some fell back, while others keeled over sideways from their horses, landing in the bloody field of battle, their arming clanging and their horses, riderless, bucking wildly.

Duncan was confused; at first, he had assumed that his men were under attack. But then he realized he was being helped. But by whom?

Duncan turned and looked to the source of the arrows and saw, high upon the ramparts of the city of Esephus, scores of men, lit up by torchlight. They were, his heart lifted to see, Esephan warriors, bows drawn, placing arrows and firing down in a high arc toward the Pandesian side. Duncan cried out with joy. Seavig, after all, had decided to risk it all and join him.

Suddenly, the gates of Esephus opened and there appeared, with a great battle cry, Seavig, riding out before hundreds of his men, all proud warriors of Escalon. Duncan was thrilled at the sight of his old friend, a man he had ridden into battle with countless times, riding at the head of his small army. Here was a soldier who had been subjugated by Pandesia for years, and who was finally making a stand. He had returned, was back to being the warrior Duncan once knew he was.

With a great surge of momentum, Seavig charged forward and joined Duncan's men, and they began to push the Pandesians back. Duncan's men let out a great shout, rushing forward, invigorated, and Duncan could see the newfound fear on the faces of the

Pandesians. Clearly, they had expected the men of Esephus to toe the line and roll over. They realized that Duncan's force had just doubled in size, and they were beginning to panic. He had seen it one too many times on his enemies' faces—and he knew what that meant: now was his chance.

Duncan surged forward, taking advantage of their fear, driving them back further as he led his men. Whatever Pandesians were spared by the arrows, Duncan and his men hacked down. Chaos began to ensue as the tide of battle began to swing the other way. The Pandesians, faltering, began backtracking—and then turned and ran.

Duncan pursued them, his men close behind, Seavig nearby as he led his men in a charge, too, the air filled with their victorious shouts. As the Pandesians tried to make it back to the safety of their stone barracks, to close the gate, Duncan reached the gate first, hacking down the soldiers who tried to yank it closed. He stabbed one in the gut, butted another in the face with the hilt of his sword, then kicked a third.

The Pandesians soon abandoned the idea of closing the gate and merely ran back for their barracks. Duncan searched for their commander, realizing he had to cut off the army's head, and he spotted him amidst the crowd, decorated with Pandesian insignias.

Duncan cut his way through the ranks of soldiers, heading for him, until finally he reached him and forced him to face off with him. They stood opposite each other, each holding out his sword, while a space was cleared and a small crowd formed around them. Duncan could feel all the eyes upon them, and he knew their match would determine the outcome of this battle.

They each charged and fought viciously. This man was a far better fighter than the others, and Duncan was surprised at the strength and speed of his blows. Sparks flew as back and forth their swords met, neither able to gain an edge, driving each other from one end to the other. Here, finally, was an opponent whom Duncan could respect; he regretted not having him as a warrior of Escalon.

Finally, Duncan, losing strength, slipped; yet as he did, he found his opening. The leader raised his sword, and Duncan lunged forward and tackled him, driving his shoulder into the man's stomach.

Duncan drove him down to the snow-covered ground, pinned him down, and drew his short sword, pressing it to his throat.

"YIELD!" Duncan commanded, as the crowd grew quiet, a lull in the fighting forming around them. "Yield, and be our prisoners, and I shall not kill you or your men!"

"Yield to you?" the man spat back. "You are no king! You are a mere slave of Escalon!"

"I shall not ask again," Duncan warned darkly.

The commander blinked several times, gasping for breath, clearly realizing Duncan's seriousness.

Finally, he nodded.

"WE YIELD!" he cried.

There came a great shout of victory amidst Duncan's and Seavig's men, as all the Pandesian soldiers, their backs to the wall, quickly laid down their arms, looking all too happy to accept the offer. None, clearly, had any heart left in the fight.

Duncan felt several strong hands clasp him on the back in admiration, as his men rushed forward and stripped the enemy of their swords and armor. One cheer after another rose, as his men all began to realize that they had achieved the impossible: Pandesia had been defeated. Esephus, one of the most important cities in Escalon, had been liberated.

The unthinkable had happened.

Against all odds, Escalon was winning.

*

Duncan walked alongside the Esephus harbor, joined by Seavig, Anvin, Arthfael and dozens of their men, all inspecting the damage. The smell of smoke hung heavy in the air as the Pandesian fleet still burned, their embers sparking in the night, punctuated by the occasional whoosh of a beam as a mast collapsed. It was like the entire harbor was alight in a great bonfire.

All about them Duncan's and Seavig's men corralled the hundreds of captive Pandesian soldiers, shepherding them, in shackles, toward the fort's dungeon. His men were also occupied with reaching over the harborside with long hooks, pulling in floating debris, valuable treasures and weaponry; they occasionally pulled in a floating corpse, too, before letting it go.

Duncan looked all up and down the shoreline, littered with bloated corpses, the greatest destruction he'd ever seen to Pandesian soldiers, and probably the greatest damage he'd ever inflicted on an invading army—and he felt a great sense of satisfaction.

Torches were extinguished, one by one, as the night sky slowly gave way to a breaking dawn, the sky brilliant with a million colors, lightening with each step they took. Duncan felt as if the world were being reborn.

"It is a thing of wonder," said Seavig, strolling beside Duncan, his voice low and gruff.

Duncan turned and looked at his old friend, with his long, wild black hair, beard and bushy eyebrows, just as he remembered him. He looked windswept, his face chaffed from too many days at sea under the open sun.

"What is that?" Duncan asked.

"What speed and surprise can do in battle," Seavig replied. "It can turn prepared men into objects of fear; it can allow a hundred to defeat a thousand."

He turned to Duncan.

"You were always the greatest of us all," he added. "What you did here, on this night, shall be recorded for all time. You have freed our great city, a city that I did not think could be freed. And you have done it in the face of a vast empire, knowing that vengeance and death would be a certainty."

Seavig clasped a hand on his shoulder.

"You are a true warrior," he added, "and a true friend. My people thank you. I thank you."

Duncan shook his head humbly.

"What I did," he replied, "I did for justice. For freedom. No more than you did yourself. I did what the old king should have done years ago. What I myself should have done years ago. And we would not have won tonight, do not forget, if it hadn't been for you and your men."

Seavig stopped and sighed.

"And now?" Seavig asked.

They came to a stop toward the harbor's end, and Duncan turned and studied his friend's earnest expression. Seavig's face, filled with lines, bore the rough, hardened look of the seasons, of this city by the sea and the rough waves and winds that shaped it.

"And now," Duncan replied, "we have but one choice. What I began, I must finish. Retreat, safety—these are things of the past. Most of Escalon remains occupied. I will not be safe in Volis—nor you in Esephus—any longer. Soon, word shall spread, the vast Pandesian army will assemble. I cannot wait; I must bring the battle to them, before they can prepare. Every city in Escalon must be freed."

Seavig slowly raised his hands to his hips and studied the water, as the early morning sun lit it a glowing aqua. They stood there and watched the dawn, two hardened warriors enjoying a comfortable silence of victory, two warriors thinking the same way.

"I know I will die one day," Seavig said. "That does not bother me. I only care to die well."

Seavig paused, examining the ebb and flow of the tide, lapping against the stone wall.

"I never knew if I would have the strength to die in trying to win back my freedom. You've done me a great service, my friend. You have allowed me to remember what matters most in life."

Seavig reached up and clasped Duncan's shoulder with his calloused hand.

"I am with you," he said, his voice solemn. "I and my men are with you. We shall ride by your side, wherever you shall go. Across all of Escalon. Stronghold to stronghold. Until every last one of us is free—even to the gates of death."

Duncan's heart warmed at his words, and he slowly smiled back, thrilled to have his old friend by his side.

"Where to next, my friend?" Seavig asked.

Duncan reflected.

"We must chop off the head first," he replied, "and the body shall follow."

Seavig looked back questioningly.

"You mean to take the capital," he then said knowingly.

Duncan nodded.

"And to take Andros," Duncan replied, "we will need the high ground. And the men who own the heights."

Seavig's eyes lit with recognition and excitement.

"Kos?" he asked.

Duncan nodded, knowing his friend understood.

Seavig looked off into the water and shook his head.

"Reaching Kos is no easy thing," Seavig replied. "The way is spotted with Pandesian garrisons. You will find yourself enmeshed in battle before you even reach the cliffs."

Duncan studied him, appreciating his insight.

"I am a man of Volis," Duncan replied. "This is your region, old friend. You know your terrain far better than I. What would you suggest?"

Seavig rubbed his beard as he stared off into the sea, clearly deep in thought.

"If you aim for Kos," Seavig replied, "you must reach the Lake of Ire first. Skirt its shores, and it will lead to The Thusius. It is the river you need. It is the only way. Go by land and you'll be trapped in a war."

He turned and looked meaningfully at Duncan.

"I know the way," Seavig said. "Let me show you."

Duncan smiled back, and clasped his friend's arm.

"I and my men will leave now," Duncan replied, satisfied with the plan. "You can join us when you are rested."

Seavig laughed.

"Rested?" he replied, smiling wider. "I fought all night—I am more rested than I've ever been."

CHAPTER ELEVEN

As dawn broke over the fort of Volis, Aidan frantically paced its ramparts, searching the horizon for any sign of his father, or Kyra, or his brothers—or any of the men. He had been up most of the night in a state of unease, tormented by nightmares of his sister falling into a pit, of his father being burned alive in a harbor. He had paced these ramparts under the night's sky, the stars aglow, and had not stopped searching the countryside for them since, anxious for their return.

Deep down, Aidan suspected they were not returning to Volis any time soon—if at all. Kyra was heading west across Escalon, through a treacherous terrain, and his father, brothers, and their men were heading somewhere south, into battle and likely death. Aidan burned inside. He wanted more than anything to be with them, especially at this time of war. He knew what was happening was once in a lifetime, and he could not stand the thought, however young he was, of sitting on the sidelines. Aidan knew he was smaller than them all, still young, weak, and untrained; yet he still felt there was much he could do. He might not be able to throw a spear, or fire an arrow, as well as the others, but he was known for his smarts, his resourcefulness, for being able to look a situation differently than everyone else, and he felt he could help his father somehow.

No matter what, he knew for certain he didn't want to be sitting here, in the nearly empty fort of Volis, far from the action, safe behind these gates with the women and the children and the geese running around the courtyard, as if nothing were happening out there in the world. He was just waiting out his days, with nothing to do but anticipate news of arriving death. He would rather die than live this way.

As dawn broke and the sky lighted, Aidan surveyed the fort, saw the dozen or so warriors his father had left behind left behind to guard the place, a skeleton force. He had been pestering these men half the night to tell him where exactly his father had ridden. But none would tell. Aidan felt a fresh wave of determination to find out.

Sensing motion out of the corner of his eye, Aidan turned to see Vidar crossing the courtyard with several men, they extinguishing torches as they went and he assigning each their posts throughout the fort. Aidan burst into action, running down the spiral staircase, twisting down level after level, determined to corner Vidar until he had the answers he wanted.

Aidan hit the ground running as he reached the snowy courtyard. He ran, ice crunching beneath his boots in the frigid morning, breathing hard as he sprinted for Vidar, who headed for the gates.

"Vidar!" he cried.

Vidar turned and, when he saw it was Aidan, looked away, rolling his eyes, clearly wanting to avoid him. He began to walk away.

"I have no answers for you, young Aidan," he called back as he walked away, he and his men marching for the gates, blowing on their hands to keep them warm.

But Aidan did not slow, running to catch up.

"I must know where my father is!" he shouted.

The men continued to march, and Aidan doubled his speed, slipping on the ice, until finally he reached Vidar's side and tugged on his shirt.

"My father is gone, and that makes me commander of this fort!" Aidan insisted, knowing he was pushing his luck, but desperate.

Vidar stopped and laughed with his men.

"Does it?" he asked.

"Answer me!" Aidan pressed. "Where is he? I can help him! My sword is as strong as yours and my aim as true!"

Vidar laughed heartily, and as all the men joined him, Aidan reddened. He shook his head and clasped Aidan's shoulder, his hand strong and reassuring.

"You are your father's son," he said, smiling, "yet even so, I cannot tell you where he went. I know that as soon as I do, you will venture after him—and that I cannot allow. You are under my watch now, and I answer to your father. You would only be a liability to him. Wait until you are older—there will be other battles to fight."

Vidar turned to go, but Aidan grabbed his sleeve, insistent.

"There will be no battle like this!" Aidan insisted. "My father needs me. My brothers need me! And I will not stop until you tell me!" he insisted, stamping his foot.

Vidar looked back at him a bit more seriously, as if surprised he could be so determined. Finally, slowly, he shook his head.

"Then you shall be waiting a long time," Vidar finally replied.

Vidar shook off Aidan's grip and marched away with his men, back through the gates, their boots crunching in the snow, each sound like a nail in Aidan's heart.

Aidan felt like crying as he stood there and watched helplessly as they all walked off, into the lightening sky, leaving him alone in the fort, behind these walls, which felt now like nothing more than a glorified tomb.

*

Aidan waited patiently behind the massive iron gates of Volis, watching as the sun rose higher in the sky and his father's men patrolled. All around him, icicles dripped as snow fell down the walls, the day slowly warming as birds began to chirp. But he did not let this distract him. He intensely watched his father's men, waiting for the change of guard he knew would come.

After he did not know how long, his hands numb and his legs stiff, a new shift of men appeared. The old guard relaxed as the new guard approached, and Aidan watched as Vidar turned and headed back to the fort, joined by his men. In the disorder that followed the change of shift, Aidan knew his opportunity had come.

Aidan stood and walked through the gates, leaving the fort casually as if it were the most natural thing in the world, whistling as he went to emphasize to anyone watching that he was unafraid of being seen. The new soldiers standing guard exchanged a puzzled glance, clearly unsure whether to stop him or not.

Aidan increased his pace, hoping and praying they didn't try to stop him. Because he was determined to leave, no matter what happened.

"And where you going?" called out one of them.

Aidan stopped, his heart pounding, trying not to seem nervous.

"Didn't Vidar tell you?" Aidan snapped back in his most authoritative voice, prepared, wanting to throw them off guard. "He asked me to get the rabbits."

The soldiers exchanged a questioning look.

"Rabbits?" one called back.

Aidan tried his best to appear confident.

"I laid traps last night, in the wood," he replied. "They are full. It shall be our lunch. Stop delaying me, or the wolves will get them."

With that, Aidan turned and continued hiking off, walking quickly, confidently, not daring to look back—and praying they bought it. He walked and walked, his back tingling, terrified the guards would run out after him and detain him.

As he hiked farther from the fort, he heard nothing behind him, and he began to breathe easy as he finally realized they were not pursuing him. His ruse had worked. He felt a thrill. He was free— and nothing would stop him now. His father was out there somewhere, and until he found him, nothing would bring Aidan back to Volis.

Aidan hiked and hiked and as he crested a hill, he saw a road stretched out before him, well-traveled in the snow, heading south. Finally out of sight of the guards, he burst into a sprint, determined to get as far away as he could before they found out and came after him.

Aidan ran as fast as his little lungs could take him, until he was gasping for air. Stung by the cold, by the vast, empty landscape, he wished that Leo was by his side now, and regretted giving him back to Kyra. He wondered how far he would get. He never found out where his father was, but he knew, at least, that he had gone south, and he would head in that direction. He had no idea how long his legs could take him before they gave out, or before he froze to death. He had no horse, and no provisions, and already he shook from the cold.

Yet he did not care. Aidan felt the exhilaration of being free, of having a purpose. He was on a journey, like his father and his brothers and Kyra. He was a real warrior now, under the protection of no one. And if this was what it meant to be a warrior, then this was what he would do. He would prove himself—even if he had to die trying.

As he hiked and hiked, it made him think of his sister. How could Kyra possibly cross all of Escalon? he wondered. Was Leo still at her side?

Aidan ran and ran, following the road until it took him to the edge of the Wood of Thorns. He suddenly heard a noise behind him, and he took cover behind a tree.

Aidan peeked out and saw a wagon approaching on the road, heading south. A farmer sat at its head, the wagon pulled by two horses and trailing a cart full of hay. It rattled and bumped on the rough road, and it looked terribly uncomfortable. But Aidan didn't care. That wagon was heading his direction, and as he pondered his already-aching legs, he knew that was all that mattered.

Aidan quickly pondered his options. He could ask the farmer for a ride. But the man would likely refuse, and send him back to Volis. No. He would have to go about it another way. His own way. After all, wasn't that what it meant to be a warrior? Warriors did not ask permission—when honor was at stake, they did what they had to do.

Aidan waited for the right moment, his heart pounding, as the wagon neared. He waited until it passed him, barely able to contain his excitement, his impatience, the sound of its jostling so loud it filled the air. Then, as soon as it passed him, he jumped out from behind the tree and ran after it.

Determined not to be discovered, he crouched low and realized how lucky he was that the crunching of snow beneath his boots was drowned out by the sound of the rattling wheels. The wagon moved just slow enough, given the pitted roads, for him to catch up, and in one quick motion he leapt forward and jumped into the back, landing in the hay.

Aidan ducked low and glanced forward to make sure he hadn't been discovered; to his immense relief, the driver did not turn around.

Aidan quickly hid beneath the hay, finding it more comfortable than he imagined—and warmer, too, sheltering him from the cold and the steady wind. It even cushioned the bumps to some extent.

Aidan sighed, deeply relieved. Soon, he even began to allow himself to relax, feeling the rhythms of the cart, banging his head against the wood, but no longer caring. He even allowed himself a smile. He had done it. He was heading south, toward his father, his brothers, the battle of his life. And nobody—*nobody*—would hold him back.

CHAPTER TWELVE

Merk stood beside the girl, watching the morning sun spread over the countryside of Ur, and as she wept quietly beside him, his heart broke for her. She stood over the bodies of her dead father and mother and brother and sobbed as she had throughout the entire night. It had taken Merk hours to pry her off so that he could bury them.

Merk went back to work, reaching out with his shovel and digging again and again, as he had for hours, his hands calloused, determined to at least bury their bodies and give the girl some sense of peace. It was the least he could do; after all, she had saved his life, and no one had done that before. He still felt the agony in his back from where he had been shot, and he remembered her stepping forward, killing that boy, then removing the arrow and healing his wound. She had nursed him back to life through a long and horrible night—and now he had strength enough to help her. Oddly, he had come here to save her—but now he felt in her debt.

Merk poked at the dirt with the shovel, digging and digging, the smell of acrid smoke from the still-burning stables filling his nostrils, needing to release the heavy night from his mind, to lose himself in something physical. He realized how lucky he was to be alive, so certain he was dead after being shot. He would have been if it were not for her. He did not like these feelings of attachment he was having for her, and as he dug, he tried to blot it from his mind. The shoveling was exhausting, his wound hurting, but it took his mind off her weeping, and off the death of these good folk. He could not help but feel he was to blame—if he had arrived sooner, perhaps they would all still be alive.

Merk dug and dug, three graves now finished, probably deeper than they needed to be. His muscles burned as he straightened his aching back, and he put the shovel down definitively, looking over at her. He wanted to wrap an arm around her, to console her. But he was not that kind of man. He never knew how to express or even understand his feelings, and he'd seen far too much death to be greatly affected by it. Yet he felt bad for the girl's emotions. He wanted her crying to stop.

Merk stood there patiently, not knowing what to do, waiting for her to place the bodies in—to do something, anything. Yet she just stood there, weeping, unmoving, and he soon realized he would have to do it himself.

Merk finally knelt, grabbed her father, and dragged him into one of the freshly dug graves. The body was heavier than he'd expected, his back was hurting now from his wound and his over-exertion, and he just wanted to get this over with.

She rushed forward suddenly and grabbed his arm.

"No, wait!" she cried out.

He turned and saw her grief-stricken eyes staring back.

"Don't do it," she pleaded. "I can't bear it."

He frowned.

"Would you rather the wolves have at them?"

"Just don't," she cried. "Please. Not now."

She wept as she dropped to her knees, cradling her father.

Merk sighed and looked out at the horizon, at the breaking dawn, and wondered if there was any end to death in this world. Some people died pleasantly while others died violently—yet no matter how they died, they all seemed to end up in the same place. What was the point of it all? What was the point of a peaceful death, or a violent one, if they all led to the same place? Did it even make any difference? And if death was inevitable, what was even the point of life?

Merk watched the sky lighten and he knew he had to move on. He had wasted too much time here already, fighting a fight that was not his. Was this what happened, he wondered, when you fought for causes that were not your own? Did you end up feeling this sense of confusion, of mixed satisfaction?

"I must go," he said firmly, impatient. "A long journey lies before me, and a new day breaks."

She did not reply. He looked down at her and felt a sense of responsibility for her, here all alone, and he debated what to do.

"Other predators roam this countryside," he continued. "It is no place for you to be alone. Come with me. I will find you protection in the Tower of Ur, or somewhere close by."

It was the first time he had ever offered anyone to join him, had ever gone out of his way to help someone for no reason, and it made him feel good—yet also nervous. It was not who he was.

Merk expected her to jump at his offer, and he was confused when she shook her head, not even meeting his eyes.

"Never," she seethed.

He was shocked as she looked up at him with eyes filled with hatred.

"I would *never* join you," she added.

He blinked back.

"I don't understand," he replied.

"This is all your fault," she said, looking back at the corpses.

"*My* fault?" he asked, indignant.

"I begged for you to come sooner," she said. "If you had listened, you could have saved them. Now they all lie dead because of you. Because of your selfishness."

Merk frowned.

"Let me remind you," he replied, "that you are alive right now because of my selfishness."

She shook her head.

"Pity for me," she replied. "I wish I had died with them. And for that I hate you even more."

Merk sighed, furious, realizing that that was what he got for helping people. Ingratitude. Hatred. Better to keep to himself.

"Fine then," he said.

He turned to walk away, but for some reason he still could not. Despite everything, for reason, he still cared for her. And he hated that he did.

"I shall not ask you again," he said, his voice quivering with anger, standing there, waiting.

She would not respond.

He turned and scowled at her.

"You do realize," he said, dumbfounded, "that staying here alone is a death sentence."

She nodded.

"And that is precisely what I hope for," she replied.

"You are confused," he said. "I am not their murderer. I am your savior."

She looked him with such contempt that Merk recoiled.

"You are *no one's* savior," she spat. "You are not even a man. You are a mercenary. A murderer for hire. And you are no better than these men—don't pretend that you are."

Her words struck him deeply, perhaps because he cared for a person for the first time he could remember, perhaps because he had let his guard down. Now Merk wished he hadn't. He felt a shiver run through his spine, felt her words ring through him like a curse.

"Then why did you save me last night?" he demanded. "Why not let me die?"

She did not respond, which agitated him even more.

Merk saw there was no reasoning with her, and he had enough: fed up, he threw down the shovel, turned, and marched away.

He hiked away from the burning compound and into the breaking sun, heading back for the woods. He could still hear the girl's crying as he went. He crested a hill, then another, and for some reason, as much as he hoped they would, the cries still did not fade. It was like they were echoing in his mind.

As he crested another hill, Merk finally turned and look back for her. His stomach clenched in a knot as he spotted her, a small figure in the distance. There she knelt, still, far in the valley below, by the graves of her family. Merk was confused by his emotions and he did not like the feeling. It clouded him.

Worst of all, Merk felt a lack of resolve. He knew she would die out there, and a part of him wanted to go back and help her. But how could he help someone who did not want helping?

Merk steeled himself, took a deep breath, and turned his back on her. He faced the woods ahead, and looked out at the pilgrimage before him. On the horizon, waiting for him, he knew, was the Tower of Ur. A place where his mission would be simple, where life would be simple. A place to belong.

Suddenly, as he pondered it, he was struck by an awful thought: what if they rejected him?

There was only one way to find out. Merk took the first step and this time he resolved to stop for nothing—for no one—until he completed his quest.

CHAPTER THIRTEEN

Kyra rode Andor at a walk, Dierdre at her side, Leo at their heels, miserable, unable to stop shivering in the freezing rain. The rain fell in sheets, so loudly she could barely hear herself think, pelting them for hours, sometimes turning to snow and hail. She could not recall the last time she had been indoors, beside a fire, in any sort of shelter. The driving wind kept at them, and she felt a chill deep in her bones which she did not think would ever thaw.

Dawn had broken long ago, though one could not tell from the sky, the clouds dark, angry, hanging low, thick, and heavy, gray, lashing rain and hail and snow, barely an improvement over the night. They had ridden through the Wood of Thorns all through the long and harrowing night, trying to get as far as they could from the Pandesians. Kyra had kept expecting them to be followed—and it drove her on without rest. Perhaps because the dark, the rain, or just having all those boys on their hands, they never tried to follow.

Hour passed hour and Kyra, freezing, scratched by branches, sleep-deprived, felt hollowed out. She felt as if she had been riding for years. She looked over and saw Dierdre equally miserable, and saw Leo whining, none of them having eaten since Volis. The irony of that whole encounter, Kyra realized, was that they had endangered their lives for food but had not managed to salvage any—and now they were even hungrier.

Kyra tried to focus on the quest ahead of her, on Ur, on the importance of her mission—but at this moment, sleep deprived, her eyes closing, all she wanted was a place to lie down and sleep, a warm fire, and a good meal. She was not even halfway across Escalon, and she wondered how she would ever possibly complete this quest; Ur felt like a million miles away.

Kyra studied her surroundings, peering through the rain, but found no sign of shelter, no boulders or caves or hollow tree trunks—nothing but this endless, mangled wood.

They rode and rode, mustering the strength to go on, Kyra and Dierdre too exhausted to speak to each other. Kyra did not know how much time had passed when she thought she began to hear, somewhere in the distance, a sound she had only heard a few times in her life: the crashing of waves.

Kyra looked up and blinked into the rain, blinded by it, wiping it from her eyes and face, and she wondered. Was it possible?

She listened closely, stopping, and Dierdre stopped beside her, each exchanging a curious glance.

"I hear ocean," Kyra said, listening, confused by the sound of gushing water. "Yet it also sounds like…a river."

She rode faster, encouraged, and as she neared heard what sounded like, perhaps, a waterfall. Her curiosity heightened.

They finally emerged from the wood and as the sky opened before them for the first time since entering the Wood of Thorns, Kyra was taken aback by the sight: there, but a few hundred yards away, sat the widest sea she had ever laid eyes upon, seeming to stretch to the end of the world. The sea was white with foam, windswept on this blustery day, pelted with rain and hail, and Kyra saw dozens of ships, taller than she'd ever seen, their masts bobbing and rocking. They were all clustered in a harbor, close to shore, and as Kyra looked carefully, she noticed a gushing river leading from the sea and winding its way through the wood. The river seemed to divide two woods, the trees on the far side a different color and glowing white. Kyra had never seen anything like it in all of Escalon, and she marveled at the sight.

They stopped there and stared, mesmerized, their faces pelted with rain and neither bothering to wipe it away.

"The Sorrow," Dierdre remarked. "We've made it."

Kyra turned and examined the river before them, and the small, wooden bridge spanning it.

"And the river?" Kyra asked.

"The River Tanis," Dierdre replied. "It divides the Wood of Thorns and Whitewood. Once we cross it, we are in the West."

"And then how far to Ur?" Kyra asked.

Dierdre shrugged.

"A few days?" she guessed.

Kyra's heart fell at the thought. She felt the hunger gnawing at her stomach, felt the freezing cold as another gale of wind lashed her, and as she shivered, she did not know how they would make it.

"We could take the River Tanis," Dierdre added. "We could find a boat. It won't take us all the way, though, and it is a rough ride. I know more than one man from Ur who has died in its waters."

Kyra examined the gushing river, its sound deafening even from here—louder even than the crashing waves of the Sorrow—and she realized its danger. She shook her head, preferring to risk whatever they might encounter on land than in those torrential currents.

She studied the contours of the river and saw where it narrowed, one shore nearly touching the other; a small bridge spanned it, clearly well-traveled, shaped in an arch to allow ships to pass through. She spotted something on its shores: a small, wooden structure, like a cottage, weathered, leaning, perched at the edge of the river. Candles burned in its sole window, and she noticed dozens of small boats tied up alongside it. It was a hub of activity. She saw men stumbling out of it, off-balance, heard a raucous shout, and she realized: it was a tavern.

The smell of food wafting in the air hit her like a punch in the gut and made it hard for her to focus on anything else. She wondered what sort of people were inside.

"Pandesians?" she wondered aloud, as Dierdre examined it, too.

Dierdre shook her head.

"Look at those boats," she said. "They have foreign markings. They're travelers, coming in off the sea. They all take the Tanis to cut through Escalon. I've seen many in Ur. Most are traders."

As Leo whined beside her, Kyra felt a hunger pang in her stomach; yet she recalled her father's warning to avoid others.

"What do you think?" Dierdre asked, clearly thinking the same thing.

Kyra shook her head, torn between a bad feeling and a desire for food and shelter, to get out of the rain and wind. She studied the tavern and her eyes narrowed in concern. She did not like the sounds coming from within its walls; they were the sounds of drunken men, she could recognize it anywhere from having grown up as the only girl in a fort filled with warriors. And she knew that when men drank, they looked for trouble.

"We will attract unwanted attention," Kyra replied, "two girls, traveling alone."

Dierdre frowned.

"Those are not soldiers," she replied. "They are travelers. And that is no garrison, but a tavern. This will not be like encountering Pandesians. That was just bad luck back there. These men will be focused on their drink, not war. We can buy the food we need and leave. Besides, we have Andor, and Leo and you and your weapons. The Pandesian soldiers could not stop us back in the wood—do you really think a bunch of drunken sailors can?"

Kyra hesitated, uneasy. She understood her point of view, and she wanted to eat as badly as she—not to mention to take shelter, even if for a minute.

"I'm weak from hunger," Dierdre said. "We all are. And I've never been so cold in my life. We can't keep going on like this. We will die out here. You are shivering so badly, you don't even realize it."

Kyra suddenly realized her teeth were chattering, and she knew Dierdre had a point. They needed a break, even if for a few moments. It was risky—yet going on like this was risky, too.

Finally, Kyra nodded.

"We'll get in and out," she said. "Keep your head down. Stick close to me. And if any man comes for you, stick this in his gut."

Kyra placed a dagger in her friend's palm and looked up at her meaningfully. They were frozen from the cold, weak from hunger, tired of running from men, and Kyra could see in her friend's eyes that she was ready.

Even so, as they rode out of the wood and into the clearing, towards the gushing river, closing in on the tavern, Kyra felt a deep foreboding overcome her—and she knew, even as she rode, that this was a very, very bad idea.

CHAPTER FOURTEEN

Duncan rode his horse at a walk, Seavig, Anvin and Arthfael beside him, their men close behind, and glanced back and saw with satisfaction that they were all one force now. Seavig's men, hundreds strong, had merged seamlessly with his own. Their force numbered well over a thousand men now, far more than Duncan had ever expected to see when he had departed the gates of Volis; indeed, he had not even expected to survive this long.

They marched south and east, trekking for hours into the new day, following Seavig's guidance through his province as they headed away from Esephus and toward the Lake of Ire. On the march since dawn, late afternoon clouds now hung heavy in the sky, none of the men, even after a long's night battle, willing to stop. They were all, Duncan could sense, filled with a sense of purpose, one that had not swept across Escalon since the invasion. Something special hung in the air, something Escalon had lacked for years, and which Duncan had thought he would never see again: hope.

Duncan felt a sense of optimism welling within him, one he had not felt since his early days as a warrior. His army had doubled in size already, villagers along the way all too eager to join him, and momentum, he felt, was building of its own accord. Volis was free; Argos was free; Esephus was free. Three of the strongholds of the northeast were now back in the hands of Escalon, and it was all happening so fast, so unexpected, like a midnight tide. The Pandesian Empire still had no idea. And that meant that Duncan still had time. If he could manage to just sweep through Escalon fast enough, maybe, just maybe, he could oust Pandesia before they could rally, before the greater Pandesia caught wind. If he could drive them all the way back through the Southern Gate, from there he was sure he could use Escalon's natural terrain to hold chokepoints and keep Escalon free once again.

The key to all of this, Duncan knew, would be rallying the strongholds, and the warlords who controlled them. With the weak king deposed and the capital in Pandesian hands, what remained of free Escalon lay in scattered strongholds, each, like his, with its own force, its own commander. And in order to convince these men to follow, Duncan, he knew, would have to give them a show of strength: he would have to take the capital. And in order to take Andros, he would need the men who controlled the heights around it: the warriors of Kos.

Kos was the key; it was also a litmus test. The men of Kos were famed isolationists, as stubborn as the goats that scaled their cliffs. If Duncan could persuade them to join him, then, he knew, the rest of Escalon would follow. But if Kos refused, or if Pandesia found out too soon, then an empire of soldiers that no one could hold back—not even the best of their men—would sweep Escalon and wipe out not only he and his men, but all the men, women and children of Escalon. Escalon would be no more, razed to a crisp. The stakes could not be higher: Duncan was gambling with all of their lives.

But freedom, his father had taught him, was more precious than anything in life. And freedom, sometimes, had to be earned repeatedly.

They marched and marched, the day cold and gray, thick clouds hanging low, snow falling all around them, a light snow which never seemed to stop. They marched in silence, these men who understood each other, who had fought many battles together, and nothing need be said between them.

Duncan watched with interest as the terrain changed the farther south they went, the salty, sea-climate of Esephus giving way to a barren stretch of plains and rolling hills. He searched for the Ire with each step, yet it never appeared; this land sprawled forever, and it did not seem as if it would ever end.

They crested a hill and a gale of wind and snow took Duncan's breath away. He blinked the snow from his eyes, and as he looked out before him, he was mesmerized by the sight. Far below, nestled in a valley, there it sat: the Lake of Ire. It shimmered even beneath a gray sky, glowing a bright red, looking like a sea of fire. Some legends, Duncan knew, told its color came from the blood of its victims, men who waded in never to be seen again; others claimed its color rose from the vicious creatures who lived in its waters; still

102

others had it that its color came from the tears of the goddess who wept in it when she first discovered Escalon.

The Lake of Ire was revered by all in Escalon as a sacred place, a place one came to to pray to the God of Birth and the God of Death—and most of all, the God of Vengeance. It was fitting, Duncan realized, that they would skirt its shores on this day.

Yet still, Duncan wished they would have taken any other route. This lake was also a cursed place, a place of death, a place one did not visit without reason. Even from here he felt a chill as he examined its shores, ringed by red, gravel-like rocks, its waters beyond it exploding with hot springs, sending off small clouds of steam as if the lake were venting its wrath. They all stopped, their armor clinking as thousands of horses rested, a sudden silence amidst the winter gale, and took in the sight before them. Duncan marveled at it, one of the wonders of Escalon.

"Is there no other way?" Duncan asked Seavig, who came to a stop beside him.

Seavig grimly shook his head, still staring out.

"We must follow its shores to the mouth of the Thusius and that is the most direct way to Kos. Don't worry, old friend," he said, clasping Duncan's shoulder with a broad smile, "the old wives' tales are not true. The lake will not eat you, and we won't be swimming in it."

Duncan still did not like it.

"Why not take the plains?" Anvin asked.

Seavig pointed.

"You see there?" he said.

Duncan looked and saw a thick fog rolling in. It came in way too fast, like a cloud in a storm, and within moments it was rushing their way, blinding. Duncan, immersed in a whiteout, had a jolt of fear as he could no longer see his men—he could not even see Seavig, just a few feet away. He had never experienced anything like it.

"It is not the Lake of Ire one fears," Seavig said, his voice rising calmly from the fog, "but the plains surrounding it—and the fog that covers them. You see, my friend, you can hear my voice but you cannot see my face. That is how men die here. They get lost in the fog and never return."

"And how could fog kill a person?" Arthfael asked, beside them.

"It is not the fog," Seavig replied. "It is the creatures that ride it."

Just as quickly, a gale of wind rushed through and blew the fog away—and Duncan felt an immense sense of relief to be able to see the lake again.

"If we take the plains," Seavig continued, "we will lose each other in the fog. If we stick to the lake's shores, we shall have a guide. Let us go quickly—the winds are shifting."

Seavig kicked his horse, and Duncan joined, as did the others, all of them proceeding at a trot downhill and toward the lake. The water's hissing grew louder as they neared, and as they reached its shores, the red gravel beneath their horses made for an eerie nose. Duncan's sense of apprehension deepened.

There came another wave of fog, and once again, Duncan found himself immersed. Again, he could not see before him, and this time, the fog did not blow away.

"Stay close and listen for the gravel," Seavig said. "That is how you know you are still on shore. Soon enough you will hear the river. Until then, do not stray from the path."

"And those beasts you speak of?" Duncan called out, on edge as they walked through the cloud of white. "If you should come?"

Duncan heard the sound of Seavig's sword being drawn.

"They will come," he replied. "Just close your eyes, and let your sword do the killing."

*

Duncan rode his horse at a walk in the fog, his men beside him, their horses brushing up against each other, the only way to navigate in the whiteout. He clutched his sword, on edge. Behind him his men sounded the horn, again and again, its lonely sound echoing through the hills, off the lake, his men following his command so that they would not lose track of each other. Yet every time a horn sounded he tensed, fearing it might provoke the creatures that lived in the fog and bracing himself for an attack. The sound was also hard to track, and if it weren't for the gravel beneath them, they might all be lost by now. Seavig had been right.

Duncan found himself getting disoriented even so, losing himself in thought, losing all sense of reality as he rode deeper into the white. It was surreal; he could see how fog could drive a man mad.

Seavig's low heavy voice rumbled, breaking the silence, and Duncan welcomed it.

"Do you remember Bloody Hill, old friend?" he asked, his voice heavy with nostalgia. "We were young. Budding warriors, with no wives and no children—just ourselves and our swords and the whole world before us to prove ourselves. That was the battle that made us men."

"I remember it well," Duncan replied, feeling as if it were yesterday.

"They outmanned us two to one," Seavig continued, "and a fog came in, much like today. We were separated from our men, just the two of us."

Duncan nodded.

"We stumbled into a trap," Duncan added.

"A hornet's nest," Seavig said. "Do you remember what you said to me on that day?"

Duncan remembered, all too well.

"You said: this is the gift I've been waiting for," Seavig continued. "I never understood what that meant until years later. It *was* a gift. It was the gift of being surrounded; the gift of being outnumbered; the gift of having no one else to rely on but ourselves. How many men get that gift?"

Duncan nodded, his heart welling with the memory of that day.

"A very rare gift indeed," Duncan said.

"I received many wounds on that day," Seavig continued after a long pause, "some of which I am reminded of every time I bend my knee. But that's not what I remember most of all—nor is it the fact that we killed them all. What I remember most are your words. And my surprise at seeing you unafraid. On the contrary, I never saw you happier than at that moment. Your courage gave me strength. That was the day I vowed to become a great warrior."

Duncan pondered his friend's words deeply, memories rushing back, as they rode in silence for a long time. Duncan hardly believed so many years had passed. Where had his youth gone?

"The kingship should be yours," Seavig said, after a long silence, his voice hard, his words rolling on the fog.

Duncan was startled by his words; the kingship was not something he aspired to, and his friend's voice felt like his darker conscious egging him on.

Duncan shook his head.

"The old King was my friend," he replied. "I have always aspired only to serve."

"He betrayed the kingship," Seavig countered. "He surrendered Escalon. He does not deserve to be King. I, for one, will never serve him again, if Escalon should ever be free—and neither will the others. We have no king—don't you see that? And what will a free Escalon be without a king?"

"That may be so," Duncan said, "and yet still he is our King, worthy or not. Surrendering a land does not forfeit a kingship."

"Doesn't it?" Seavig replied. "If not that, then what? What is a King who does not defend his land?"

Duncan sighed, knowing his friend was right. He had thought this through many times himself. Speaking to his friend was like arguing with himself; he was unsure what to say.

"Even if we had a new king," Duncan replied, "why should it be me? There are many worthy men out there."

"We all respect you," Seavig replied. "All the warlords. All the great warriors who remain, scattered across Escalon. You represent what is best in all of us. When the Tarnis surrendered the land, we all expected you to assume the kingship. But you did not. Your silence spoke louder than all. It was your silence, my friend, your sticking by the old King's side, that enabled Pandesia to take our land."

The words struck Duncan deep, like a dagger in his heart, as he wondered if his friend were right. He had never considered it that way.

"I wanted only to be loyal," Duncan replied. "Loyal to my land, loyal to my people, and loyal to my king."

Seavig shook his head.

106

"Loyalty can be the greatest danger of all, when it is blind, when it is misplaced."

Duncan thought about that. Had he been blinded by loyalty for the sake of loyalty?

"You taught me a great deal, Duncan," Seavig continued. "Now allow me to teach you. It is not loyalty and devotion that make a man. It is knowing *who* to be loyal to—and *when*. Loyalty is not forever. Loyalty must be earned, every moment of every day. If the man I was loyal to yesterday does not earn it today, then that loyalty *must* be changed—or else that loyalty means nothing. Loyalty is not a birthright. To be the recipient of loyalty is a very sacred thing; and if recipients are unworthy, they must face the consequence. Blind devotion is a crutch. It is passive. And a warrior must never be passive."

They continued on in silence, Seavig's words ringing in Duncan's ears, striking home to his very heart and soul, making him rethink his entire life. They stung him; they provoked him; and while he wished he had never heard them, he also knew that on some level he needed to.

"What will you do once Escalon is free?" Seavig continued, after a long silence. "Shame all the warriors who fight for you, and hand the kingship back to the man who does not deserve it? Or honor those who have honored you, and give them the leader they demand?"

Duncan did not know how to respond. He had been raised by his father to value loyalty above all else; *men come and go, but loyalty is for life*, he had been told. He had never betrayed those close to him, and had never forgotten a debt. He had also been raised to appreciate his place in life, and to not strive to reach a station that was too great for him.

All of what Seavig was saying went against the very grain of who he was, of what he knew. Yet at the same time, he could see his point: the weak king had let them all down, had hurt their great land, and Duncan knew there was some truth hidden in Seavig's words, even if at the moment he could not fully process it.

They fell back into silence as they continued around the Lake of Ire, gravel crunching beneath their horses' feet, the fog still so thick that Duncan could not see his hands. And as they went, his foreboding deepened. He feared no man, yet he did not like to fight what he could not see. He felt something evil in this wind, something coming, and he gripped his sword tighter. He hoped he was not leading his men to slaughter.

Duncan stiffened as he thought he heard a muffled shout. He stopped and stared into the fog, wondering, when suddenly, it came again. One of his men cried out, and this was followed by a thud, as if a man had fallen from his horse.

"Fog walkers!" shrieked Seavig, his voice cutting through the air.

There suddenly came shouts from all around him, and Duncan turned every which way, gripping his sword, trying to spot the foe—and then all was chaos.

Duncan suddenly felt an icy grip around his throat and he looked down to see what appeared to be a skeleton, but nearly translucent, like ice, its long claws digging into his throat and piercing his skin. He looked up to see a ghoulish creature, skeleton-like, with empty sockets for eyes, its face inches away, slowly becoming visible in the fog. It opened its mouth impossibly wide, leaned in, and placed it on Duncan's chest and began to suck.

Even through the creature was toothless, still, the fog walker was suctioning him, like a leech, and he could feel it beginning to suck his body out of him, even through the chainmail. Duncan cried out in pain. With all the energy he could muster, he reached down, grabbed the creature's skull with both hands, and squeezed. It was a monumental struggle, his arms shaking, as he felt himself getting weaker, feeling as if his heart would be sucked out of his chest.

Finally, the creature's skull burst, its brittle bones falling all around him.

Duncan breathed hard, rubbing his chest, feeling his skin burning, realizing what a close call that was.

Shouts rose up all around him and Duncan peered through the fog, struggling to see, never having felt so helpless in battle. He could barely make out a thing; all he could sense was motion. He kicked his horse and charged into the mist, realizing he could not sit there; he had to help his men and he would just have to feel his way.

Duncan rode into one of his men and made out a fog walker clinging to his chest, its mouth suctioning him, and he watched in horror as the fog walker suctioned out the man's heart. It was still pumping in the air as the soldier shrieked and fell, dead, to the ground.

A gale of wind passed through, and for a moment the fog lifted and Duncan spotted hundreds of fog walkers flying through the air, many rising from the Lake of Ire itself. His heart dropped at the sight. He knew if he did not act quickly his men would die on these shores.

"DISMOUNT!" he shouted to his men. "Take the low ground!"

His order carried on the wind, and there came a great rankling of armor as his men all dismounted, and he did, too. Duncan crouched down low to get a better angle on these creatures as they came flying at him in the wind, and as one neared, he raised his sword and slashed. His sword cut it across the torso and there came the sound of clattering bones as it collapsed into pieces all around him.

Another came at him, opening its mouth wide, and he stabbed it in the chest, shattering it. One came at him from the side and no sooner had he smashed it with his shield then another came from his other side.

Duncan spun and slashed left and right, shattering these things in every direction as their claws reached for him. Anvin found him, and the two fought back to back in the fog. Anvin swung his flail, its spiked balls swinging overhead and smashing fog walkers as they collapsed in heaps all around them.

Seavig hit the ground beside Duncan's, rolling on his back and swinging with an axe, chopping fog walkers out of the sky. The group stuck together, guarding each other's backs, fighting as one as they fended off the creatures.

Yet all around them the cries of agony continued, too many of their men getting killed by these things which came out of nowhere, as if they were one with the fog. There seemed to be a never-ending stream of them, as if the lake were churning them out in its vapors. Duncan spun and slashed one, sparing Seavig right before he was bitten in the back—but as he did, Duncan suddenly felt sharp claws digging into his back. He reached around and grabbed the creature and threw it over his head, stepping on it and smashing it. But as soon as he did, another latched onto him and began suctioning his arm. Seavig stepped forward and smashed it to bits with his axe—while Anvin lunged forward and stabbed another through its open mouth before it landed on Duncan's neck.

The air was filled with the sound of bones clattering as men fought back bravely. A wind blew in and lifted the fog for a moment and as it did, Duncan saw piles of bones, hundreds of dead fog walkers littering the shores. Yet in the distance, he was horrified to see thousands more fog walkers emerging from the mist and flying towards them, howling their awful high-pitched howl.

"There are too many!" Anvin yelled out.

"To the waters!" Seavig yelled. "Into the lake! All of you! It is our last chance!"

Duncan was horrified at the thought.

"The Lake of Ire?" Duncan called back. "Does it not swarm with creatures?"

"It does!" Seavig called. "But a possible death is better than a certain one!"

"TO THE WATERS!" Duncan commanded, shouting out to his men, realizing their situation was helpless otherwise.

Horns sounded and as one, their men ran for the lake. Duncan ran with them, wading in, a great splashing noise rising up as they all could not get in fast enough. As he entered, Duncan was surprised to find the red waters to be warm and sticky, thick, as if he were running into quicksand. He waded in deeper, up to his chest, and the water grew hotter as he did, bubbling and hissing.

Fog walkers flew through the air toward them, but as they neared the water, this time they flew up and avoided them, as if afraid. They circled overhead in a huge swarm, like bats, howling in frustration. Duncan felt a moment of relief as he realized Seavig had been right: they were, indeed, afraid of the waters. It had saved them from the swarm.

Finally, realizing they could not get close, the fog walkers let out a great howl and as one, the flock flew off, disappearing for good.

Duncan's men raised their arms in the water and let out a shout of victory, elated. Duncan himself finally let down his guard for the first time.

No sooner had he done so when Duncan suddenly felt something slimy wrapping itself around his ankles, like seaweed. His heart slammed as he tried to kick it off. He looked down, studying the thick waters, but could not see what it was. It tugged at him, all muscle, and with a sudden yank, Duncan began to feel himself being dragged down.

He looked down and suddenly saw the water teeming, alive with thousands of creatures resembling sea snakes.

Shouts arose all amongst his men as one by one, on all sides, his men began to disappear, to get sucked down beneath the murky waters, to a terrible, terrible death.

CHAPTER FIFTEEN

Kyra's foreboding deepened as she rode across the soggy clearing, Dierdre and Leo by her side, wind and rain whipping her face, heading for the tavern beside the gushing river. She felt a knot in her stomach, sensing this was a mistake—yet she also felt unable to turn back. Rationally, Kyra knew she should follow her father's advice, stay clear of people, stick to the road and keep the sea in sight until they reached Ur.

Physically, though, she was just too hungry, too tired, and unable to resist the impulse that was driving her out of the rain and toward warmth, shelter, and the smell of food. After all, Dierdre had a point: there were risks involved in not finding food, especially with Ur still several days away.

As they approached, there came more shouts of drunken men, louder this time. A few pigs and stray chickens rooted around outside its walls, and a shingle hung crookedly, swaying in the wind.

"What does it say?" Dierdre asked her, and she realized her friend was unable to read. That should not have surprised her, she realized, as most of Escalon could not. She had had a very special upbringing.

Kyra raised a hand to her eyes and struggled to read in the rain.

"The Inn at Tanis," she replied, thinking how unoriginal a name it was.

This place, named after the river, looked as if it had been constructed from the forest clearing in a few days' time. There came another shout, and Kyra tried not to imagine the crowd awaiting them.

"You're lucky," Dierdre said.

"Why's that?" Kyra asked, confused.

"Only highborn can read," she said. "I wish I could."

Kyra felt sorry.

"My brothers cannot," Kyra replied. "I was the only one who insisted. I can teach you, if you like."

112

Dierdre's eyes lit up.

"I would like that," she replied.

As they approached, Kyra reached down and was reassured to feel the gold jingling in her pocket, knowing it would be more than enough to get the provisions they needed. They would stay just long enough to thaw out their frozen hands, to buy feed for the horse and Andor, and move on. How much could happen in a few minutes' time?

She looked and saw no sign of Pandesian horses or boats outside, and she felt a bit of relief. Fellow Escalons would likely not attack their own; after all, they were all in this war together. But travelers?

They headed around the side of the structure, searching for the front door, and Kyra found it ajar, crooked, facing the gushing river and near the wooden bridge that crossed it. Bobbing in the river were dozens of small boats, some long and narrow, like canoes, others wide and flat; to the north she saw the mouth of the harbor leading to the sea and the many large ships flying the colors of all different lands. She figured all these sailors probably stopped here for the same reason she did: to replenish their provisions and get some warmth.

They dismounted, Kyra tying Andor alongside the structure, while Dierdre tied up her horse. Andor, resentful, stomped uncomfortably and snarled.

Kyra reached up and stroked his head.

"I'll be right out," she said. "I'm just going to get you some food."

Andor stomped again, as if he knew bad things lay inside.

Leo whined, wanting to join, too, but Kyra knelt down and held him in place, stroking his head.

"Wait with Andor," she said, feeling guilty as the rain picked up.

"Let's go," Dierdre said.

Kyra stood, following Dierdre as they walked up the creaky wooden plank toward the door, and as they did, it suddenly slammed open, a man stumbling out so quickly they had to get out of his way. The man hurried to the side rail, leaned over, and threw up.

Kyra, revolted, tried not to look; she turned back for the door and hurried inside, wondering if that was an omen.

As the door opened, Kyra was struck by a wave of noise and by the smell of stale beer, body odor, sweat, and food. She nearly gagged. She looked around and saw a narrow bar, behind which was a tall, skinny bartender with a gaunt face, perhaps in his forties. Inside the room were dozens of men, sitting and standing, of all different appearances, their dress foreign, men clearly from all over the world. She heard languages she did not recognize, and accents she could not understand. All of them were immersed in drink.

As they entered the tavern, all the men stopped and turned, the place falling silent. Kyra felt uncomfortable as they looked her up and down, felt more conspicuous than ever. It was not every day, Kyra realized, that two women walked into a place like this alone. In fact, as she looked around at the grime and filth, she figured a woman's foot had probably never stepped foot in here once.

Kyra looked back at their faces, and she did not like what she saw. They were the faces of drunk men, of desperate men, foreigners, most with heavy stubble, others with thick beards, few of them shaven. Some had beady eyes, many eyes were bloodshot, and most were tainted by drink. Their hair was long, unkempt, greasy, and they all had a hunger in their eyes—and not for food. It was for violence. For women.

It was exactly the sort of situation Kyra had wanted to avoid. A part of her wanted to turn and walk out, but they needed the provisions and it was too late now.

Kyra put on her toughest face and strutted through the crowd, right for the bar, keeping her eyes fixed on the barkeep and trying not to seem afraid. Dierdre followed close behind.

"Those chickens behind the bar," Kyra said to the bartender, speaking in a loud and firm voice, "I'll take four. I'll also need four bags of feed, two sacks of water, and one slab of raw meat," she added, thinking of Leo.

The bartender looked back with surprise.

"And you have money to pay for all that?" he asked, in an accent she had not heard before.

Kyra, keeping her eyes fixed on him, reached into her sack and extracted one large gold coin, which she knew would be enough to

114

pay for all that and more. She set it down on the bar, and it rang with a distinctive clink.

The barkeep glanced warily at her and picked up the coin and examined it, holding it up to the candlelight. Kyra could feel the eyes of all the patrons on it, and she knew it was drawing even more attention than she would have liked.

"These markings," the barkeep observed. "Are you from Volis, then?"

Kyra nodded back, her heart pounding, feeling a tension rise within her, more on guard than ever.

"And what are two girls from Volis doing all the way on the River Tanis? Alone?" came a harsh voice.

Kyra heard a commotion and turned to see a large man, taller than most of the others, with green eyes and brown hair, staring back at her as he approached. She tensed, not knowing what to expect, debating how much to tell him.

"I'm on my way to see my uncle," she said vaguely, leaving it at that.

He narrowed his eyes.

"And where is your uncle?" he asked. "Perhaps I know him."

"Ur," she replied flatly.

He looked back at her skeptically.

"Ur is far from here. Are you two crossing Escalon alone then?"

Kyra hesitated, debating whether to reply. She owed this man no answers and just wanted to be out of this place.

She turned and faced him, squaring her shoulders.

"And who are you that you should demand answers from me?" she replied firmly.

A few men in the bar groaned, and the man's face reddened.

"For a girl alone, in your situation, you should show more respect to your elders," he said darkly.

"I give respect to those who give it to me," she replied, not backing down. "And so far, I have seen none from you. As for being in a vulnerable position," she added, "I daresay it is *you* who are in that position. I have a very fine weapon strapped to my back, and I see you have but a knife on your waist. Do not underestimate me because I am a girl. I can slit your throat before you finish speaking."

There came a low grumble from the crowd, as the tension raised several notches.

The man stared back, shocked, and raised a hand to his hips.

"Big words for a girl," he said. "Much less for one traveling alone." He looked her over. "You are a brave one, aren't you?" he asked. "I suspect you're not an ordinary girl." He rubbed his chin. "No, by the looks of you, I'd say you are someone important. Furs like that are reserved for warlords. What are two girls doing wearing a warlord's furs?"

He stared back darkly, demanding a response, as the tavern quieted. Kyra decided it was time to tell them.

"They are my father's furs," she said proudly, glaring back. "Duncan. Warlord of Volis."

For the first time, the man displayed true shock and fear. His expression softened.

"Duncan, you say?" he said, his voice quivering. "Your father?"

The room grumbled in surprise.

"And would he let you travel alone?" he added. "And not with a company of a hundred men?"

"My father has faith in me," she replied. "He has seen what I can do. He has seen how many men's throats, like you, I have already cut. It is *they* he fears for, not myself," she replied boldly, knowing she must show no weakness if she were to survive this place.

The man stared back, shocked, clearly not expecting that response.

Slowly, his face broke into a smile.

"You are your father's daughter then," he replied. "And a fine man he is. I met him once. The boldest, bravest warrior I'd ever known."

He turned to the barkeep.

"Everything they asked for," he said, "double it! It's on me!"

He threw another gold coin on the bar as the barkeep grabbed it and quickly scrambled to get the provisions.

Kyra watched, relieved and surprised. Slowly, she relaxed her shoulders and loosened her grip on her staff.

"Why should you pay for our food?" Dierdre asked.

"Your father saved my life once," the man said to Kyra. "I owe him. Now you can tell him we're even. Plus, I hear a rumor that your father has killed some Pandesians," he said. "Rumor has it that war is brewing in Escalon."

Kyra looked back him, her heart thumping, wondering how much to say.

He summed her up, and nodded to himself.

"I suspect that is what your journey's about," he said. "And by the looks of you, I suspect you may have already shed some Pandesian blood yourself."

Kyra shrugged.

"There may have been one or two who crossed my path," she said. "But nothing unprovoked."

The man's smile widened, and this time he leaned back and laughed.

"Anyone who kills Pandesians is a friend of mine," he said heartily. "Don't worry, girls, you shall not be harmed here. Not by me or any of my men!"

Kyra began to feel a sense of relief—when suddenly a dark voice boomed from across the room.

"Speak for yourself!"

Kyra turned, as did the rest of the men in the room, to see a brute of a man appear, twice as wide as the others, and flanked by several friends. They all wore chain mail, covered by dark brown cloaks, and had a yellow hawk insignia branded on them. They stared darkly at Kyra and Dierdre as they approached.

The other men stepped aside as they walked across the tavern, floorboards creaking, menace in their eyes, hands on swords and daggers. Kyra's stomach tightened; she sensed this was real trouble.

"I don't give a damn about who your father is," the oaf muttered, coming closer. "My land lies far across the sea, and I don't give a damn about Pandesians, or Escalons, or any of your politics. I see two young girls, traveling alone. And I am hungry. My *men* are hungry."

He stepped closer, smiling widely, missing teeth, stinking, his face grotesque as he smiled, with his elongated jaw. Kyra's heart thumped madly as she tightened her grip on her staff, sensing a confrontation and wishing she had more room to maneuver in these close quarters.

"What do you want?" Dierdre asked, fear in her voice.

Kyra silently fumed, wishing her friend had remained silent; the fear in her voice was evident, and that, she knew, would only embolden them.

"Many things," the man replied, looking at her, licking his lips. "The gold in your sacks. And even more—the money I will get for selling you. You see, where I come from, two young girls demand a very high price." He grinned a wide, creepy grin. "I will be many, many times richer than I was when I woke this morning."

He stepped even closer, a few feet from Kyra, and Kyra saw the friend of her father look back and forth from her to the foreigners, as if unsure whether to get involved.

"Don't try to protect her," the foreigner said to him. "Unless you want to end up dead, too."

Her father's friend, to Kyra's disappointment, raised his hands and backed away.

"I said I owed her father a favor," he said. "I fulfilled it. I won't harm her. But what anyone else does with her, well….that's not my business."

Kyra lost all respect for the man as he slinked back into the crowd. Yet it also emboldened her. It was just her now, and she liked it that way. She needed to rely on no man.

As the men closed in on her, preparing to grab her and Dierdre, Kyra tightened her grip on her staff and steeled herself. No matter what happened, she would not be taken alive by these men.

CHAPTER SIXTEEN

Alec marched across the plains of northern Soli, the hills rising and falling, staring into the rising sun, bleary-eyed, weary with exhaustion, numb with cold, and no longer feeling the hunger in his belly. He and Marco, beside him, had hiked all night through Whitewood, neither, after their encounter with the Wilvox, willing to take a chance at sleep. Alec could feel the exhaustion in his legs, and as he hiked, watching the horizon, the clouds began to part and the morning sun broke through, lighting the green hills he remembered from childhood—and he felt so grateful to have emerged from the forest. There was nothing like being under open sky. He marveled that he had survived the long trek, so many long and nights, all the way from The Flames.

Alec, still smarting from his wounds, reached up and felt his stiffening leg and arm, the wounds still raw from where the Wilvox had bitten him. He walked more slowly than he had been, yet Marco was walking slowly now, too, he, too, recovering from wounds and slowed by exhaustion and hunger. Alec could not remember the last time he rested, the last time he ate, and he felt as if he were entering a dreamlike state.

Seeing the open sky, the breaking dawn, the familiar hills he knew so well, knowing he was, finally, close to home, Alec, overcome with exhaustion and emotion, felt tears run down his cheeks. It took him several minutes to realize he was crying. He quickly wiped the tears away. He supposed they had sprung from his delirium from his wounds, his hunger, and his joy at seeing his homeland—a place he had never thought to set eyes upon again. He felt as if he had escaped the jaws of death and had been given a second chance at life.

"Where is your village?" Marco's voice rang out beside him, startling him in the deep silence.

Alec looked over and saw Marco studying the landscape with wonder, eyes filled with exhaustion, dark circles beneath them. They crested a hill and both paused, looking out, the grassy hills

119

covered in a low mist, sparkling in the dawn. Before them lay three hills, identically shaped.

"My village lies beyond the third hill," Alec said. "We are close," he sighed with relief. "Hardly an hour's hike away."

Marco's eyes lit with joy.

"And a very welcome arrival it will be," Marco replied. "I doubt my legs could carry me much farther. Will your family have food for us?"

Alec smiled, reveling in the thought.

"Food and much more," he replied. "A warm fire, a change of clothing, any weapons you could want, and—"

"And hay?" Marco asked.

Alec smiled wide.

"Hay enough to sleep a thousand years."

Marco smiled back.

"That is all I want."

The two set off at a brisk walk downhill, with renewed vigor, a bounce in their step. Alec could already, in his mind's eye, smell the cooking from his mother's kitchen, could already anticipate the look of approval in his father's eyes as he came home a hero, having sacrificed his life for his brother's. He envisioned the look on his brother's face when he walked through the door, and he could already feel his embrace. He could see the look of wonder on his parents' faces, the joy at seeing their son return. Now, perhaps, they would appreciate him. Before, he had been the second-born son, the one they always took for granted; but now, finally, they would realize how much he meant.

The final stretch of the hike flew by, Alec no longer feeling his pain or exhaustion, and before he knew it, they crested the final hill and he found himself looking down at Soli. He stopped, his heart pounding madly, looking out with great anticipation at the sight of his village below. He immediately recognized its familiar contours, the ramshackle stone cottages, and he searched for their brightly colored roofs, the usual activity of children playing, chickens and dogs chasing each other, cows being led through the streets.

But as he studied it closely, he realized immediately that something was awry. He felt a knot in his stomach as he peered down in confusion. Before him was not the sight of his village as he

120

had expected—but rather a scene of devastation. It was an ugly picture, one he barely recognized. Instead of the familiar cottages, there were burnt-out structures, razed to the ground; instead of trees and paths, there was a field of ash and rubble, smoldering, smoke still rising.

His village was no more.

There was no sound of joyous screams of children playing, but rather the distant wails of old women, kneeling on the ground before mounds of dirt. Alec followed their glances and saw, with a jolt to his heart, that the mounds were all fresh graves, rows and rows of them, all marked with crooked crosses—and he felt himself sinking. He suddenly knew, with an awful premonition that swept over him, that everyone and everything he ever knew and loved was dead.

"NO!" Alec shrieked.

Without thinking, without even being aware of what he was doing, Alec stumbled down the hill at a sprint, nearly tripping over himself as he gained speed. It was as if he were stumbling toward a nightmare.

"Alec!" Marco called out behind him.

Alec tripped and fell in the grass, rolling, covered in mud but not caring as he got to his feet again and continued to run. He could barely feel the world around him, could hear only his own heart pounding madly as he ran.

"Ashton!" he cried out as he ran into what was once his village.

Alec ran past house after house, everything burnt to a crisp, nothing but smoldering fires. Nothing was recognizable. He could not fathom what on earth had happened here. Who could have done this? And why?

Alec could not find anything left of his own house as he sprinted by it with dread, now just a pile of embers. All that remained was one stone wall of what used to be his father's forge.

Alec followed the wailing and ran to the end of town. Finally, he reached the rows of freshly dug graves, the air thick with the smell of soil, smoke, and death.

He reached the rows of old women, kneeling, weeping, dirt on their hands, in their hair, wailing their mournful prayers. Alec stumbled forward and scanned all the bodies, his heart pounding inside, praying it couldn't be.

Please, he prayed. *Don't let my family be there. Please. I'll give anything.*

Alec suddenly stopped cold and felt his knees go weak as he saw a sight he wished he had never seen: there, laid out before him, untended, were the corpses of his father and mother, too pale, frozen in a look of agony. He felt everything inside him die at that moment.

"MOTHER! FATHER!"

He collapsed by their side in the dirt, embracing them, and his knees sank into the fresh earth as he wept, unable to understand what was happening.

Alec suddenly remembered his brother. He sat bolt upright and searched everywhere, and he could not see him. He had a glimmer of hope: had he survived?

Desperate, he ran over to a kneeling woman and grabbed her arm.

"Where is he!?" he asked. "Where is my brother!?"

The woman looked back at him and shook her head wordlessly, too overcome with grief to respond.

Alec jumped up and ran, searching.

"ASHTON!" he cried out.

Alec ran up and down the graves, searching everywhere, his heart thumping, desperate to know, wondering if he could have made it. Finally, he heard something.

"Alec!" called a weak voice.

Alec felt a wave of relief as he recognized his brother's voice, albeit a weaker version of it, and he turned and ran to the edge of the graves.

There lay his brother, wounded, seeping blood, unmoving, and Alec's heart sank as he saw him lying in the dirt, blood trickling from his mouth, gravely wounded.

He rushed forward and collapsed by his brother's side, grabbing his limp, cold hand as he wept. He saw the grievous gash across his brother's stomach, and he knew immediately that he was dying. He had never felt so helpless, seeing his brother staring back up at him, looking partially at him and partially at the sky, his eyes glazed, the life force leaving even as he watched.

"Brother," Ashton said, more of a whisper.

He smiled weakly, despite his wounds, and Alec's heart broke inside.

"I knew you would come," Ashton said, smiling. "I was waiting for you…before I died."

Alec clutched his brother's hand, shaking his head, unwilling to accept this.

"You will not die," Alec said, knowing even as he said his words that they were untrue.

Ashton smiled back.

"I never had a chance to thank you," Ashton said. "For going…to The Flames."

Ashton tried to swallow, while Alec blinked away tears.

"Who did this?" Alec insisted. "Who did this to you?"

Ashton fell silent for a long time, having difficulty swallowing.

"The Pandesians…" he finally replied, his voice weaker. "They…came…to teach us …for vengeance…"

Alec was surprised to feel his brother's sudden strong grip on his arm, to see his brother clutching his forearm with a surprising strength. His brother stared up at him with one last look of strength, of intensity, the desperation of a dying man.

"Avenge me," he said, his voice a whisper. "Avenge…all of us. Our parents. Our folk. Kill…Pandesians…. Vow to me…"

Alec felt a fresh sense of purpose, of determination, rise up within him as he had never felt in his life. He clasped his brother's hand and looked back into his eyes with an equal ferocity.

"I vow to you," Alec replied. "I vow to you with everything that I am. I will kill every last Pandesian—or I shall die trying."

His brother looked at him with a fierceness in his eyes which Alec had never seen, for a long time. Finally, his expression turned into one of satisfaction.

Ashton's face slackened, and he slid down and lay back his head, unmoving. He stared up at the sky with blank eyes, and Alec felt himself dying inside as he knew that at that moment, his brother was dead.

"NO!" Alec shrieked.

He leaned back and wailed to the heavens, wondering why everything he had loved in this world had to be taken from him—and knowing that his life was about to be consumed, to be driven, by one thing and nothing else.

Vengeance.

CHAPTER SEVENTEEN

Kyra stared back at the oaf confronting her, this foreigner with his low forehead, wide body and black eyes, smiling creepily at her, his sharpened teeth showing.

"You have no one to protect you," he said to her. "Do not struggle: it will only make it worse for you."

Kyra forced herself to breathe, to focus, drawing all the intensity she had when in battle. Inside, her heart was thumping, fire pumping in her veins, as she prepared herself for the confrontation of her life.

"If anyone needs protection," Kyra replied boldly, "it is you. I shall give you one chance to step out of my way, before you learn what the people of Escalon are made of."

The oaf stared back and blinked in shocked silence.

Then a moment later, he began laughing, a coarse, ugly sound, and all his men joined in.

"You are bold," he said. "That is good. More fun to break. I might even take you as my personal slave. Yes, the men on my ship can use a good plaything. Our trips at sea can be so very long."

Kyra felt a chill as he looked her up and down.

"Tell me something," he said. "There are ten of us and two of you. What makes you think you can survive?"

An idea began to form in Kyra's mind; it was risky, but she had no choice. She turned her back slowly on the man, determined to catch him off guard and to show him that she was unafraid.

Kyra, heart slamming, hoping he didn't jump her from behind, turned to the barkeep, looked out at the sacks of feed laid out on the bar, and out of the corner of her eye gave Dierdre a knowing look as she slowly reached out and grabbed a sack.

"Are these ours?" she asked the barkeep, casually.

He nodded back, looking scared, sweating.

"Is my payment sufficient?" she asked.

He nodded again.

"Girl," barked the foreigner behind her, annoyed, "you are about to be taken captive for life, and all you care about is your feed? Are you mad?"

Kyra felt a fire burning inside her, about to explode, but she forced herself to stay rooted in place, to wait until the moment was right. Her back to him, she addressed him:

"I am not a girl," she replied. "But a woman. And those who assume they will win merely because they are male, because they are bigger, because they outnumber their victims, seem to forget the most important thing in battle."

There came a long silence, until finally, he asked:

"And what is that?"

Kyra took a deep breath, steeling herself, knowing the moment of truth had come.

"Surprise," she said flatly.

Kyra quickly spun, still clutching the sack, and hurled it with all her might. As she did, the sack opened and the feed went flying through the air, spraying all of her attackers' eyes.

The men shrieked, clutching their eyes in the dust storm, all temporally blinded, while Dierdre, picking up on Kyra's cues, did the same, swinging the other sack in a wide arc and blinding the rest of the men. It all happened so quickly, before the startled men could react. Clearly, they had not anticipated that.

Without hesitating, Kyra drew the staff from her back, stepped forward, and with a great shout, brought it down hard on the leader's head, smashing him in a downward strike. The man fell to his knees and as soon as he did, she kicked him in the chest, sending him to his back. She then brought her staff straight down, breaking his nose.

In the same motion, Kyra spun her staff sideways and behind her, cracking another oaf across the jaw; she then sidestepped and jabbed straight back, breaking the nose of another. She then clutched her staff with both hands, rushed forward, raised it high overhead, and brought it down sideways into the faces of two men before her, knocking them both down.

While the others still clawed at their eyes, trying to extract the feed, Kyra rushed forward and kicked one between the legs, then raised her staff back and struck him downward across the face,

126

knocking him down. She then grabbed her staff with both hands, raised it high and brought it down like a knife into the chest of another man, sending him stumbling back, crashing into a table and knocking it over.

Kyra whirled through the group like lightning, so fast that the stunned men didn't have a chance to react. She was in such harmony with her weapon, all of her sparring lessons with her father's men coming back to her, it was as if she and her staff were one. Her countless nights of sparring alone, long after the other men had left, came flooding back. Her instincts took over, and within moments several of her attackers, cracked by her staff, lay writhing on the floor, bloodied, groaning.

After the chaos, only two men were left standing, and these two, grain finally cleared from their eyes, stared back at Kyra with death in their eyes. One drew a dagger.

"Let's see how that stick of yours does against a knife," he growled, and charged.

Kyra braced herself for the attack when suddenly there came a crashing noise and she was surprised to see him collapse, face-first, at her feet. She looked up to see Dierdre standing behind, holding a broken stool, hands shaking, staring down as if in shock at what she had just done.

Kyra sensed motion and turned to see the final attacker rush for Dierdre. He must have realized that she was the weak point, and Kyra saw he was about to tackle her and pin her to the ground. She could not allow that. If Dierdre were taken hostage, Kyra knew, it would make defeating these men infinitely more complicated.

Kyra, knowing she had no time, raised her staff, took aim, stepped forward, and hurled it.

Her staff went flying through the air like a spear, and Kyra watched with satisfaction as it hit the running man in his temple, right in his pressure point. His legs fell out from under him and he collapsed to the ground right before he reached Dierdre.

Dierdre looked down in gratitude, then picked up Kyra's staff and threw it back to her.

Kyra caught it and stood in the silent room, surveying the damage, all the men laid out, unmoving. She could hardly believe what she had just done. The rest of the tavern-goers stared back, mouths agape, clearly not believing what they had just witnessed, either. Her father's friend gulped, looking scared.

"I would have helped you," he said lamely, fear in his voice.

Kyra ignored the coward. Instead, she turned slowly, stepped over the unmoving bodies, and walked casually back to the bar, where the barkeep still stood, staring back, amazed. She grabbed her chickens and meat from the bar, while Dierdre took their sacks of water. This time Kyra would not leave without food for her or the others.

"Looks like I'll need more feed," she said to the barkeep.

The bartender, stunned, slowly reached down and handed her more sacks of feed.

The two girls walked back across the room, through the tavern, and out the door, none of the other men daring to approach them now.

As they walked back outside, into the freezing, pelting rain, Kyra no longer felt the cold. She was warm inside, warm with the certainty that she could defend herself, that she was no longer her father's little girl. Those men had underestimated her, as had all the men in her life—and more importantly, she realized, she had underestimated herself. Never again. She felt a confidence rising up within her. She was becoming herself. She did not know what the road ahead held, but she knew, no matter what, she would never back down to anyone again. She was as strong as these men.

Even stronger.

CHAPTER EIGHTEEN

"BLOOD EELS!" Seavig cried.

Duncan raised his sword and hacked at the thick, red eels twisting their way up his leg, as the Lake of Ire seemed to come alive with them. He felt them squeezing his flesh as all around him his men cried out and fell into the waters, splashing, flailing; yet as he swung, he was unable to gain enough momentum to slash through the thick waters and do any real damage to the creatures.

Desperate, feeling himself being dragged down, Duncan reached into his belt, grabbed his dagger and jabbed straight down. There came a screeching noise, follow by bubbles shooting to the surface, and the eel wrapped around him went limp.

"DAGGERS!" Duncan shouted to his men.

With the fog walkers gone, the fog finally began to lift all around them, and Duncan could see, all around him, his men following his command, jabbing their daggers at the eels as they were being pulled down. Hisses and shrieks rose up, as one by one the eels were killed and the men began to extricate themselves.

"MAKE FOR THE SHORE!" Duncan shouted, realizing the fog had lifted.

The men all made for the shore, splashing wildly as they waded their way out as quickly as they could. Duncan was dismayed to see that many of his men, unable to stab the eels quickly enough, were sucked down, shrieking, beneath the murky waters—dead before anyone could reach them.

Duncan heard a shout and looked over to see Anvin being dragged down behind him. He turned back and splashed for his friend, leaping into action.

"Take my hand!" Duncan yelled, wading into the eel-filled waters, hacking with one hand while extending a hand to Anvin with the other. He knew he was risking his life, but he could not leave his friend behind.

He finally grabbed Anvin's hand and pulled with all his might, trying to extricate him from the nest of eels. He was making progress when suddenly several eels leapt from the water and wrapped around Duncan's forearm; instead of helping his friend, he felt himself being sucked under.

There came a splashing, and Duncan turned to see Arthfael and Seavig and several of their men rushing back to help them. They swung with daggers and swords, chopping at the eels, swinging expertly, just missing Duncan's and Anvin's arms. The eels hissed all around them, and soon Duncan felt himself extricated again.

They all turned and waded back for shore, splashing as fast as they could, and this time, Duncan reached it, finding himself on shore, gasping for breath, aching all over from the sting of those creatures. He dropped to his knees, exhausted, and kissed the sand. The fog was gone, the eels hissed in the waters, a safe distance away, and Duncan had never felt so grateful to be on dry land again.

Finally, one nightmare after the next was behind them.

*

Duncan raised his ax and hacked away at the small red tree before him, chopping as he had been for hours, worked up into a sweat, his hands raw and calloused. All around him the air was filled with the sound of his men chopping, of the small trees falling in the clearing. With one final hack his tree fell, too, landing with a whoosh before him.

Duncan leaned back and rested on his ax handle, breathing hard, wiping sweat from his forehead, and he surveyed his men. They were all hard at work, some chopping trees, others carrying them and lining them up beside each other, and others were binding the logs to each other with thick ropes, creating rafts.

Duncan grabbed one end of his tree while Anvin grabbed the other, a log about fifteen feet long, and they hoisted it, surprisingly heavy, onto their shoulders. They marched through the muddy banks of the Thusius and dropped it in a pile by the river's edge.

Sprayed by the gushing currents of the river, Duncan stood and examined his handiwork. That log had been the final piece needed for his impromptu raft. All up and down the banks of the Thusius, his men were engaged in the same activity, dozens of rafts being hastily erected, all of them preparing. It would be a great army moving downriver.

130

Duncan examined the gushing currents of the Thusius, and he wondered if his boat would hold. Yet he knew this was the only way, if he were to get all of his men to Kos undetected. He turned and saw the last of the rafts being tied, and he knew the time had come.

Seavig stepped up beside him, flanked by several men and, hands on his hips, looked downriver.

"Will they hold?" Duncan asked, surveying the rafts.

Seavig nodded.

"I've spent more time on sea than land," he replied. "Not to worry. If it's one thing my people understand, it is water. Those rafts may look shoddy, but they are secure. That is Esephan twine, stronger than any Volis rope. And those logs may seem small, but don't be fooled: the Red Pine of the Thusius is the hardiest in the world. It may bend, but will never give."

Duncan looked at his legions of men, battle-hardened, but few of them sailors. The rafts were slippery, with not much to hold onto, and the men wore armor, too easy for them to sink. Seavig was used to leading men at sea, but in Duncan's eyes, the conditions were far from ideal.

"How far to Kos?" Duncan asked.

Seavig nodded to the horizon.

"You see those mountains?"

Duncan looked out and on the horizon he saw the jagged, white peaks rising impossibly high, disappearing into the clouds, higher than any mountain should ever reach. From the looks of them, they appeared to be days away.

"If the current flows," Seavig replied, "we may reach the base in a day. That is, if we all make it."

Seavig gave him a concerned look.

"Advise your men to stay in the center of the rafts; the Thusius teems with creatures that make those we left behind seem pleasant. Above all, have them avoid the swirls."

"The swirls?" Duncan asked, not liking the sound of it.

"Whirlpools abound in this river," Seavig said. "Stick close together, and we should be fine."

Duncan furrowed his brow; he was a man of the land, and he did not like this.

131

"Is there no safer way to Kos?" he asked again, studying the land.

Seavig shook his head.

"There is no more direct way, either," he replied. "We can take the plains, if you wish, but a Pandesian garrison guards it. That would mean a battle now. If you want to reach Kos in peace, the Thusius is the only way."

Duncan still had speed and surprise on his side, and he could not risk alarming Pandesia to his revolt; it was a chance he simply could not take.

"The river, then," Duncan said, decided.

Duncan had one thing left to do before they all embarked. He turned and walked over to his war horse, a great friend to him in battle for as long as he could remember. It pained him to leave his side—but they could not take their horses on the rafts.

"Good friend," Duncan said, stroking his mane, "lead the other horses. They are your army now. Lead them south. To Kos. To the mountain base. Wait for us there, on the way to Andros. I will be expecting you—and I know you will be waiting for me."

Duncan spoke to his horse as he would one of his men, and with a gentle nudge, he watched him neigh, rear his fierce legs high in the air, then turn and suddenly gallop proudly away, a leader in his own right. As he did, all the other horses—hundreds of them—turned and followed him, a great stampede, all racing south in one massive heard, the earth shaking with their rumble. They kicked up a cloud of dust and Duncan watched them go with a mix of sadness and pride. His horse understood him better than any man alive.

"If only my men would heed me the same way," Seavig said wistfully, coming up by his side.

"Let us hope he has a master left for him when he arrives," Duncan replied.

Duncan nodded and Anvin sounded the horn as Seavig's men sounded theirs. Their army came alive, all the men stepping forward, shoving their rafts onto the waters, and jumping aboard. Duncan shoved his, too; it was heavier than he thought, he and several others pushing it through the mud until it floated in the water. As it floated, he was relieved to see that Seavig had been

132

right: the Red Pine became buoyant in the water, and the twine held firm.

Duncan jumped aboard with the others, then reached out with the long pole he had carved and jabbed it into the dry ground, shoving, pushing them farther out, away from shore, and into the middle of the river.

The Thusius, perhaps fifty yards wide, ran with crystal clear water, and he could see straight down to the bottom of it, perhaps twenty feet below, its bed sparkling with rocks and gems of all different shapes and colors. It was a sight to see. Soon the currents caught them, and they all began to move, slowly at first, hundreds of rafts carrying thousands of men as one. They were a floating army.

They gained momentum quickly and soon the pace quickened. Duncan was satisfied to feel the waters moving at a fast pace beneath them, all of the rafts holding, gaining more speed than they ever would have on land—and not having to strain any horses or men. He searched the land and spotted his horse, galloping in the distance, leading the army of horses, and he felt a wave of pride.

Duncan, standing on the raft with several men, felt the river racing beneath him, the wind in his hair, the spray of the water reaching him on occasion. He used the pole to steer their raft, and they fell into a comfortable groove on the wide and smooth river.

He eventually relaxed and let down his guard as the river took them twisting around one bend after the other. He looked out and studied the ever-changing landscape. They passed purple forests and plains bleached white; they passed herds of exotic creatures, looking like gazelles, but with heads at each end of their body. They passed plains of rock, sprawled in odd shapes, as if some ancient civilization had plopped them down and left. It was an uninhabited stretch of Escalon, dominated more by nature than man.

Duncan looked up and studied the mountains of Kos, their white peaks ever present, looming larger the closer they came. Soon enough, they would reach them. If he could rally the warriors who lived at its peak, it would be the turning point, what he needed to stage an attack on the capital. He knew his chances were slim, but that was what it meant, in his eyes, to be a warrior: to wage battle, despite all odds.

His heart beat faster at the idea of freeing Escalon, of ridding it of the Pandesians, of waging the war they should have waged years ago. Win or lose, at least, finally, he was riding into his destiny.

"How long since you've seen Kos?" Seavig called out over the sound of the current, his raft coming up beside Duncan's as he steered it with his pole, the two rafts cruising downriver side by side.

Duncan crouched down low as his raft suddenly dropped two feet, rocking violently in the rapids before leveling out again. The water was getting rougher, and as Duncan tried to concentrate on the currents, he marveled at how poised Seavig and his men were—water people, they stood tall, well-balanced, as if standing on dry land.

"Many years," Duncan finally called back. "I was a young man then. Still, it was a time I can never forget. I remember...the climb...the altitude...its people—a hard people. Brave warriors, fearless—but hard. They were reclusive. They were with us, but never quite with us."

Seavig nodded.

"Nothing has changed," he replied. "Now, they are more reclusive than ever. They were always separatist—now, after Tarnis' betrayal, they are like a nation of their own."

"Maybe it's the mountain air," joked Anvin, his raft coming up beside theirs. "Maybe they look down on all of us."

"They don't," Seavig replied. "They just don't have much interest in others."

Duncan looked up and studied the white peaks, getting closer with each bend in the river.

"They hide up there," Seavig replied, "from the Pandesian strongholds below. If they came down, they would be attacked. And the Pandesians don't dare breach those heights—they know it would be folly. So the men of Kos fancy themselves free—but they are not free. They are trapped."

Duncan studied the mountains, and he wasn't so sure.

"The men of Kos whom I met feared nothing," Duncan replied. "Certainly no Pandesians. I doubt they fear coming down."

"Then why haven't they descended since the invasion?" Seavig asked.

It was a mystery that Duncan had wondered at himself.

"Maybe they feel the old king does not deserve their respect," Anvin offered. "Maybe they feel we are not worth coming down for after surrendering Escalon. The mountains are their home—to come down would be to fight our battles."

"To come down would be to fight for Escalon, their land, too," Seavig countered.

Duncan shrugged.

"I don't know the answer," Duncan called out. "But we shall find out."

"And if they refuse to join us?" Seavig asked. "Then what? Climbing those peaks is no small risk."

Duncan looked up and studied the steep ascent, and he wondered the same thing. He would be leading his men up a perilous path—what if it was all for naught?

"They will descend," Duncan finally said. "They will join us. Because the men of Kos whom I know would not refuse an invitation to freedom."

"Whose freedom?" Seavig asked. "Theirs or ours?"

Duncan pondered his words as they all fell back into silence, the rapids gaining speed, bringing them ever farther down the Thusius. It was a fine question, indeed. Climbing those peaks would indeed be a risk—and he prayed it would not all be for naught.

Duncan heard an unfamiliar noise and as he looked over at Seavig, wondering. He was surprised to find his friend studying the river, fear in his eyes for the first time.

"The swirls!" Seavig cried.

His men all blew their horns at once, and Seavig shoved with his pole, desperately trying to move his raft to the far side of the river. Duncan and his men followed, steering their rafts to the far side of the river, and as they did, Duncan looked over to the middle of the river and was shocked by what he saw. There were a series of small whirlpools, twisting and turning, making a great noise, sucking everything in their path down into it. It consumed much of the river, leaving only a narrow strip to navigate past, forcing their great army to cruise alongside the edge of the river single file.

Duncan looked back over his shoulder, taking stock of his men, and his heart dropped to see one of his rafts not get out of the way fast enough. He watched with horror as it was sucked into the whirlpool, his men shrieking as they spun again and again, instantly sucked down to the bottom of the river.

Duncan reflexively tried to jump in after them, even though he was a good fifty yards away, but Seavig reached out with his pole and held it against his chest, stopping him, while Duncan's men grabbed his shoulders.

"You jump in, you're a dead man," Seavig said. "The more who follow, the more will die. Without you, far more men will die. Is that what you wish?"

Duncan stood there, torn inside, feeling as if he were going down with his men. Deep down, he knew Seavig was right. He had no choice but to grit his teeth and watch his men, from afar, disappear in the currents.

Duncan turned back, reluctantly, looked ahead, downriver, as the swirls disappeared and the currents went back to normal. He cursed this place. Nothing pained him more than to watch the death of his men—and to be helpless to do anything about it. It was the price of being a leader, he knew. He was no longer just one of the men; he was responsible for each and every one.

"I am sorry, my friend," Seavig said with a heavy voice. "It is the price of the Thusius. The land would, I'm sure, carry its own dangers."

Duncan noticed the fear in the faces of the soldiers on the raft with him, including his two sons, and he could not help but think of Kyra. He wondered where she was now. Had she reached Whitewood yet? Had she made it to the sea?

Most of all, was she safe?

He had a pit in his stomach as he thought of her, practically alone out there. He remembered, of course, her power, her incredible skills in combat; yet still, she was but a girl, hardly a woman yet, and Escalon was an unforgiving place. It was a quest she needed to take, for her benefit, yet still, he doubted himself. Had it been a mistake to send her on the journey alone? What if she didn't make it? He would never be able to live with himself again.

Most of all, he wondered: who would she become during her training? Who would she be when she returned to him? He was both in awe of the powers he knew she had—and afraid of them.

Duncan looked out and watched the ever-changing landscape, the climate cooling as they neared the immense mountains. The grass shores bordering the river slowly gave way to bogs the further south they went, long stretches of river bank bordered by reeds, marshes. Duncan saw exotic, brightly colored animals raise their heads in the reeds and snap at the air before disappearing just as quickly.

Hour followed hour, the Thusius ever twisting and turning. The weather grew colder, the spray stronger, and soon Duncan felt his hands and feet growing numb. The mountains loomed ever larger, closer and closer, feeling as if they were just an arm's reach away, though he knew they still had hours to go. Duncan searched for his horses out there, hoping, but saw none.

Duncan did not know how many hours had passed, holding his pole, studying the currents, when suddenly he noticed Seavig gesture in the raft beside him. As they rounded a bend, he noticed a disturbance in the water up ahead. Something was foaming and churning in the waters, even though the water here was calm. It was as if a school of fish might be beneath it.

Duncan studied it, confused, and as they neared, he thought he saw something leap from the water. He looked over to Seavig, and for the first time since they began this journey together, he saw real fear in his friend's face.

"River sharks!" Seavig shrieked. "Get down!"

His men dropped to their stomachs on their rafts while Duncan watched, puzzled. Before he and his men could get down, he suddenly looked out and saw, with horror, what they were talking about: there, up ahead, was a school of massive sharks, thirty feet long, leaping from the river, soaring through the air in a high arch and crashing back down. There were dozens of them, and as the churning moved, they were all clearly heading upriver—right for them.

Duncan watched, mesmerized, horrified, as he saw their massive jaws, their rows of sharpened teeth, their glowing red eyes, filled with fury as they sailed through the air and came upriver, right for them. Everything inside him told him to get down—but it was too late. It all happened too quickly, and by the time he understood, there was no time to react.

He stared a shark in the face as it began to descend right for him, jaws wide open, and he knew that here, on this river, he had finally met a foe he would not defeat. Here, amidst these currents, his end had come.

CHAPTER NINETEEN

Kyra sat in the cave before the crackling fire, leaned back against the warm rock wall and breathed deep, finally relaxed. Finally, they were dry, warm, out of the wind and rain, her belly was full, and she was able to feel her hands and feet again. Her muscles ached, slowly coming back to themselves. The cave was filled with the smells of roasting chickens, and the fire in this small space emitted more warmth than she had expected. For the first time, she felt she could let her guard down.

Beside her, Dierdre leaned back, too, also full, content, while Leo, his head in her lap, was already snoring. At the entrance to the cave, just outside, in the night, Andor stood guard with Dierdre's mare, each tied up and happily munching on their sacks of feed, the rain having finally stopped. Kyra had tried to get Andor to come inside and rest, but he had no interest.

Kyra closed her eyes for a moment, exhausted, having been awake for she did not know how many days, and she reflected. After they'd left that tavern they had crossed the River Tanis and had entered Whitewood, another forest, although this one filled with beautiful white trees and leaves and having a more peaceful energy. The Wood of the West, Dierdre had called it. Kyra had been so relieved to be out of the darkness of the Wood of Thorns, and to now, at least, have the ocean in hearing distance. It would be her guide, she knew, all the way to Ur.

They had continued in Whitewood until Leo had spotted this cave, and Kyra thanked God for it. She did not know how much longer they all could have gone on without a rest, a chance to dry off, to eat. She had just meant to stay for a few minutes, but they all, once settled, felt so rested here, on the soft earthen floor, the fire crackling at their feet, that they all settled in. Kyra realized the wisdom in staying put: she did not see the point of continuing on at night, and with everyone so exhausted.

Kyra closed her eyes and let herself drift off into her thoughts. She thought first of her father, wondering where he was now. Had he made it south? Did he reach Esephus? Was he in combat right now? Was he thinking of her? Did he care about her? And most of all: would he be proud of her?

And what of Aidan? Was he all alone in Volis?

Kyra, eyes heavy, so tired, let them close for just a moment. She was drifting in and out of sleep, when a sudden noise awakened her. She opened her eyes and was shocked to see that dawn had broken. She could not believe she had slept that long.

She realized the source of the sound: Leo. He stood beside her, snarling, hair rising on his back, protective of her, staring at the entrance to the cave.

Immediately, Kyra sat up, heart pounding, on guard.

"Leo, what is it, boy?" she asked.

But he ignored her, instead creeping toward the entrance, his hair stiffening as his snarling became more vicious. Kyra sat bolt upright, gripping her staff, listening. But she could not hear a thing.

Kyra wondered what could be lurking outside, how long she had slept. She stood and poked Dierdre with her staff, until Dierdre woke and sat up, too. They both watched Leo as he crept toward the entrance.

"LEO!" Kyra cried.

There suddenly came a horrific snarling noise, followed by a stampede of hooves and a great cloud of dust racing past the cave. Kyra and Dierdre raced for the entrance as another stampede came, Kyra wondering what on earth that was.

Kyra reached the entrance, Andor snarling, too, and looked out and saw several deer running past the cave. She realized, with dread, that they were fleeing something. Something bigger.

Kyra turned to her right and spotted, about a hundred yards away, a pack of beasts running her way. At first she thought she was seeing things, yet the coming cloud of dust and thunderous noise told her it was no illusion. The creatures were each the size of a small rhino, with a black hide adorned with yellow stripes and two slim horns at the tip of their nose that ran straight up, a good ten feet. There were six of them, and they all charged right for them, their eyes glowing red, filled with fury.

"Hornhogs!" Dierdre cried out. "They must have smelled our food!"

140

Dierdre quickly mounted her horse while Kyra mounted Andor—and they all took off, Leo beside them, heading into the wood, hoping to outrun them.

As she rode, Kyra scratched by branches still wet from the long rain, she marveled at how different the wood was on this side of the river. The trees were all white, the branches white, the leaves white, quite beautiful, the world glistening as they rode, catching her eye even as she rode for her life. They rode south, using the River Tanis as a guide, hearing its gushing as they went. Kyra had hoped to wake rested and refreshed, but now she was startled, still unsure if she were awake or having a terrible dream.

Kyra checked back over her shoulder, hoping the hornhogs would be out of sight, especially given Andor's speed—yet was dismayed to see they were not. They were, in fact, closer. They were incredibly fast creatures, especially for their size, and they bore down right for them, like hornets on a trail.

Kyra kicked Andor, but it was no use. Andor was faster than Dierdre's mare, and Kyra gained some distance on her—yet even so, he was not fast enough to outrun the beasts. Kyra realized she could not let too much distant come between her and her friend.

No sooner had she had the thought when suddenly Kyra heard a cry, followed by a horse's shriek and a rumble. She looked back and was horrified to see the lead hornhog, faster than the others, had caught up to Dierdre and her mare. It pounced, piercing the mare with its long horns, then sank its fangs into the mare's back.

The mare went tumbling down, and Kyra was horrified to see her friend go down, too. She flew off the mare and rolled into the wood, while the hornhog, preoccupied, attacked the mare, tearing it to shreds as it shrieked. Kyra knew it was only a matter of time until it set its sights on Dierdre.

The pack soon caught up, all of them distracted as they pounced on the mare and tore it to bits.

Kyra could not let her friend wallow there. She turned Andor around and charged for Dierdre, Leo at her side. She rode up beside her, reached down, grabbed her hand, and yanked her up. Dierdre sat behind her and they all turned and took off, while the hornhogs, preoccupied, continued to devour their kill, fighting over the pieces of the horse.

Kyra tore through Whitewood at a gallop, and Kyra was sure, given Andor's blazing speed, that they would soon put a great distance between them.

But her heart dropped as she heard a familiar sound behind her: a hornhog broke away from the pack, its face covered in blood, and hunted them down, still not satisfied.

The creature bore down them, and Leo, snarling, suddenly stopped, turned and charged.

"LEO!" Kyra shrieked.

But Leo would not be deterred. He leapt into the air and met it head on, sinking his fangs into the hornhog's throat, catching it off guard and driving it to the ground, despite its size.

Kyra watched in shock, so proud of Leo's courage, but was amazed to see that, for the first time, her wolf's razor sharp fangs were unable to puncture a creature's hide, as thick as it was. The hornhog merely rolled on its back and threw Leo, who went flying onto his back. The hornhog then charged for the prone wolf.

Kyra, horrified, saw that it was about to kill Leo, and that she would not reach him in time.

"NO!" Kyra shrieked.

Her reflexes kicked in. Without thinking, she grabbed her bow, placed an arrow, raised it, and took aim.

Her heart slammed as she watched the arrow sail through the air, praying that it hit its mark, with barely time to take aim.

The arrow hit the hornhog in its eye, a powerful shot that would have felled any other beast.

But not this one. The hornhog shrieked in agony and, furious, turned away from Leo and set its sights, instead, on her. It reached up with its paw and merely snapped the arrow in two, then snarled at her, death in its eyes. At least Leo's life had been spared.

It charged and Kyra had no time to reload another arrow; it was too close, and too fast, and she knew that in but a moment it would tear her apart.

There came a vicious snarl, even more vicious than that of the hornhog, and Kyra suddenly felt Andor lunge beneath her. Andor snarled, lowered its horns, and charged with a ferocity unlike any Kyra had ever seen. As it bucked, it was all Kyra could do just to hang on.

A moment later there came a tremendous impact as the two creatures met, like the world shaking beneath her. Andor's horns gored the hornhog in the side, and the hornhog shrieked in true despair. Kyra was shocked to witness Andor lift the immense creature high in the air, impaled on its horns, overhead, as if displaying a trophy of his kill.

Andor threw it, and it flew through the wood and landed with a thud, lifeless.

Whistling at Leo to follow, Kyra kicked Andor, and the group of them turned and took off at a gallop, running back through the wood, Kyra trying to get as much distance as she could from the rest of the pack, knowing this was a battle she did not want to fight—and a battle they all could not win. She hoped and prayed that the hornhogs were gorged, and that with one of their own dead, maybe they would think twice about pursuing any further.

She was wrong. Kyra heard a familiar sound behind her, and her heart dropped as she soon realized the rest of the pack was after them. Relentless, they chased them down through the rustling leaves, all as determined as ever. The death of one of their own only seemed to embolden them. These tenacious creatures did not seem as if they would ever quit.

Given their numbers, Kyra knew their situation was desperate: there was no way Andor and Leo could defeat all of them at once. She felt a sudden panic as she knew they would all die by these creatures' hands.

"We won't make it!" Dierdre cried out, fear in her voice, as she looked back at the pack, snarling and closing in.

Kyra wracked her brain, thinking hard as they galloped, realizing they needed another way—and fast. She closed her eyes and focused, forcing herself to tune in, to draw on all her faculties to save them. Despite the chaos all around them, she grew very quiet inside.

Kyra suddenly began to hear a noise, one she had not heard before. She opened her eyes as she focused on the sound of gushing water, and she remembered: the River Tanis. They were heading parallel to it, and it was hardly a hundred yards to her left. She suddenly had an idea.

143

"The river!" she shouted to Dierdre, remembering all those flat, wooden rafts she'd seen tied up along its shores. "We can take the river!"

Kyra suddenly pulled Andor's reins, making a sharp left, heading toward the water; as she did, the hornhogs, but feet behind them, leapt through the air and missed, falling flat on their faces on the ground. The sharp turn bought them some time.

Kyra dug her heels into Andor and they galloped at full speed, as the sound of water grew louder. She raced past branches, weaving in and out of trees, scratched and no longer caring, breathing hard, hearing the pack behind them and knowing their time was limited.

Come on, she thought, urging the river to appear. *Come on!*

They finally burst out of the wood, into a clearing, and there, before them, the river lay in sight, hardly thirty yards away.

"What about Andor?" Dierdre cried out as they neared.

Kyra set her sights on a wide, flat boat, tied up at its shore and realized it would serve their needs.

"That will hold us all!" she cried back, pointing.

Kyra yanked Andor to a stop near the shoreline, and they all dismounted immediately. Kyra hit the ground running and raced for the shore, jumping onto the wildly rocking boat, Leo at her side, Dierdre beside her. She made room for Andor, yanking on his reins, but she was shocked as she felt him resist.

Andor stood on shore and refused to follow, bucking like crazy, and Kyra wondered what it could be. At first she thought that perhaps he feared water. But then Andor gave her a meaningful look and she suddenly understood: he was not afraid. He meant to stay behind and guard their rear, to fight the hornhogs to the death, alone, so that they could all escape without him.

Kyra was overwhelmed by his loyalty, but she could not leave him behind.

"No, Andor!" Kyra cried.

She went to get back off the boat and get him.

But Andor suddenly lowered his head and used his sharp horns to sever the rope. Kyra felt the boat jerk out from under her and immediately it was carried away by the rough tides, drifting quickly away from shore.

144

Kyra stood at the edge of the boat and watched, helpless, as Andor turned around, on shore, and faced off against the pack. She saw one of the hornhogs race past him, and was amazed to watch it leap into the water, swimming as fast as it ran, and treading right for their boat. She was shocked to see these hornhogs could swim, and she suddenly realized: Andor knew. He knew that if he didn't stay behind, they could all be attacked in the water. He was sacrificing for them all.

As the hornhog approached, Leo snarled, snapping at the water as he stood at the edge of the boat. Kyra raised her bow, took aim, and fired, aiming right for its open mouth.

The arrow lodged itself in its open mouth, and the hornhog sucked in water and flailed as it drowned.

Kyra looked back to shore and saw Andor charge boldly for the pack, even though he was outnumbered. He must have known he could not win—and yet he did not care. It was as if fear did not exist within him. She was in awe of him; he was like a great warrior charging alone against an army.

Kyra could not stand the sight of him fighting alone—especially on their behalf. It went against everything inside her.

"ANDOR!" Kyra shrieked.

"It's too late," Dierdre said, placing a hand on her arm, as their boat drifted farther and farther from shore, the rapids more violent. "There is nothing we can do."

But Kyra refused to accept that. She could not allow her friend, her partner in battle, to be left behind.

Without thinking, Kyra let her impulses take over. She rushed forward and leapt off the boat, into the raging river, instantly submerged in the freezing waters.

Kyra tried to swim, desperate to reach shore, to reach Andor—but the rapids were just too intense. She could not make it upstream; she could not even catch her breath.

"KYRA!" Dierdre yelled, as Leo whined at the boat's edge.

A moment later, Kyra found herself flailing, sinking—and realizing, after all that, she would die by drowning.

CHAPTER TWENTY

Aidan tossed and turned as he dreamt troubled dreams. He saw his father gushing downriver, drowning in rapids; he saw another river and his sister, Kyra, flailing as she tumbled down over waterfalls; he saw the entire Pandesian army invading Escalon, setting it aflame; and he saw an army of dragons swooping low, breathing fire over Escalon and burning it to a crisp. The flames of the dragons met the flames of the Pandesians, and soon Escalon was nothing but one giant conflagration. Aidan saw himself caught in the middle of it, shrieking, burned alive.

Aidan woke with a start, gasping, breathing hard, wanting to cry out; yet some part of him stopped himself, warning him to stay silent. He felt himself moving, bumping, and felt hard wood behind his head. He twisted, supremely uncomfortable, and tried to figure out where he was.

Disoriented, Aidan looked about, felt a clump of hay in his hand, and noticed hay in his mouth. He spit it out and as he heard the clatter of horses and felt another bump, it all came rushing back to him: the wagon.

Aidan remembered he had been crammed back here, hiding beneath the straw, riding south for what felt like days—though he knew it could not have been that long. He felt the hunger gnawing in his stomach, felt the cold in his bones, and realized he had fallen asleep somewhere along the way. The dreams had seemed so real it took him a moment to collect himself, and as he began to sit up, he checked himself, realizing not to sit too high so as to remain undetected. The last thing he'd want would be to lose his only ride out here, far from home, in the midst of the Wood of Thorns. There remained a long way to go, he knew, until he reached his father and his men—wherever they were.

Aidan pondered the dreams, trying to shake them off but unable to. His heart pounded as he considered it all. Was his father in danger? Was Kyra? Was Pandesia attacking? Were the dragons coming to kill them all? He felt more of an urgency to reach his father than ever.

Aidan leaned back and looked up at the sky, relieved to see it was still night, giving him more cover from being detected. The sky jostled by as they rode, the millions of stars far away, and he wondered about them, as he often did. Aidan had studied astronomy—along with philosophy, history, reading and writing—as had his siblings, all of them so fortunate, he knew, to have been given a rare education typically reserved for the royal family. He was lucky the weak king's historian had fled Andros to stay with his father in Volis.

His tutor had drilled him for years about the star systems, and as Aidan studied them he recognized the Four Points, and the Seven Daggers; he saw which way they were turned and he took comfort in realizing he was indeed heading south—though also a bit west. That could only mean one thing: they were heading to Andros. Exactly as Aidan had hoped.

Aidan knew his father was heading south, but was still unsure where. The capital had been his first guess. After all, wouldn't his father want to go to the capital first, to win the old king's support? And was that not south? That was where Aidan would find him, he decided. Andros.

The last time Aidan had been to the capital he had been too young to remember. He imagined himself entering it now, on the back of this wagon, dismounting and taking it all in, the greatest city in Escalon, a sight, he knew, which would not disappoint. He would enter it boldly, fearlessly, make his presence known and demand to know where his father was. He would be taken right to him, and would arrive as a welcome hero.

Aidan was disappointed his father did not have faith in him to let him know where he was going, to invite him along; he felt certain he could help his cause somehow. After all, he knew more about the great battles of history than most of his father's men. Could he not counsel them on strategy, at least? Why did his father think one had to be a grown man to achieve great things? After all, hadn't Nikor the Great conquered The Plains at fourteen? Hadn't Carnald the Cruel taken the Western Half when he was but twelve? Of course, those were centuries ago, in another time and place. But Aidan refused to be discounted. He was still a great warrior's son, even if the youngest and weakest of them.

Aidan was jostled as the horses hit a ditch, and as he banged his head in the carriage, he grunted involuntarily.

The carriage came to a sudden stop, and Aidan immediately slid down beneath the bales of hay, his heart thumping, terrified, praying he was not discovered. If he was kicked off this carriage, as far as he was from anything, he knew he could very well die out here.

Aidan peeked out and saw the driver, a heavyset, middle-aged man with broad shoulders and a bald spot on the back of his head, turn and peer back in the night, examining his carriage. He had a bulbous nose, wide jaws, a low forehead, and the look of a man who wanted to kill something.

Stupid, Aidan thought. *Why didn't you stay put? Why did you make a noise?*

He lay there, in a cold sweat, praying he was not discovered. And as he waited in the night's silence, he expected to hear the man jumping down, coming back and grabbing him.

A moment later, to Aidan's surprise, he felt movement and heard the horses walking again. He was flooded with relief, and he thanked God he had the cover of darkness. He let out a deep breath, and vowed not to move again all the way until they reached Andros.

Hour followed hour, Aidan resting as comfortably as he could with the carriage jostling, and slowly he found himself drifting back towards sleep. His eyes heavy, he was nearly dreaming again—when suddenly he felt something moving against his leg.

Aidan lay there, frozen in fear, wondering. It moved again. Something was in there, in the hay, with him. Something alive. Could it be a snake had found its way into the hay?

Aidan knew he should stay still, but he couldn't help it. He slowly lifted the hay, just enough to see—and he saw a sight that he would never forget. There, beneath the hay, were several dead animals—a dead deer, three dead fox, and a dead boar, all bound by their paws, bound together with coarse twine. Yet that was not what stunned him; there was one other animal, bound to them, too, that lay there, bloody, wounded: a small dog. Aidan was even more stunned to see it move its paw.

It was no ordinary dog, Aidan could see right away, but a Wood Dog, a wild breed that lived in the woods, nearly twice the size of a normal dog and rumored to be a fierce animal. This one had a white coat, short hair, a thick muscular body, a long, narrow jaw, and piercing, soulful green eyes which stared up helplessly at Aidan. It lay on its side, breathing hard, clearly in pain, moving its paw limply. It was, Aidan was pained to see, dying. Aidan saw the gash across the animal's leg and saw it look at him with a look of desperation. It was a plea for help.

Aidan's heart broke. There was nothing he hated to see more than a wounded animal. He immediately recalled the banner of his house, a knight holding a wolf, and he knew it was also his family's sacred obligation to save any animal in need. Obligation or not, he could not let any animal suffer.

Aidan recalled that Wood Dogs, despite their tame appearance, were even more dangerous than wolves. He had been cautioned not to go near one. And yet as Aidan studied it, he did not sense it wished to harm him; on the contrary, he felt a connection to this animal. He burned with anger that it had been treated this way, and he knew he could not let it die.

Aidan sat there, torn up inside. He knew that if he tried to free it, or help it, he would be discovered. That would mean his being abandoned here in the middle of this wood—which, in turn, would mean death. The cost of saving this creature would be high—it would be his own life. And for a dying animal.

Yet Aidan didn't care. What mattered most to him was doing the right thing.

Aidan crawled through the hay, trying to stay low, reached over, and stroked the dog's fur. He expected it to bite him, given what he knew about the breed, but he was shocked to see the dog, perhaps because it was wounded, whine and lick his hand.

"Shhh," Aidan tried to soothe him. "You'll be okay." Aidan examined its white hide, and said, "I shall call you White."

White whined, as if in approval.

Aidan glanced up, relieved the driver had not spotted him, and examined White's wound. He tore a strip off his tunic and wrapped it around the dog's leg, and as it did, White whined louder. Aidan quickly pulled a piece of dried meat from his sack and placed it in his mouth, trying to quiet him.

White chewed weakly, his eyes half closed, and Aidan sensed he was very weak. He seemed to be gravely injured, and Aidan wondered if he would live.

Yet after he swallowed it, to Aidan's surprise, White opened his eyes wide and appeared to have a burst of energy. He looked directly at Aidan with a grateful look, and Aidan felt they were bonded for life. Aidan knew he could not walk away from this animal—whatever the cost. He had to free it.

Aidan removed his small dagger from his belt and quickly severed the ropes binding White's paws, and a moment later, he was free.

White sat up and looked at Aidan with what appeared to be a look of surprise. He began to wag his tail.

"Shhhh," Aidan said, "don't move. Or we shall both be discovered."

But White was too excited—and Aidan could not control him as he burst to his feet, sending hay everywhere in a big commotion. Aidan's heart stopped, knowing they would be discovered.

Sure enough, a moment later the carriage came to a jolting stop, slamming Aidan's head on the wood rail. Hardly had the horses stopped when the driver jumped down and came running around the back.

Aidan saw an angry man standing there, hands on his hips, scowling down at them both. He appeared surprised to see the dog alive, more surprised to see him free, and furious to see Aidan sitting there.

"Who are you, boy?" the man demanded. "And what are you doing on my cart?" The man then scowled at the dog. "And what have you done with my kill?"

"I have freed him," Aidan said back proudly, standing, chest out, an indignant feeling overtaking him and giving him courage. "He is a beautiful animal you tried to kill. Shame on you."

The man fumed, turning bright red, visible even beneath the starlight.

"How dare you talk back to me, you insolent little boy!" the man said. "That is my game to do with as I wish!"

"He is not!" Aidan "He is a dog! And he is free now!"

"*Free*, is he!?" the man spat, apoplectic, taking a threatening step forward.

But Aidan felt an unfamiliar strength overcoming him as he thought of saving the dog. He knew he was in a precarious position, and he realized he needed to make his best effort to scare this man away once and for all.

"My father is warlord of Volis!" Aidan stated firmly, proudly. "He has a thousand men at his command. If you lay a hand on me, or on this creature, I shall have you imprisoned!"

The man huffed, and Aidan was disappointed to see he was unimpressed.

"Stupid little boy. Do you really think I care who your father is?" the man shot back. "You are in my cart. And that is my game. I am going to kill him—and when I'm done I'm going to give you a proper pounding."

The man rushed forward, raised his fist, and before Aidan could react, he brought it down quickly on the dog's skull.

Aidan was horrified to watch White yelp and slide backwards, off the cart, landing on the frozen ground with a thud.

The man reached up to punch the dog again, death in his eyes, and this time, Aidan reacted without thinking. He held out his dagger and lunged forward, and before the man could hit White, he sliced the man's armpit.

The man shrieked, stumbling back, grabbing his armpit, dripping blood. He slowly turned and scowled at Aidan, death in his eyes.

"You're a dead boy now," he said darkly.

The man lunged forward, too quick for Aidan to react, grabbed Aidan's wrist, shook the dagger from it, then grabbed him from behind and threw him.

Aidan felt himself go flying through the air, off the cart. He landed face-first in the mud, winded, pain rippling through his body.

Aidan tried to scramble to his knees, but before he could, the man rushed forward and kicked him in the ribs with his huge boot.

Aidan had never felt such pain his life, feeling as if all his ribs were cracking as he rolled in the mud. Before he could catch his breath, he felt rough hands grabbing him as he was hoisted into the air.

"Stupid," the man said. "To risk your life for a dog—and a dead one at that."

He threw him, and Aidan, airborne, hit the ground, tumbling, harder than before, seeing stars, unable to breathe.

Aidan turned on his back, groaning, and looked up. He saw the man step forward, raise his boot, aim it for his face, and he could see from the look in his eyes that this man was evil, a cruel man, a heartless man. He would be good to his word: he would kill Aidan. And Aidan would die out here in the woods, alone, far from everyone, on this black and cold night—and not a soul would ever know.

His trip to see his father had come to an abrupt end.

CHAPTER TWENTY ONE

Kyra tumbled end over end in the gushing rapids of the River Tanis, trying to catch her breath as the icy water pierced her bones. It was the coldest water of her life—yet it was not the cold that bothered her, or even the pain as she slammed into rocks, bouncing off them like a twig. Nor was it fear for her own well-being. What upset her most was her regret over Andor, leaving him behind, being able to reach him, to save him—while he made a heroic stand against those hornhogs, while sacrificing his own life for hers. She had never encountered an animal more noble, more fearless. The idea of abandoning him while he fought her battles was too much for her. Even while tumbling, she fought against the current with all she had, desperate to make it back to him.

But she just could not. The current gushed and carried her downriver with a tremendous force, and she could barely stay afloat, much less swim backwards. She knew, with a pain in her heart, that Andor was gone forever.

Kyra suddenly slammed against a rock and this time, weakened, reeling from the pain, she felt herself begin to submerge. She felt herself sinking lower and lower, dragged down by the currents, and unable to stop it. She looked up and saw the sunlight from the surface becoming more faint, and a part of her, overcome with remorse, did not want to go on. The quest to Ur felt insurmountable, so many obstacles at every turn, a land so filled with cruelty and inhospitality—and Ur still so far away.

Yet as Kyra looked up she saw shadows, saw the outline of her raft, and she remembered Leo and Dierdre. If she let herself die here, those two would be left alone, floating away into danger themselves—and she could not allow that to happen. She had to live, if not for herself, then for them. And for her father, and for Aidan. For all those who cared about her. Regret was a terrible thing, but life had to go on. She could simply not allow herself to be swallowed by guilt and remorse. It was selfish. Other people needed her.

Kyra snapped out of it, and with one great kick she swam back up, towards the surface, overcoming her pain, her exhaustion, the biting cold. She kicked again and again, fought back against the currents, clawing at the icy water with her hands. She felt as if her lungs were going to burst, each kick bringing her closer and yet each taking an effort she did not know if she had.

Finally, with her last ounce of strength, Kyra broke through the surface. She gasped as she flailed in the currents, pushed downriver, but this time, managed to stay afloat as she tread water.

"Kyra!" cried a voice.

Kyra looked over to see the raft floating toward her, Dierdre holding out a hand and Leo barking at its edge. Kyra swam for it, kicking, and as the current spun the raft in her direction, she reached out and just managed to grab Dierdre's hand. Dierdre's hand was surprisingly strong for a frail girl, clearly determined to save her friend, and with one big yank, Kyra found herself back on board, lying on her stomach, wet and shivering.

Kyra rolled onto her stomach and spit out water, gasping for breath, shaking from the cold, numb. Leo licked her, and she got to her hands and knees and she turned and looked back upriver, searching for Andor on the horizon.

But, she was dismayed to see, the river had twisted and turned and she could no longer see beyond the bends of the river. Andor was nowhere in sight.

Kyra closed her eyes and tried not to picture those hornhogs encircling her friend and tearing him to pieces. She felt pained at the thought.

Kyra felt another lick on her face, and she turned to see Leo, whining, nudging his face up against hers, and she hugged and kissed him back. She looked up and clasped Dierdre's hand, pulling herself to a sitting position.

"Thank you," she said to Dierdre, meaning it.

Kyra brushed water from her eyes and felt a warmth around her shoulders, and she looked over to see Dierdre had taken off her own furs and draped them over her shoulders.

"I can't take this from you," Kyra said, trying to remove them.

Dierdre shook her head.

"You need it more than I do."

154

Kyra clutched the furs, shaking, desperate for its warmth, and she slowly felt herself drying off, returning to normal. The currents calmed, now bringing them downriver at a slow and gentle drift, and the Tanis widened here, too, finally free of boulders. Kyra looked out before her, saw smooth waters ahead as far as she could see, and finally she took a deep breath and relaxed.

"The Tanis winds toward Ur," Dierdre said. "It won't bring us all the way, but within a day's hike. We can make the final leg on land."

"How do we know when to get off?" Kyra asked.

"Don't worry," Dierdre said. "I'll know. I am from here, remember? It's not for a while, anyway—we must still cross much of Escalon. You can rest easy now—the worst stretch is behind us."

Kyra did not need to be told twice. She was too exhausted to ponder it. She knew she should think about their provisions, should take stock of what weapons she had, should examine everyone's wounds. But she was just too tired.

Kyra leaned back, wrapped in her furs, and lay her head on the raft, just for a moment. She looked up at the sky, and high up she saw passing scarlet clouds, drifting by. She heard the trickling beneath her—and it was all deeply relaxing.

Kyra, eyes heavy, told herself she'd only close her eyes for a moment—but before she knew it, overcome with exhaustion, she felt her eyes closing on her, and moments later she found herself, drifting downriver, fast asleep.

*

Kyra stared into the glowing, yellow eyes of a dragon, each as large as her, and was completely hypnotized. It flew down from the sky and swooped right for her, its wings spread wide, its ancient, scarlet scales aglow, its talons hanging low as if to pick her up. She lay there, immobile, on her raft, floating downriver, watching it descend.

Theos, she called out in her mind, recognizing him, so relieved to see him again. *Where did you go? Why did you leave me? Why did you come back?*

Kyra heard his response, his ancient voice reverberating in her mind, shaking her entire world.

I've come for my child.

Kyra could hardly believe his words. His child? What could that mean?

She stared back, her heart racing, desperate to know.

"Child?" she asked.

But Theos did not respond; instead, he flew lower and lower, his talons approaching as if they might tear her to pieces.

As Kyra felt the great wind of his approach, she did not brace herself—rather, she awaited it eagerly. She wanted more than anything to be scooped up by him, to be carried away, to understand who he was, to understand who *she* was.

But as quickly as he had descended, Theos suddenly rose back up in the sky, just missing her, flying higher and higher. She craned her neck and watched him go, flapping his great wings as he disappeared into a cloud, screeching.

Kyra opened her eyes with a start. She felt something cold and wet on her face, and she looked over to see Leo lying by her side, licking her face, looking at her with his soulful eyes—and she remembered.

Kyra sat up at once, feeling the boat moving beneath her, swaying gently, and she looked about, stroking Leo's head. She craned her neck and searched the skies, looking for a sign of Theos, listening for his cry, hoping it was not just a dream.

But she saw and heard nothing.

Kyra was confused. It had seemed so real. Was it just a dream? Or had it been something more?

Kyra looked over and saw Dierdre, sitting on the raft beside her, looking out at the waters of the Tanis, steering them along, steady and smooth. She was surprised to realize how much time had passed—it had been morning when she'd fallen asleep, and now the sky was darker, aglow with amber and orange, clearly late in the day. She sat there, rubbing her eyes, so disoriented, hardly believing she had slept most of the day. She felt as if her dream of the dragon had transported her to another realm.

"Have I slept all this time?" she asked.

Dierdre turned to her and smiled.

"You needed it. You kept speaking in your sleep...something about a dragon. Something about an egg."

"An egg?" Kyra asked, unable to recall.

Kyra looked up at the late-afternoon sky, now streaked with purple and orange, and as she looked around, she noticed how different the terrain was. They had emerged from Whitewood, had left behind a landscape of snow and ice, and entered one of grass and plains. She realized they must be much farther south, as it was warmer here, too; she marveled at how much the climate had changed in such a short distance. She removed Dierdre's furs, remembering, and draped them back over her friend's shoulders.

"Thank you," Kyra said. "And sorry. I had no idea I had fallen asleep in them."

Dierdre pulled the furs tight, clearly pleased to have them back. She smiled.

"You needed them more than I did."

Kyra stood and marveled at how quickly they moved, how much ground they were covering, and how easily.

"Much smoother than traveling by land," she observed, studying the passing landscape. They had covered so much distance, had crossed so much of Escalon, and had done so without the danger of savage creatures or humans. She stroked Leo's head and turned and looked at Dierdre.

"Were you sleeping all this time, too?" Kyra asked.

Dierdre shook her head, studying the waters.

"Thinking," she replied.

"Of what?" Kyra asked, curious. Yet she realized, the moment she asked it, that perhaps she shouldn't have inquired, given what Dierdre had just been through. She could only imagine what dark thoughts were haunting her friend.

Dierdre paused, staring out at the horizon, her eyes bloodshot, from exhaustion or crying, Kyra could not tell. Kyra could see the lingering pain and sadness in her eyes, could see she was trapped in memory.

"Of going home," Dierdre finally replied.

Kyra wondered. She did not want to pry, but she couldn't help herself.

"Do you have anyone awaiting you there?"

157

Dierdre sighed.

"My father," she replied. "The man who gave me away."

Kyra felt a pit in her stomach, understanding how Dierdre felt.

"He did not fight for me," Dierdre continued. "None of them did. All of those brave warriors, who put so much stock into chivalry, did nothing when one of their own was taken away, right out from under them. Why? Because I was a woman. As if that gave them the right not to care. Because they were following a law written by men. If I was a boy, they would have fought to the death before I was taken away. But because I was a girl, somehow it didn't matter. It was men whom I lost all respect for on that day— my father most of all. I trusted him."

Kyra remained silent, understanding all too well her feeling of betrayal.

"And yet you are returning to them," Kyra noted, confused.

Dierdre teared up. She fell silent for a long time.

Finally, she wiped away a tear and spoke with difficulty.

"He is still my father," she finally said. "I don't know where else to go." She took a deep breath. "Besides, I want him to know. I want them all to know what they did. I want them all to be ashamed. I want them to understand that the value of a girl is as great as that of a boy. I want them to understand that their actions— their lack of caring—had consequences. I don't want to give them all the chance to avoid me, to be able to forget what they did or what happened to me. I want to be there, in their presence, a thorn in their side that they cannot avoid—and be a living testament to their shame."

Kyra felt a deep sorrow as she pondered how her friend felt.

"And then?" Kyra asked. "When you're done shaming them?"

Dierdre slowly shook her head, tears in her eyes.

"I don't know what is left for me," she replied. "I feel washed up. As if my childhood was taken from me. I used to dream of being taken away by a prince—yet I feel that no one would want me now."

Dierdre began to cry, and Kyra leaned over and draped an arm around her shoulder, trying to calm her, while Leo came over and laid his head in her lap.

"Don't think that way," Kyra said. "Sometimes, life can be filled with horrible things. But life goes on. It must go on. And sometimes, even years later, it can also be filled with amazing things. You just need to hang in there, to give it time, to give life a chance to be born again. If you can hang in there long enough, life will give you a fresh slate. It will become brand new. The horrors of your past will disappear, as if they never happened. Old memories will fade so much that one day you won't even be able to remember what it was that troubled you."

Dierdre studied the river, listening quietly.

"You are not your past," Kyra continued. "You are your *future*. Horrible things happen to us not to trap us in the past, but to help us decide on our future. They make us stronger. They teach us we have more power than we knew. They show us how strong we are. The question is: what will you choose to do with that strength?"

Kyra saw her friend pondering her words, and she fell silent, allowing her her space. Speaking of past struggles, she could not help but think of her own pain and suffering, and she realized she was speaking as much to herself as she was to her friend. It seemed everyone she knew, now that she thought about it, young and old, was suffering in some way, was haunted by some memory. Was that the way of life? She wondered.

Kyra watched the river pass by and the sky grow darker, changing color again and again. She did not know how much time passed when she was snapped out of her reverie by the sound of a splashing and a snapping noise. She examined the waters and saw small, yellow, fluorescent creatures floating on the surface, like jellyfish, their tiny teeth snapping at the air. They all floated toward the river bank, and she looked over and watched the exotic creatures lodge themselves in the mud, swarming with them, making the muddy banks glow yellow. It made Kyra not want to leave her raft.

They turned a bend in the river and a new noise filled the air, setting Kyra on edge. It sounded like rapids—yet she was confused as she looked out and saw none. Dierdre turned, too, standing, hands on her hips, studying the horizon with a face filled with concern.

Suddenly, her face fell.

159

"We must turn back!" she cried out, panicked.

"What is it?" Kyra asked, alarmed, jumping to her feet.

"The Great Falls!" Dierdre cried out. "I did not think they existed!"

Dierdre grabbed an oar and rowed backwards frantically, trying to slow their descent. Their raft slowed, but not enough. The noise grew louder, and Kyra could begin to feel the spray, the clouds of mist even from here.

"Help me!" Dierdre cried.

Kyra jumped into action, grabbed the other oar, and began rowing. But the currents grew stronger and, try as she did, she was unable to reverse course.

"We can't fight it!" Kyra yelled out, shouting to be heard over the noise of the falls.

"Row sideways!" Dierdre yelled back. "For the river bank!"

Kyra followed Dierdre's lead, and they rowed sideways with all they had; soon, to her relief, the raft began to change course, drifting sideways for the muddy banks. The falls were growing louder, too—now hardly twenty yards away—a great white spray rising into the sky, and Kyra knew they had little time.

They were closing in on the river bank, about to make it to safety, when suddenly, their raft rocked violently. Kyra looked down, confused, not comprehending what had happened—there were no boulders she could see below.

It happened again, and this time Kyra stumbled and fell down to the raft as it rocked from side to side. She knelt there and looked down at the waters, wondering—when her heart plummeted to see a yellow tentacle rise up out of the waters and latch onto the raft. There emerged another tentacle—then another—and Kyra watched with horror as an enormous squid-like creature emerged, its tentacles reaching out and spreading across their boat. Bright yellow, luminescent, it opened its jaws right for her.

Kyra and Dierdre rowed frantically, trying to get away, but the creature was too strong, pulling them right toward it. Kyra realized they would never make it to shore, even though it was only feet away. They would die at the hands of this beast.

Worse, they were now back in the current, drifting closer to the falls, hardly ten yards away.

Desperate, Kyra reached back, grabbed her staff, released it into two parts, and raised it high. She brought down its sharp blades on the creature's tentacles as hard as she could.

The creature screeched, an awful noise, as green pus emerged from it. Yet still, it did not release their boat. It raised its jaws higher, and Kyra knew that in moments it would swallow them whole.

Kyra knew they had no choice—and she had to make a quick decision.

"Drop the oars!" she cried to Dierdre, who was still frantically try to row away. "We have to jump!"

"Jump!?" Dierdre called back, frantic, her voice barely audible over the deafening roar of the falls.

"Now!" Kyra shrieked, as the beast's jaws were but feet away and closing in.

Kyra grabbed Leo and grabbed Dierdre's hand, and she turned and jumped, pulling them both overboard and into the rapids.

A moment later they were all submerged in the icy waters of the Tanis, the currents pulling them for the falls. Kyra saw the squid, glowing beneath the water, too and turned and saw the falls but feet away. The fall might kill them—but that creature certainly would.

Water gushing, Kyra felt herself propelled downriver and she braced herself as she began to go over the falls. Beside her, she saw Leo and then Dierdre go over, airborne, shrieking—when suddenly something wrapped around her leg, keeping her back. She looked upriver to see a glowing tentacle wrapped around her leg, pulling her back.

Kyra was horrified to realize she was stuck on the precipice, and to see the creature's jaws closing in on her as it pulled her close, using its magnificent strength to keep her from going over. She looked back and saw the falls behind her and ironically she wished for nothing more than to go over.

About to be eaten, desperate, Kyra thought quickly. She raised the two halves of her staff, still in her hand, and with one last desperate effort, she threw them at the beast. She watched them sail through the air, and she prayed her aim was true.

161

There came an awful shriek, and she watched with satisfaction as the short spears landed in the squid's eyes.

The creature released its grip on her foot—and a moment later, Kyra felt herself gushing downriver, over the falls, plummeting through the air and mist and spray, and hurtling down to the rocks a hundred feet below.

CHAPTER TWENTY TWO

Merk jabbed his staff into the moist forest floor, poking leaves beneath his feet, hiking as he had been for days back through Whitewood, and determined to stop at nothing this time until he reached the Tower of Ur. As he walked, he closed his eyes and, try as he did, he could not stop seeing that scene of grief flashing through his mind, the girl, her family, her weeping.... Her final words still rang in his ears. He hated himself for returning for her—and he hated himself for leaving.

Merk did not understand what was happening to him; all his life he had been unsusceptible to guilt, to rebuke, to anyone else's problems. He had always been his own man, on his own island, his own mission. He had always made it a point to keep himself at arm's length from the world, not to involve himself in anyone else's troubles—unless they needed his special skills and there was hefty payment involved.

But now, for some reason, Merk could not stop thinking of this girl he barely knew, of her rebuke of his character, even though he had done the right thing. He didn't know why it bothered him, but it did.

He, of course, could not return for her again. She had her chance. What bothered him was why he had turned back at all. He longer knew what was right: to live a life for himself, or to live a life of others? Had his encounter with her been a lesson? If so, what was the lesson learned?

What was wrong, Merk wondered, with just living a life for yourself? For your own selfish needs? For your own survival? Why did people have to get entangled in other people's lives? Why should they care? Why couldn't other people count on themselves for survival? And if they could not, then why should they have a right to survive?

Something was poking at his consciousness, an awareness, perhaps, that there was a greater world out there, a realization that his having only looked out for himself his entire life had lead him to a deep loneliness. It was a realization that helping other people might be the best way to help himself, too. He realized it gave him some feeling of connection to the greater world without which he felt he would eventually shrivel up and die.

It was a *purpose*. That was it. Merk craved purpose the way a starving man craves food. Not the purpose of some other man who was hiring him, but a purpose of his own. It wasn't a job he needed—it was *meaning*. What was meaning? He wondered. It was elusive, felt always just out of reach. And he hated things he could not easily put his finger on.

Merk looked up as he hiked through Whitewood, its stark white leaves shimmering in the late afternoon sun, the golden rays of an early sunset cutting through them and casting them in a beautiful light. This place was magical. A warm breeze blew, the weather finally turning, the rustling sound filling his ears, and as leaves fell from trees they showered down all around him. Merk forced himself to turn his thoughts back to his hike, his destination. The Tower of Ur.

Merk already saw himself as a Watcher, entering the sacred order, protecting the kingdom from trolls and anyone else who dared tried to steal the Sword of Fire. He knew it was a sacred duty, knew the fate of Escalon depended upon it, and he wanted nothing more than that sense of duty. He could not wait for his talents to be put to use for a good cause, not a selfish one. It was the highest order he could imagine.

Yet Merk was struck with sudden worry as a terrible thought crossed his mind like a shadow: what if they turned him away? He had heard the Watchers were a diverse group, made up of human warriors, like he, but also of another race, an ancient race, part human and part something else—famed for turning people away. He had no idea how they would react to his presence. What would they be like? he wondered. Would they accept him? And what if they did not?

Merk crested a hill and as he did, a valley spread out beneath him and in the far distance, a great peninsula reached out into the Sea of Sorrow, water sparkling all around it. He gasped. At its windswept end, there it sat: the Tower of Ur. Merk's heart beat faster at the sight. Surrounded by ocean on three sides, huge waves crashing into the rocks and sending up sprays of mist, sparkling in the sunlight, the tower was set in the most haunting, beautiful landscape he had ever seen. A hundred feet high, fifty feet wide, shaped in a perfect circle, its stone was ancient, a shade of white he had never seen before, looking as if it had stood for centuries. It was capped by a smooth, round golden dome, reflecting the sun, and its entrance was marked by soaring doors, thirty feet high, arched, they, too, made of shining gold.

It was the sort of place Merk expected to see in a dream. It was a place he'd always wondered about, and a place he could hardly fathom was real. Seeing it now, in person, took his breath away. He did not believe in energy, yet still, he could not deny that there was some sort of special energy radiating off the place.

Merk set off downhill with a new bounce to his step, elated to be on the final leg of his journey. The forest opened up and he found himself a smooth, green countryside, the entrance to the peninsula, warmer here than the rest of Escalon. He felt the sun shining down on his face, heard the crashing of the waves, and saw the open sky before him, and he felt a deep peace. He felt, finally, he had arrived.

Merk hiked, the tower looming in the distance, and he was baffled to see no one standing guard around it. He had expected to find a small army guarding it on all sides, protecting the most precious relics of Escalon, and he was perplexed. It was as if it were abandoned.

Merk couldn't understand. How could a place be so well-guarded, and yet have no one standing outside? He sensed this place was unlike any other he had been, that he would learn things here about the art of combat that he would never learn elsewhere.

Merk continued hiking and reached a broad plateau of grass before the tower. Before him sat a curious sculpture: a stone staircase, circular, rising perhaps twenty feet high, its steps intricately carved in ivory. The steps turned and twisted and led, oddly, to nothing but air. It was a freestanding spiral staircase, and Merk could not understand its meaning or symbolism—or why it was placed here in the midst of this grass field. He wondered what other surprises lay ahead.

Merk continued on and as he approached the tall, golden doors to the tower, hardly twenty yards away, his heart pounded in anticipation. He felt dwarfed by this place, in awe of it. He walked reverentially up to the doors, stopping before them, and slowly reached up his palms and laid them on the gold. The metal was cold and curiously dry, despite the ocean breezes; he could feel the contours of the intricately carved symbols, smooth in his palm. He craned back his neck and looked straight up at the tower, and admired its height, its immaculate design. Rarely in his life had he felt in the presence of something greater than himself—architecturally, physically, and spiritually—yet now, for the first time, he did.

Merk studied the ancient golden doors, like a portal to another world, guarding, he knew, the greatest treasure in Escalon. They gleamed in the sun, and Merk was taken not only by their power, but also their beauty. This tower doubled as a fortress and as a work of art.

He saw an ancient script etched into the gold, and wished desperately that he could understand the meaning. He felt a deep regret that he could not read or write, felt ashamed as he tried. Those who lived inside would know more than he ever could. He was not of the noble class, and while never before had he wished that he was, on this day, he did.

Merk searched the doors for a knob, a knocker, some point of entry—and he was surprised to find none. This place seemed to be perfectly sealed.

He stood there, wondering. This place was a deepening mystery. There came no noise, no activity inside or out, there were no Watchers, no humans—nothing but silence. He was baffled. There came only the sound of the wind, a gale whistling through, rippling off the ocean, blowing so hard it nearly knocked him off balance before it disappeared just as quickly. It felt as if this place had been abandoned.

Not knowing what else to do, Merk reached up and began to pound the door with his fist. It barely made a sound, echoing then fading away, drowned out by the wind.

Merk waited, expecting the door to open.

But there came no response.

Merk wondered what he had to do to make his presence known. He stood there, thinking, then finally had an idea. He extracted the dagger from his belt, reached high, and slammed its hilt into the door. This time, the sharp noise reverberated throughout the place, echoing again and again. There was no way they could not hear that.

Merk stood there and waited, listening to the echo slowly die down, and he began to wonder if anyone would ever appear. Why were they ignoring him? Was this some sort of test?

He was debating whether to walk around the tower, to look for another entrance, when a slit in the door suddenly slid back, making him flinch. He was caught off guard to see, staring back at him at eye level, two yellow, piercing eyes, as inhuman eyes as he had ever seen, staring right through his soul. It instilled a chill in him.

Merk stared back, not knowing what to say in the tense silence.

"What is it that you wish here?" the voice finally came, a deep, hollow voice which set him on edge.

At first, Merk did not know how to respond. Finally, he replied:

"I wish to enter. I wish to become a Watcher. To serve Escalon."

The eyes stared back, unflinching, expressionless, and Merk thought the creature would never respond. Finally, though, a response came, its voice rumbling:

"Only the worthy may enter here," it replied.

Merk reddened.

"And what makes you think I'm unworthy?" he demanded.

"In what way can you prove that you are?"

The slit slid shut as quickly as it had opened, and with that, the doors were completely sealed again.

Merk stared back in the silence, baffled. He reached up with his dagger hilt and slammed the door again and again. The hollow sound echoed, ringing in his ears, filling the desolate countryside.

But no matter how long and how hard he banged, the slit did not open again.

"Let me in!" Merk shrieked, a cry filled with despair, rising to the heavens, as he leaned back in agony and realized that those doors might not ever, ever open again

CHAPTER TWENTY THREE

Duncan braced himself as the enormous red shark—thirty feet long—leapt out of the river and came down, jaws wide open, right for him. He knew that in a moment it would land in his boat, smashing it to pieces and tearing him apart. Worse, all around him a school of these sharks leapt through the air, aiming for his men and their rafts on all sides.

Duncan reacted instinctively, as he always did in battle. He drew his sword and prepared to meet his foe head on. He would die with nobility, and if he could distract this creature, have it focus only on him, then he might be able to save the other men on his raft.

"JUMP!" Duncan commanded his other men in his fiercest voice. The other soldiers on his raft did as he commanded, leaping overboard, none needing any prodding as the massive shark came their way.

Duncan grasped his sword in two hands, stepped forward, and with a great battle cry raised his sword and met the shark head-on. As the shark descended he squatted low and raised his sword straight up, aiming beneath the shark's lower jaw. He stood as he did so, plunging his sword up through the shark's lower jaw and through the roof of his mouth, clamping its jaw shut with his long sword. He was surprised at how tough its skin was, how enormous its weight, as it took all of his might to drive the sword upward.

Blood gushed down all over Duncan as the shark, flailing, began to fall on him. Duncan, still holding the sword, could not get out of the way in time, and he saw its tremendous weight coming down and he knew he would be crushed.

Duncan's shout was muffled as the shark landed on top of him. It must have weighed a thousand pounds, and as it landed on him, Duncan felt himself being pounded into the raft. It felt as if his ribs were being crushed as his world was engulfed in black.

There came a great splintering of wood as the raft beneath him shattered to pieces, and Duncan suddenly felt himself, mercifully, plunging through the water, free of the weight of the beast. If he were on land, he realized, he would have been crushed to death, but because water was beneath him, and because the raft shattered, he was still alive.

Submerged, getting his bearings, still sinking beneath the shark, Duncan tried to swim away as the shark continued to come at him. Luckily, with its jaws clamped tight, it was unable to bite him.

Duncan kicked and swam out from under it, releasing his sword and taking several strong strokes away. He turned and expected it to follow, but blood gushed everywhere, and he watched as the shark finally sank to the river bed.

Duncan swam through the frigid waters, every part of his body aching, the current taking him downriver as he looked up for sunlight and headed for the surface. As he looked up through the clear water he could see the school of sharks leaping through the air high above, could hear the muffled sounds of their crashing all around him—and of his men shrieking. He flinched inside, seeing the waters turn red with blood, watching the bodies begin to sink, knowing that good men up there were dying.

Duncan finally broke the surface, gasping, treading water, trying to orient himself. He looked upriver and saw the school of sharks had already passed through, leaping like salmon upriver, smashing into random rafts as they went. He was relieved to see they weren't targeting his men; rather, they just continued upriver, oblivious to what lay before them, leaping and landing, smashing whatever was in their way—eating a man if he was in their way, but if not, then continuing to swim. They clearly were driven to go somewhere, and the school stuck together, disappearing from sight as fast as it had appeared.

Duncan, treading water in the currents, surveyed the damage. About a third of their fleet had been destroyed, pools of blood filling the river, bodies floating, logs everywhere. Dozens of men were dead or injured, some moaning, writhing, others floating lifelessly on the surface. Duncan spotted the men from his own raft, saw his sons, saw Seavig, Anvin and Arthfael, and was relieved to see they had survived. Their rafts had been smashed, too, and they tread water not far from him.

All around him men fished out the survivors, yanking them up onto rafts, salvaging the wounded and allowing the dead to float downstream. It was an awful scene of carnage, a wave of death that had come out of a clear blue sky. Duncan realized that they were lucky to have survived at all.

Duncan felt the sting in his arm, and looked over to see that his right shoulder had been scraped badly from the shark's skin. It bled, and though it was painful, he knew it was not life-threatening. He heard splashing and turned to see Seavig treading next to him, and he was horrified to see blood pouring from his friend's hand, and to see he was missing two fingers.

"Your hand!" Duncan called out, shocked that Seavig seemed so stoic.

Seavig shrugged. He gritted his teeth as he tore a piece of cloth from his shirt and wrapped it around his bleeding hand.

"Just a scratch," he replied. "You should see the shark," he added with a grin.

Duncan felt strong hands grabbing him from behind and soon he felt himself being pulled up onto a raft. He sat there, breathing heavily, slowly regaining his composure. He looked up to the skyline and saw, closer than ever, the mountains of Kos, and he felt a fresh determination. His army, whatever of it survived, was still floating inevitably downriver, and nothing would stop them now.

The Thusius twisted and turned as they neared Kos, and the landscape changed dramatically. The towering mountains dominated this region of Escalon, their snow-covered peaks, covered in mist, looming over everything. The climate was colder here, too, and Duncan felt as if he were entering a different country.

Duncan just wanted to get off this river, to get back on land where he felt most at home. He would fight any man, any army, any beast or creature—he only wanted to do it on land. He did not like to fight where he could not stand his ground, and he did not trust this cursed river, its creatures or its whirlpools. As indomitable as those mountains appeared, he would choose them anytime and have solid ground beneath his feet.

As the river gushed on, they neared the base of the mountains and Duncan saw the vast, empty plains surrounding it. On the horizon, stationed on these plains, Duncan was concerned to see garrison after garrison of Pandesian troops. The river was luckily far enough to keep his men shielded from view, especially with the

170

trees bordering its banks. Yet between the trees Duncan could spot the Pandesian soldiers, far off, guarding the mountains as if they owned them.

"The men of Kos may be some of the best warriors of Escalon," Seavig said, drifting up beside him in his raft, "but they are trapped up there. The Pandesians have been waiting for them to descend ever since they invaded."

"The Pandesians will never risk ascent," added Anvin, drifting in close. "Those cliffs are too treacherous."

"They don't need to," added Arthfael. "Pandesia has them trapped and will wait until they force their surrender."

Duncan studied the landscape, pondering.

"Then perhaps it's time we liberate them," he finally said.

"Shall we not have a fight on our hands before we reach the mountains?" Anvin asked.

Seavig shook his head.

"This river winds to the mountain's base, through the narrow pass," he replied. "We shall disembark on the other side and climb the mountains unseen. It will spare us a confrontation with the Pandesians."

Duncan nodded, satisfied.

"I wouldn't mind confronting them now," Anvin said, hand on his sword as he peered out through the trees towards the distant plains.

"All in good time, my friend," Duncan said. "First we rally Kos—then we attack Pandesia. When we fight them, I want us to be unified, one force—and I want it be on our own terms. It is as important to choose *when* and *where* to fight as it is *who*."

As the boats drifted underneath a natural stone outcropping, the river narrowing, Duncan looked up and studied the mountains, reaching straight up to the sky.

"Even if we reach the peaks," Arthfael said, turning to Duncan, "do you really think Kos will join us? They are mountain people—they are famed to never come down."

Duncan sighed, wondering the same thing. He knew the warriors of Kos to be a stubborn lot.

"For freedom," he finally replied, "a true warrior will do what is right. Your homeland lies in your heart—not where you live."

The men fell silent as they pondered his words and studied the ever-changing river before them. The mountains closed in on them now, blocking them completely from the open plains, from the Pandesian garrisons, as the river continued to gush its way south.

"Do you remember when we rode the Thusius to the end?"

Duncan turned to see Seavig looking out at the waters before him, lost in memory. He nodded, having a memory he'd rather forget.

"Too well," he replied.

Duncan remembered the awful journey, all the way to the Devil's Finger and on to the Tower of Kos. He tried to shake it from his mind, the memories of that barren wasteland in which he'd almost died. They called it the devil's country—and for good reason. He had vowed to never return.

Duncan studied the mountains closing in on the river banks, white with snow and ice. They had arrived, and he wondered where Seavig would disembark. Seavig, too, studied the landscape, on alert. Finally, he nodded, and Duncan held up a fist, signaling to his men to stop—and not to sound the horns.

One raft at a time steered over to the river bank, the air filled with the gentle sound of wood rafts bumping against each other, then grounding on a rocky shore. Duncan jumped ashore the second they did, thrilled to be back on dry land, and his men followed his lead. He turned and kicked his raft back out into the water, making room for the other rafts to follow, as did all of his men, and he watched as the now-empty rafts drifted away with the current.

"Will we not need our rafts?" Arthfael asked with concern.

Duncan shook his head.

"We will descend these cliffs on foot," he replied, "on the other side, with an army in tow and attacking the capital—or not at all. There is no retreat—we succeed or we die."

Duncan knew the power of burning his bridges when he needed to—it sent a powerful signal to his men that there would be no turning back—and he could see that they respected it.

Hundreds of his men soon congregated at the base of the mountains, and Duncan took stock: he could see they were all shaken, exhausted, cold and hungry. He felt the same, but did not dare show it: after all, the worst of their journey still lay before them.

"MEN!" Duncan called out as they gathered around him. "I know you have all suffered much. I shall not lie to you: the worst is yet to come. We must climb these cliffs, and do it quickly, and we may not find a hospitable welcome at the top. There will be no rest, and the hiking will be hard. I know some of you are wounded, and I know you have lost close friends. But ask yourselves as you climb: what is the price of freedom?"

Duncan examined all of their faces, and could see them reassured by his words.

"If there is any man here who is not up for the journey ahead, step forward now," he called out, studying them all.

He waited in the thick silence and there was not a single man, he was relieved to see, who came forward. He knew there would not be. These were his men, and they would follow him to the death.

Satisfied, Duncan turned and prepared to climb the cliffs— when suddenly, there came a noise, and he turned to see there emerge from the trees a dozen boys. They held in their arms hundreds of large snowshoes, spikes at the bottom, along with icepicks and bundles of rope.

Duncan shot a curious look at Seavig, who looked back knowingly.

"Mountain traders," he explained. "This is how they make their living. They want to sell us their wares."

One boy stepped forward.

"You will need these," he said, holding out a snowshoe. "Anyone who climbs these mountains needs these."

Duncan took it and examined its sharp spikes. He looked up at the cliffs and pondered the icy ascent.

"And how much do you wish for these?" Duncan asked.

"One sack of gold for the whole lot," one boy said, stepping forward, his face covered in dirt.

Duncan looked at the boy, near the age of his own sons, looking as if he hadn't eaten in days, and his heart broke for him; clearly, he had a hard life here.

173

"One sack for this junk?" asked Brandon derisively, stepping forward.

"Just take them from them, Father," added Braxton, stepping up beside him. "What are they going to do—stop us?"

Duncan looked at his own sons with shame. They had everything, and yet they would deny these poor boys their livelihood.

Duncan stepped forward and pushed back his two sons, then looked at the boys and nodded back soundly.

"You shall have two sacks of gold," Duncan said.

The boys gasped in delight, wide-eyed, and Duncan then turned to his sons:

"And the money shall come from your personal coffers," he said sternly. "You can each hand me one sack. Now."

It was not a question but a command, and Brandon and Braxton looked crestfallen. They must have seen the determined look in their father's eyes, though, since they reluctantly reached into their waists and each pulled out a sack.

"That is all my gold, Father!" Brandon called out.

Duncan nodded, uncaring.

"Good," he replied. "Now hand it to the boys."

Brandon and Braxton grudgingly stepped forward and hand the sacks to the boys. The boys, delighted, rushed forward and handed Duncan and his men the shoes and ropes.

"Take the eastern face," one of the boys advised Duncan. "There is less melting. The north seems easier, but it narrows— you'll get stuck. Remember—don't remove the spikes. You will have more than one cause for them."

With that the boys turned and scurried back into the woods, as Duncan was left to wonder at their words.

He and his men put on the shoes and secured the climbing ropes over their shoulders, and as Duncan put them on, he realized how much he would need them.

They all turned to ascend the mountain when suddenly another man rushed forward from the woods, dressed in rags, perhaps in his thirties, with long greasy hair and yellow teeth. He stopped before them and looked nervously from man to man before he addressed Duncan.

"I'm a tracker," he said. "I know the best routes to Kos. All who ascend trust me. Hike without me, and you hike at your own peril."

Duncan exchanged a look with Seavig.

Seavig stepped forward casually and laid a hand on the man's shoulder.

"I thank you for your offer," he said.

The man smiled back nervously, and Seavig, to Duncan's shock, suddenly pulled a dagger from his waist and stabbed the man in the gut.

The man groaned and keeled over, slumping to his feet, dead.

Duncan stared down at the body, stunned.

"Why did you do that?" he asked.

Seavig raised his boot and pushed over the man's body until he was lying on his back. He then kicked the man's shirt, and out clinked several gold coins. Seavig reached down and held one up—and Duncan was shocked to see the insignia of the Pandesian Emperor.

"A man of Escalon once, perhaps," Seavig said. "But no longer. The Pandesians paid him well. If we had followed him, we would all be dead right now."

Duncan was amazed, never expecting such treachery here.

Seavig threw the Pandesian gold back down to the ground.

"These mountains," Seavig said, "hold more danger than one."

CHAPTER TWENTY FOUR

Kyra plummeted through the air so fast she could barely catch her breath, the icy mist of the waterfall engulfing her as she tumbled end over end, her screams drowned out by the roaring waters. Down below she could faintly make out Leo and Dierdre, landing somewhere in the huge clouds of white foam, could see their bodies tumbling as they went gushing down the rapids of the River Tanis. She had no idea if they had survived the fall—but it did not look good.

Kyra saw her life flashing before her eyes. Of all the ways she might die, she had never expected to die like this. She looked down and saw a group of boulders at the base into which the water landed, sending up waves of foam. She also dimly saw a narrow opening between the rocks; if she could land there, then maybe, just maybe, she would not break her neck when she landed, and have a remote chance to survive this.

She flailed and twisted, contorting her body as best she could, doing whatever possible to aim for the crevice.

And then it happened. Kyra felt herself submerged as she hit the water so hard, winded, she was unsure if she hit water or rock.

She kept sinking, deeper and deeper, falling like a stone even beneath the surface of the river; she did not think it would ever end. The currents were also pushing her sideways from the tremendous energy of the falls, and as she sank, she knew, at last, that she had not landed on rock. She had made the crevice; she knew she should be grateful for that.

Yet she was still sinking, tumbling underwater, the air pressure killing her ears, as she tried to gain control, to swim. It took her a good thirty seconds until she finally felt her feet hit the bottom of the river, bouncing off the sandy bed.

Kyra reflexively kicked off it, using her momentum to launch her back up for the surface. She got caught in the current, and after swimming with all her might, was finally able to gain control. She kicked and kicked, feeling her lungs would burst from the effort.

But there was no choice. To give up meant death. And she was not ready to die.

Just as she felt she could go no further, Kyra gave one final kick and finally exploded onto the surface. She heaved, immediately pushed back under by the currents, then surfaced again, gulping another breath of air before being pushed back down.

Finally, after drifting a good thirty feet more downriver, the tides slowed enough for Kyra to stay above the surface. As she tread water she saw something rush by her and realized it was a log. She swam for it, reaching and missing several times, until finally she grabbed hold of it and managed, slipping, to pull herself up.

Kyra gasped for air as she lay across it, trying to collect herself while the river pulled her downriver, holding on as she bumped off rocks. She wiped water from her eyes and spotted in the distance what appeared to be Dierdre and Leo, floating and flailing in the currents. She kicked, heading toward them, trying her best to direct herself in the rapids.

As she neared she saw it was indeed Leo, alive, she was relieved to see; he was kicking his legs, keeping his head above water, and she was amazed to see he had survived. But her joy was tempered by the sight of Dierdre, lying on her stomach, face in the water, motionless. Her heart dropped as she suspected the worst.

"DIERDRE!" she shrieked.

Kyra yanked Leo up onto the wide, flat log, his paws draped across it, whining, and then she immediately kicked over to Dierdre and yanked her up, too. She turned her over and was horrified to see her friend's face was turning blue.

"Dierdre!" Kyra cried, shaking her.

Kyra thought quickly. She turned her over the log and slapped her back several times, trying to revive her.

"You can't die now!" she cried.

She felt a sudden panic at the idea of losing her new friend, and she slapped her back again and again—and suddenly, Dierdre began to throw up water. To Kyra's great relief, Dierdre grabbed hold of the log, balancing herself as she gagged.

Kyra beamed as her friend slowly came back to life. Dierdre, spent, turned and looked at her, arms trembling, and while no words came out, she could see the gratitude in her friend's eyes.

Kyra noticed something rush by in the rapids, and she turned and saw it was a piece of their shattered raft. More pieces floated by, the raft now useless, and Kyra realized that this log in the river was all they had.

As their log cruised downriver, Kyra, Dierdre, and Leo instinctively climbed up onto it, sitting on the broad, flat surface, just wide enough for them all to fit. Leo lay down on his stomach, whining, clearly suspicious of the log—luckily it was too heavy and wide to spin. It straightened out and cruised like a spear down the rapids, and the current, fortunately, slowed enough to make it manageable as a vessel.

"It's not roomy," Kyra smiled to Dierdre, "but I suppose it will do."

Dierdre smiled back, looking exhausted but alive.

"We haven't much farther," she replied, studying the horizon ahead. "See that fork?" she asked, pointing. "Where the river splits, that's where we get off. From there on, we are back on land, on foot."

Kyra saw the fork in the distance and was relieved there was an end in sight; she'd had more than enough of this river, and was eager to get back onto dry land.

She took a deep breath for the first time. She glanced back over her shoulder and saw the waterfalls, now far behind, and she could hardly believe they had all survived. She realized how lucky they were to be alive, and in one piece. She looked back ahead and wondered what other perils lay in store for them.

They continued downriver as hours passed, Kyra watching the changing landscape with awe. The trees shimmered, all shades of white, as they crossed through the Whitewood, white leaves falling everywhere, lending the place a magical feel. Kyra watched it all, shivering, her clothes wet from the spray, and Dierdre finally reached out and pointed.

"There," she said. "See those two boulders? They mark the road to Ur. We must get out here."

Kyra and Dierdre did their best to direct the log for shore, reaching over and stroking and kicking the water. But despite their efforts, nothing worked. This big stubborn log refused to be directed.

178

"We'll have to jump!" Kyra said, realizing they were about to fork the wrong way downriver.

They stood and as they did, Leo barked at the water, clearly reluctant.

"It's okay, Leo," Kyra reassured him. "Stay by my side and we'll swim to shore together."

Kyra looked up ahead and saw the rapids forking, gaining speed, and as reluctant as she was to jump back in, she knew it was now or never. She and Dierdre exchanged a look and at the same time they both jumped into the roaring river, Kyra grabbing Leo as she did.

Kyra found herself submerged, frozen again, her skin pierced by a thousand small needles as she swam for shore. While the currents carried them downriver, they swam sideways, fighting their way toward the river bank. The water slowed and became more shallow, and finally, Kyra was amazed to find herself standing on the river bed, then crawling on her hands and knees as she emerged from the waters and onto the sand.

Kyra collapsed on the sand, Dierdre and Leo beside her, dripping wet, exhausted, sand in her face and hair—and no longer caring. She breathed hard, spitting up water. She lay there, unmoving for several minutes, her arms shaking from the exertion. She wanted to sleep for a million years. Would this quest ever end? she wondered.

Kyra did not know how much time had passed when she felt a hand beneath her arm, helping her up. She looked up to see Dierdre standing over her, smiling down.

"You saved my life—again," Dierdre said.

Kyra stood and smiled back, brushing off sand and feeling the weariness in her bones.

"Well, I guess if a waterfall can't kill us, nothing can," she replied.

Kyra brushed the mud and sand off her body and off Leo, too, as he came close and licked her palm. The three of them turned and faced the white wood before them, an endless stretch of ancient white trees shimmering in the late afternoon sun.

"Through these trees leads the road to Ur," Dierdre remarked.

"How far do you suppose it is on foot?" Kyra asked.

Dierdre shrugged.

"A few days more."

Kyra studied the darkening woods, devoid of shelter, heard the strange animal noises calling out beyond, and she searched everywhere, filled with sadness, for Andor, hoping beyond hope that he had somehow made it.

But he was nowhere to be found, of course. They were alone, utterly alone, the three of them, without provisions, without a horse, with nothing but the weapons still strapped to Kyra's back.

Kyra knew there was no time to waste. She took the first step into the wood, joined by her friends, back onto the long and lonely trek to the Tower of Ur.

*

Kyra, Dierdre, and Leo hiked through Whitewood, leaves crunching beneath their feet as the white trees swayed all about them, walking quietly for hours as they headed west, into the setting sun. Kyra wondered if they would ever reach Ur. She was relieved, at least, to be on this side of the River Tanis, and she was beginning to allow herself a sense of optimism. She felt her heart beat faster as she realized that Ur was not that far away now. With no more unexpected encounters, she could reach it in a few days' time. They even had food now, thanks to Leo, who bounded behind them happily, holding three dead rabbits in his mouth that he had killed along the way. Selfless, he did not eat them, waiting for all of them to share them together.

Kyra thought of her father as they went, wondered where he was now, if he was winning his battles—or, she dared not imagine, if he were already dead. She thought of Aidan, even of her reckless brothers who annoyed her. She wondered if she would even have a Volis left to return to, or if the Pandesians had laid it to waste. She knew it was only a matter of time until the great armies of Pandesia heard what they did, until they all came searching for her. She knew it was a race against time until she reached the safety of Ur.

Why? she wondered. Why was she needed in Ur? Who was her uncle? Who was her mother? What powers did she have that could help her father? And why had it all been kept secret from her? Were

180

the prophecies true? Would she truly become a powerful warrior like her father?

There came a rustling of branches, snapping her from her reverie, and Kyra suddenly felt Dierdre's arm against her chest, stopping her. The three of them stood at the edge of the wood line, and Kyra looked out and was surprised to see a road before them, winding through the forest. She was even more surprised, as she studied the wide, well-traveled forest road, to hear someone coming on it. There was a great rustling followed by the creaking of wooden wheels. It was, she realized, a carriage.

Kyra's heart pounded as she saw, rounding the bend and coming toward them, a large carriage with the blue and yellow of Pandesia emblazoned on its side. The carriage neared, the horses trotting by, and as it passed them, Kyra looked up into the carriage and saw, behind bars, the faces of several girls, terror in their eyes. They looked to be about her age.

Kyra felt a rush of indignation.

"They're taking them," she remarked. "They're taking them to their Lord Governors."

Kyra watched it race by, and it was quickly followed by another carriage, filled with armed Pandesian soldiers on the lookout. The horses moved by at a quick trot, leaving a cloud of dust as they turned a bend and disappeared as quickly as they had come.

Kyra and Dierdre exchanged a look, and Kyra could see the shared indignation in her friend's eyes.

"I know what you're thinking," Dierdre said. "But if we go after them, we will never make it. You realize how badly outmanned we are, don't you?"

Beside them, Leo snarled.

Kyra did know; she also knew in her heart that, whatever the odds, whatever the risk, there was no way she could let that carriage go. It would haunt her for the rest of her life. Injustice had crossed her path, and she could not choose to let it go.

"Who would I be," Kyra asked, "if I turned an eye away?"

Kyra looked at her friend and she could see the fear in her eyes, but also the inspiration—and finally, the shared resolve. She nodded, and she knew her friend was with her.

Kyra reached back, tightened her grip on her staff, and before she knew it, before she even thought it through, she was running, bursting out of the tree line, joined by Dierdre and Leo, the three of them sprinting, away from Ur, away from their quest—and toward justice.

CHAPTER TWENTY FIVE

Alec knelt in the soil, not feeling the mud on his hands, the cool breeze on his face—not even feeling his own body—as he knelt there, numb, bent over his brother's grave. He wept and wept beside the mounds of dirt, hands raw from having dug all night long, from having buried his brother himself.

Alec felt nothing now; he felt nothing but raw, hollowed out, kneeling there, before his family, all alive just days ago—and now all dead. It was surreal. There, before him, was the brother he had sacrificed for, had sent volunteered to The Flames for. But Alec did not feel a hero; on the contrary, he was overwhelmed by guilt. He could not help thinking that this was all due to him.

Pandesia had swept through his village for one reason only: for vengeance. Alec had shamed them when he had escaped The Flames, and they had come here to send a message to all those who dared defy them. If he had never escaped, Alec realized, his family would be alive today; ironically, he had set out to sacrifice his life for his brother's, but had ended up killing him instead. He wished for nothing more than to be there with them, beneath the earth, dead and buried with the family he loved.

Alec felt a strong hand on his shoulder and he looked up to see Marco standing over him, reassuring, looking down with a face filled with sadness and compassion. It was also a face of strength, a face silently urging him to go on.

"My friend," Marco finally said, his voice hesitant and deep, "I understand your grief—no, in truth, I cannot understand it. I have never had a loss like yours. But I know what it's like to have nothing. To feel like nothing. To have what you love taken from you."

Marco sighed.

"But I also know that life pushes on, whether we want it to or not. It is the tide of a river that cannot be stopped. You cannot kneel here forever; you cannot collapse and die. You must go on. Life *demands* you go on."

Alec wiped away tears, embarrassed to be crying before his friend as he slowly became aware of his presence.

"I don't see how I can," Alec said.

"To want to go on living, you must have a reason, a purpose," Marco said. "A will. Can you think of no reason? No purpose? Not one reason to live?"

Alec tried to think, his mind a blur, spinning. He tried to concentrate, but he found it hard to focus on any one thought.

Alec stared down at the earth, cast red by the sunrise, and he saw his life flashing before him. He was overcome by memories of he and Ashton playing when they were kids; of pounding steel in his father's forge; of his mother cooking; of happy times in this village when it seemed as if they would all live here forever. Life was perfect, it seemed, and always would be—before Pandesia invaded.

As he had that last thought, slowly, something began to crystallize in his mind. Alec slowly remembered Ashton's final words. He recalled the look in his brother's eyes, the feel of his hand clutching his wrist.

Avenge me.

They were more than words. They were a command. A life sentence. His brother's look at that moment, the fierceness in his eyes, a fierceness he had never seen in his life, still haunted Alec. It was unlike his brother to ever condone violence, to condone vengeance. Yet in his dying moments he wanted it, more than Alec had ever seen anyone want anything.

As his words rang in Alec's mind again and again, like a bell tolling, Alec began to hear them, like a mantra, rising up in his mind. They ignited a fire that began to course through his veins as Alec turned and looked away from the graves, from his village, and out, toward the horizon. Toward Pandesia.

They drove him to stand.

Alec looked out, eyes red from crying, and slowly, his sadness gave way to a tide of anger, as his jaw set. It felt good to stand: it allowed the heat of anger to pulse up within him, until it coursed through to his very fingertips. It was anger driven by purpose. A desire to kill. A need for vengeance.

Alec turned and looked at Marco, and he felt his muscles bulging, muscles he had developed from years of striking the anvil, and he knew that he, indeed, had something left to offer this world. He had strength, a knowledge of weaponry—and a desire to use them both.

"I do have a reason," Alec finally responded. "I have one thing left to live for."

Marco stared back questioningly.

"Death," Alec continued. "I must find the Pandesians who murdered my family, and give them the same death they gave my family."

As he uttered the words, Alec felt his own conviction, and it felt good. It was as if he were speaking outside of himself.

Marco nodded back, seeming satisfied.

"That is reason indeed," he replied, "as fine a reason as anyone has to live. Finer indeed than I myself have. You have a cause now, my friend. That is more than most people have in life. Consider it a gift."

Marco clasped his shoulder.

"You are not alone," he said. "There are others, too, who crave vengeance. Others who want to cast off the yoke of Pandesia. I know of them. They are my friends. They hail from my city: the city of Ur."

Marco gave him a knowing look.

"If you want vengeance against a vast army, you will need help," Marco continued. "I want this vengeance, too, and these men can help us."

Alec felt a resolution growing within him.

"Pandesians are everywhere," Marco said. "Stay here, and we shall be captured, sent back to The Flames. We must make it to Ur, and quickly."

As his friend spoke the words, they resonated within him. Alec was ready, ready for the first day of the rest of his life: a life of vengeance. Doing for his brother what Ashton could not do for himself.

"I am ready," Alec replied.

The two of them turned and began to march back through his village. They began the long hike into the plains, heading south and west, their backs to the rising sun, on their way for death, for vengeance, and for the city of Ur.

CHAPTER TWENTY SIX

Kyra sprinted down the forest path, Dierdre and Leo beside her, adrenaline pumping through her veins as she chased after the Pandesian carriage. It turned and disappeared from view, and she increased her speed, lungs burning, determined not to lose it. There were girls trapped in there, girls like her, girls being shipped off to an awful life, as she nearly had been. No matter what the cost, she could not sit by and allow that.

She rounded the bend Kyra and was thrilled to spot the carriages, slowed by a muddy stretch of road, and she increased her pace. As she bore down on them, the reality sank in of what she was doing, of how reckless this was; she knew they could not kill all of these professional soldiers, and that they would likely be captured or killed by them. Yet the strangest thing happened to her. For some reason, Kyra felt her fear dissolving. In its place, she felt a rush of adrenaline, felt a great sense of purpose, and she did not think of herself, but only of these girls. She imagined the battle to come and she felt comfortable that, no matter what happened, even if she should die here on this day, her cause was true.

Kyra glanced over at Dierdre, running beside her, and she could see the fear in her friend's face. Dierdre seemed unsure what to do.

"Make for the wood line and circle around, behind them," Kyra commanded her. "On my signal, attack them from behind."

"Attack them with what?" Dierdre called back, her voice filled with fear.

Kyra realized her friend was weaponless, and she studied the soldiers on the back of the carriage, and singled out the ones with tall spears, riding closer to the wood line, and she came to a decision.

"We'll use their weapons against them," she said. "On my signal, you shall unlock the carriages and free the girls. I shall aim for the men with the spears, and when they drop, you shall gather one for yourself. Go!"

Dierdre veered off into the wood line, leaving Kyra and Leo alone on the road. Kyra, about twenty yards away, was close enough now to be in range with her arrows and she stopped in the muddy path, took aim, and released her first arrow, aiming for a particularly large soldier on the last carriage, who appeared to be their leader. He sat high up on the carriage, whipping the horses, and Kyra knew if she could take him out, the carriage would lose control, and all would be chaos. She aimed high, taking into account the wind, and aimed for his back.

Kyra released, feeling all the tension leaving her body, and she watched breathlessly as the fateful arrow sailed through the air, whistling. She held her breath, as she always did, praying it did not miss.

It hit its target, and she felt a flood of relief as she saw it was a perfect shot. The soldier cried out and slumped over and tumbled down, the carriage immediately veering, directionless, until it smashed into a tree—sending several soldiers falling off of it, into the mud.

Before the stunned soldiers could regroup, Kyra planted and fired again, this time aiming for the other carriage driver. The arrow landed in the back of his shoulder, sending him flying off the carriage and sending his carriage, filled with the girls, keeling over on its side. There came the shouts of the girls, along with the cries of two Pandesian soldiers crushed by the weight of it. Kyra hoped she had not hurt the captives.

Kyra felt a thrill of satisfaction: two shots, and both carriages were stopped, and four Pandesian men down. She quickly took stock and realized that left her ten soldiers to reckon with.

The remaining soldiers began to collect themselves, looking about the woods in every direction, clearly wondering who was attacking them. One of them looked back and noticed Kyra, and he turned and shouted to the others.

As they turned her way, she dropped two more.

That left eight. The remaining soldiers, now keen to her presence, raised their shields and crouched low as Kyra continued to fire. These men were professionals, though, and she was unable to find room for an open shot. One soldier stood, took aim and hurled his spear—and she was surprised at his speed and strength.

The spear flew through the air and just missed her head; that left the soldier exposed, and Kyra immediately fired back, and before he could take cover, she felled him, too.

Of the seven men left, six of them let out a battle cry, drew their swords, raised their shields, and surprised her by all charging for her at once in a well-coordinated attack. Only one remained behind, guarding the locked carriage, on its side, filled with shrieking girls.

"Dierdre!" Kyra shrieked to the wood line.

Dierdre, on the far side of the clearing, emerged from the woods and she, to Kyra's surprise, ran fearlessly for the one soldier standing guard. She ran up behind him, jumped on his back, wrapped a piece of twine around his throat and squeezed, holding on with all her might.

The soldier gasped and writhed, trying to break free. Yet Dierdre was determined, holding on for her life as the man, twice her size, bucked and stumbled. He slammed her into the iron bars of the carriage and Dierdre cried out—yet still she held on.

The soldier threw himself backwards, landing on the ground, on top of her, and Dierdre cried out, crushed by the weight of him. She let go of her grip as he spun around and reached for her face, raising his thumbs, Kyra saw with horror, to gouge out her eyes. Kyra saw, with a sinking heart, that her friend was about to die.

Suddenly there came a shriek, and the girls from the carriage, right beside Dierdre, rushed forward and stuck their arms through the bars, grabbing the soldier by the hair and face. They managed to yank him back, against the bars, off of Dierdre.

Dierdre, freed up, scrambled to her feet, grabbed the soldier's dropped spear from the mud, and plunged it with two hands into his gut, as the girls held him in place.

The soldier went limp and fell face-first to the mud, dead.

Kyra saw the six soldiers charging her, but yards away, and she focused on them. With little time to react, she raised her bow and fired, this time aiming low, beneath their shields, to their exposed legs. She felled one more soldier, as her arrow went through his calf.

The five remaining closed in on her, too close now for her to fire again. Kyra dropped her bow and instead reached around and

189

grabbed her staff off her back. She turned it sideways as a fierce soldier raised his sword high with both hands and brought it down for her head, and prayed that the staff held.

Kyra blocked the blow, sparks flying, both hands shaking from the force, relieved her staff was in one piece. She then spun around and used her staff to jab the soldier in the jaw, a clean strike, breaking his jaw and knocking him down to the mud.

The four remaining soldiers closed in. As one held his sword high, she spun and jabbed him in the solar plexus, making him keel over, then in the same motion raised her staff and cracked him in the side of the head, sending him to the ground.

Kyra ducked as a soldier swung for her head, then spun around and jabbed him with her staff in the kidneys, making him drop his sword and collapse.

Another soldier came her way, and Kyra crouched down low, then came up with an uppercut, connecting the staff under his chin and snapping his neck back, sending him to his back.

Of the two men left, one slashed at her and she raised her staff and blocked it. He was quicker and stronger than the others, and as he slashed again and again, she blocked, swinging her staff around, sparks flying as he drove her back in the mud. She could not find an opening.

As Kyra found herself losing strength, being dominated by this soldier, she felt she was going to lose. Finally, as she stumbled back, she had a realization, as her father's words from one of their endless sparring sessions rang in her head: *never fight on another man's terms.*

Kyra realized she was fighting to this man's strength, not to hers. Instead of trying to go blow for blow with him, this time, as he swung, she no longer tried to resist. Instead, she sidestepped and got out of his way.

This caught him off guard and he stumbled in the mud—and as he went past, Kyra swung around and smashed him in the face with her staff, knocking him down, face-first in the mud. He tried to get up, and she brought her staff down on his back, knocking him out.

Kyra stood there, breathing hard, taking stock of the bodies all around her, lying in the mud, and as she stood there, taking in the scene, she momentarily let her guard down and forgot—the final soldier. Kyra noticed, too late, movement out of the corner of her eye and she watched in horror as he brought his sword down for the back of her neck. She had been careless, and now there was no time to react.

A snarling noise tore through the air as Leo leapt into the air and landed on the soldier's chest, sinking his fangs into his throat right before he could kill Kyra. The man shrieked as Leo pinned him to the ground and tore him to pieces.

Kyra stood there, realizing how much she owed her life Leo, and so grateful he was at her side.

Kyra heard a commotion and looked across the clearing and saw Dierdre reaching up with the soldier's sword and slashing at the chains to the carriage. It broke in a shower of sparks and a dozen girls rushed out, overjoyed, thrilled to be free. Dierdre then slashed the chains on the second carriage, and more girls rushed out. Some of them kicked the lifeless soldiers, venting their anger on them, while others cried and hugged each other. The sight of these girls' freedom made it all worth it to Kyra. She knew she had done the right thing. She could hardly believe she had survived, had defeated all these men.

Kyra joined Dierdre as they embraced the girls, all running over to them, eyes filled with tears and gratitude. She saw the look of trauma in their eyes, and she understood it too well.

"Thank you," one girl after another gushed.

"I don't know how to repay you!"

"You already have," Dierdre replied, and Kyra could see how cathartic this was for her.

"Where will you go now?" Kyra asked, realizing they were all still here, in the middle of nowhere. "It is unsafe for you here."

The girls looked at each other, all clearly stumped.

"Our homes are far from here," one said.

"And if we return, our families may send us back."

Dierdre stepped forward.

"You shall come with me," she said proudly, determined. "I am going to the city of Ur. You shall find safe harbor there. My family will take you in. *I* will take you in."

As she spoke the words, Kyra could see a new life begin to blossom within Dierdre, one of purpose, of fearlessness, as if her old self had a reason to live again. The girls, too, brightened at the idea.

"Very well then," Kyra said. We shall ride together. There is strength in numbers. Let us go!"

Kyra went over and snatched a sword from a dead soldier and handed it to one of the girls, and one at a time, the other girls did the same, canvassing the battlefield for weapons.

Kyra severed the ropes of the Pandesian horses bound to the carriages and mounted one, thrilled to have a ride again. The other girls rushed forward, each mounting a horse; there were so many of them they had to ride two or three to a horse, yet somehow, crammed as they were, they all fit, all of them armed, mounted, and ready to go.

Kyra kicked her new horse and the others joined in, all of them taking off at a gallop, down the road, back in the other direction, finally, toward Ur. The wind in her hair, a horse beneath her, companions beside her, Kyra finally knew that the home stretch was before her, and nothing in the world would stop her now.

The Tower of Ur was her next stop.

CHAPTER TWENTY SEVEN

Duncan lowered his head to the wind as he hiked up the steep mountainside of Kos, the wind whipping his face with a fresh, driving snow, wondering how much worse conditions could become. The sky, so clear but hours ago, had turned a dark, angry gray, snow and wind driving them back, this mountain as unpredictable as it was famed to be. They had been hiking for hours, but now the elevation had become rapidly steeper.

Duncan, hiking beside Seavig, Anvin and Arthfael, glanced back over his shoulder to check on his men. They all hiked with heads down, side-by-side two men wide in the narrow trail, all of them snaking their way up the mountain like a long line of ants. The wind and snow had worsened enough so that Duncan could no longer see all of his men, and he felt a pang of anxiety. He was for all of them, and a part of him felt that this was madness, marching them all straight up a mountain of ice and snow. There was a reason the Pandesians had never tried to ascend and take Kos: it was folly.

Duncan ascended through a narrow stretch of rock and as he emerged, he looked up and his stomach dropped: the trail disappeared in a wall of ice. From here on in, it was a climb—straight up. He and his men would have to switch from walking to climbing by ice and pick. And they were still hardly halfway up the mountain.

"Can we climb it?" Anvin asked, fear in his voice.

Duncan looked up, squinted into the wind, and as he took stock, he thought he detected motion. There came a loud cracking noise, and suddenly, a huge icicle, perhaps twenty feet long, begin to separate. His heart plummeted as it released and came straight down for them, like a bolt of lightning from the sky.

"MOVE!" Duncan shrieked.

Duncan shoved his men out of the way then jumped himself, rolling several feet down the mountain as there came an enormous crash behind them. He looked back to see the icicle, like a giant sword, thrust into the earth and shattering into pieces. Fragments flew everywhere, and he covered his head with his hands, deflecting them, the chips painfully scratching him.

The icicle then tumbled down the cliff, towards his men, and Duncan looked back over his shoulder and watched with dread as his men jumped left and right to get out of its way. More than one man slipped to his death, while one soldier, he saw, was impaled by it, his shrieks filling the air as he was crushed.

Duncan lay on the ground, shaken, and looked over to Seavig, who exchanged a look with him. It was a look of dread.

Duncan turned and looked back up the cliff, and he noticed hundreds more icicles, all perched warily along the edge, all with their tips pointing straight down at them. He was finally beginning to understand just how treacherous this ascent was.

"No point waiting here," Seavig said. "Either we climb now, or we wait for more of those things to come down and find us."

Duncan knew he was right, and he regained his feet. He turned and walked back down the mountain and took stock of the dead and wounded. He knelt beside a soldier, a boy hardly older than his own, and reached up and lowered his eyelids, a pain in his heart.

"Cover him," Duncan ordered his men.

They rushed forward and did so, and Duncan moved on to the wounded, kneeling beside a young soldier whose ribs had been pierced by the icicle. He clasped his shoulder.

"I'm sorry, sir," the boy said. "I can't make it up the mountain. Not like this." He gasped. "Leave me here. Go on without me."

Duncan shook his head.

"That's not who I am," he replied, knowing that, if he did, the boy would die out here. He came to a quick decision. "I shall carry you myself."

The boy's eyes widened in surprise.

"You'd never make it."

"We'll see about that," Duncan replied.

Duncan squatted down, slung the soldier over his shoulder as he groaned, and then walked back through his ranks of men, all of them looking at him with wonder and respect.

Seavig stared back at him as he reached the front, as if wondering how he could attempt this.

"As you said," Duncan said to him, "we have no time to lose."

194

Duncan continued marching forward, right for the sheet of rock, the soldier groaning over his shoulder. As he reached the ice, he motioned to his men, who stepped forward.

"Tie him to my back," Duncan said. "Make the ropes tight. It's a long climb, and I don't plan on either of us dying."

Duncan knew this would make a hard climb even harder, yet he also knew he would find a way. He had been through worse in his life, and he would rather die himself than leave one of his men behind.

Duncan put on his snow shoes, feeling the spikes beneath his feet, grabbed his icepicks, threw back his arm and struck the ice wall. The pick settled into it nicely and he pulled himself up and jammed his foot into the ice below, which also settled in. He took another step, then slammed the ice pick in, and up he went, one step at a time, surprised at the effort it took as he climbed and praying that his tools held. He was, he realized, putting his very life into the fate of their craftsmanship.

All around him his men did the same, and the air was suddenly filled with the sound of a thousand small picks chipping away at ice, rising up even over the howling of the wind. Like an army of mountain goats, they slowly ascended the ice face together. Each step was hard work for Duncan, especially with the wounded soldier on his back, but he never considered turning back. Giving up was not an option.

Duncan climbed and climbed, arms shaking from the effort, the wind and snow occasionally blinding him. As he was breathing harder and harder, trying not to look up and see how much was left to go, he was relieved to see, after about fifty feet, a plateau up ahead.

Duncan pulled himself up on it and momentarily collapsed, breathing hard, resting his shaking arms and shoulders.

"Sir, leave me here," the soldier implored, groaning on his back. "It's too much for you."

But Duncan merely shook his head and got back to his knees, joined by others all around him as they reached the plateau. He looked up and was grateful to see the mountain face level off a bit, not such a steep climb. Duncan dug his pick and shoes in again and continued on, taking it one step at a time, trying not to think of the journey ahead.

Duncan wondered how the men of Kos ever came down off this mountain. He had fought beside them in battle more than once, yet he had never seen them up here, in their element, in these mountains. They were truly a different breed of man, he realized, living amidst such heights, winds and snow.

They climbed for what felt like hours more, Duncan looking up now and again and checking, the peak always seeming to be further and further away, always out of reach. As they went, a cloud drifted in and consumed them, and before long, there was a complete whiteout.

Duncan continued to climb, knowing this was crazy but that now they had no choice. He hoped only for the safety of his men below, and as soon as another gale blew the cloud away, he looked down, checking on his men. There they were all still there, hiking behind him, all slowly but surely scaling their way up the mountain. He caught a glimpse of the magnificent view, all of Escalon spread out below, between majestic peaks capped in white. He felt like a king up here, atop the world, able to see the entire country from one end to the other. Escalon was a beautiful country, with its rolling hills, wide-open plains, dotted with lakes, intersected by rivers and waterfalls. It was a land of bounty and goodness, one that had been robbed from them since the Pandesians had arrived. Duncan knew he had to find a way to get it back.

Duncan looked back up the mountain face, arms shaking as he slammed the pick in and pulled. This appeared to be the last stretch of ice before him, the wall straight and smooth, with perhaps another hundred feet to climb. Duncan, exhausted, was dreading it, but it had to be done. He just prayed his arms did not give out.

Duncan climbed higher, the wind picking up, when another cloud appeared, consuming them in a whiteout, then disappeared just as quickly. He stepped with shaking legs, then paused and let the sweat sting his eyes, not daring to wipe it. He looked up and saw he had only gone a few feet, although it had felt like hours. These few feet might as well have been a few miles.

Duncan stopped and listened as, over the sound of the wind and snow, there slowly arose another sound, like a squealing. It seemed to grow louder by the moment. He froze, wondering what it could be.

Duncan detected motion out of the corner of his eye, and as he turned, he was horrified to see a swarm of creatures flying right for him, small, nearly translucent, resembling a flock of bats. The creatures opened their jaws and squealed their awful noise, revealing three crystal fangs. They flew in an odd way, leaning from side to side, and thousands of them all suddenly descended right for Duncan and his men, vulnerable, perched on the cliff.

"Ice bats!" Seavig yelled out. "Take cover!"

Duncan ducked, holding the pick with one hand and covering the back of his head with the other, and a moment later he was engulfed. These creatures descended on him, screeching in his ears, clawing at him. The wounded soldier on his back shrieked out in pain.

Duncan looked down below and was relieved to see most of his men taking cover on the plateau, lying on their stomachs, raising their hands over their heads. But Duncan and Seavig were too high up, way out in front of the group, and they could not make it back down in time. Duncan knew he was alone up here, and that he would have to fight it out on his own.

Duncan fought back. He grasped the other pick and swung around his head, chopping at them, swinging wildly. Screeching arose as he killed more than a few of them, the things dropping all around him.

Yet, Duncan soon realized, it was but a drop in the bucket; for every one he killed, ten more appeared. He was getting scratched and bit in every direction, and as the pain ripped through his body, Duncan, growing weaker, did not know how much longer he could hang on.

An ice bat sunk his fangs deep into his shoulder and Duncan shrieked out in pain, losing his balance as he reached around with his free hand and pried it off him, crushing its head. He was growing lightheaded, and, dizzy, felt himself about to fall. He suddenly knew he would die here, in this place, beside his brothers. He did not regret dying. He only regretted dying this way, up here, so far from the home he loved. But death, he knew, came for you when it did, and it had come knocking, definitively, for him.

CHAPTER TWENTY EIGHT

Merk woke to the smell of the ocean, to the feel of ocean mist spraying his face, to the sound of crashing waves, and he opened his eyes slowly, disoriented, wondering where he was. He tried to shake off the cobwebs of his mind, having had a long night filled with dreams he did not understand. He had dreamt of rescuing the girl from her burning farm, her family's faces haunting him, pointing at him, accusing him, only to see them all go up in flames—and he with them. His last dream had been of his ascending the tower, running up a circular staircase for what felt like hours, only to reach the top and slip and come hurtling down to the ground.

Merk opened his eyes to see the sun rise over the windy, desolate peninsula that housed the Tower of Ur and slowly, he remembered where he was. The vast Sea of Sorrow stretched out to the horizon, its waves rolling and smashing into the soaring cliffs that framed Escalon high above the sea. Feeling a stiffness in his back and neck, Merk sat up and looked around, trying to get his bearings. He felt cold hard metal against his back, and he turned and saw what he had slept against all night: the silver doors of Ur.

It all came rushing back: after being rejected from the tower, Merk had circled around, searching for another way in, and he had found this other set of doors, on the far side of the tower, identical to the doors in the front, except these made of silver. These, too, were carved with writing and symbols he could not read. He remembered slamming against these doors half the night, refusing to be turned away. But no one had answered his slamming—and finally, he had fallen asleep.

Merk rose to his feet, his knees stiff from the long night, his body aching, and as he looked at the morning sun he felt a fresh determination. He was not a quitter. He had known it would not be easy to enter here—after all, the Watchers were an elite, sacred sect, famed for turning people away. He sensed, though, that this was

198

part of their ritual, their way of weeding out those who were not meant to be here.

Merk looked back up at the tower, awe-inspiring, rising to the sky, its ancient stone so smooth, its silver doors shining, tinted scarlet in the morning sun, and he knew he had no choice but to try again, however long it took.

Merk raised his dagger and once again slammed its hilt on the door, pounding again and again and again. The slams echoed in the still morning air, the tower sounding hollow. He slammed and slammed until his arms were weary, falling into a monotonous rhythm. The vibrations shook his hand, his wrist, his arms and shoulders until they were numb. He no longer cared.

As he slammed, Merk pondered his previous encounter, pondered the words of the creature who had opened the slot in the door: *Only the worthy may enter here* the man had said. What had he meant? What did it mean to be worthy? What was the answer they were hoping for? What answer would open those doors?

The riddle circled in his mind, again and again, echoing with each slam. Merk was determined to answer correctly next time it opened—if it ever opened again.

After hours of slamming, so long that he could no longer think straight, suddenly, to Merk's surprise, a slot slid open in the door, as it had in the front.

Merk stopped, stunned, and he stared back, his heart pounding to see the two yellow eyes appear again, realizing he had another chance and determined not to lose it. The eyes were filled with intensity as they stared back, silently summing him up.

"Please," Merk said, breathing heavily. "Let me in. Let me join you. I demand to be let it!"

There came a long silence, so long that Merk began to wonder if the man would ever respond.

Then finally, he spoke:

"Only the worthy can enter here. Are you worthy?" he asked, his voice deep, ancient.

Merk felt a rush of excitement.

"I *am* worthy!" he called back confidently.

"Why?" the voice asked. "Why are you worthy?"

Merk wracked his brain, thinking, desperate to say the right thing.

"I am worthy because I am a fearless warrior. Because I am loyal. Because I want to join your ranks and help your cause. I am worthy because I want to protect the tower and protect the sword. I am worthy because I am a better killer than anyone here. Let me in and allow me to prove it to you."

The eyes stared back for a long time, and Merk stood there, heart pounding, feeling certain he had answered correctly and that the man would let him in.

But to his shock and disappointment, the slot slammed closed as quickly as it had opened, and he heard footsteps walking away. He could not believe it. He was crestfallen.

Merk stared back at the silver doors, shaken. It couldn't be possible.

"No!" Merk cried in anguish. "You must let me in!"

Merk slammed on the door again and again, wondering what he had done wrong.

Why was he worthy?

Merk pondered what worthiness meant. What did it really mean to be worthy? Was anyone really worthy? Who could even determine that?

Merk, torn up inside, turned his back on the tower. Without this place, without this chance at a new start in life, he could not imagine any other life for himself, any other place to go.

Merk strutted across the plateau, burning with frustration, until he reached the edge of the cliff. He stood there, looking down at the crashing of the great waves beneath him and suddenly, in a bout of frustration, he hurled his dagger, his most precious possession, his only means of slamming on those doors.

He watched as it tumbled down over the cliff, falling hundreds of feet below into the sea, disappearing in a great crashing of waves.

He leaned back and shrieked a cry of agony, of loneliness. It rose to the heavens, echoed by a lonely seagull, and disappeared into the next crashing wave, as if mocking him, as if letting him know that, no matter what he did, he would never be allowed into the Tower of Ur.

200

CHAPTER TWENTY NINE

Kyra clutched her horse's mane as they galloped through Whitewood, the wind in her hair, two girls seated on the horse behind her, and surrounded by the girls she and Dierdre had freed, all of them riding, Leo at their heels. Kyra felt a great sense of satisfaction as she saw all of their faces, so thrilled to be free, so thrilled to be alive. She had rescued them from a dark future, and that meant more than anything to them.

Finally, Kyra had a horse beneath her, the final stretch before her, and a sense of optimism, a sense that her long quest would soon be over—and that she was actually going to make it. They all rode together, a unified force, all of them invigorated. They galloped, as they had for hours, and Kyra took a deep breath, filled with a rush of excitement as they burst out of the shimmering leaves of Whitewood and into the open plains. The huge sky stretched before her and Kyra felt as if the world had been unveiled. After so many days of being trapped in the dark woods, she felt a sense of freedom and exhilaration as she had never before.

The gorgeous countryside of Ur opened up before her, and it was a place unlike any she had ever seen. There were magnificent rolling hills, covered in orange and purple flowers, this part of Escalon much warmer than Volis. The late afternoon sun shone down, illuminating it all in a scarlet light, making this land look as if it had been forged by the hand of God.

Kyra kicked her horse and egged him on faster, invigorated. They hadn't stopped for hours, none of them wanting a break, all wanting to escape the woods, to escape their dark past, and to look to the future. Kyra rode up and down hills, breathing in the Ur air, feeling as if a whole new life were opening up before her.

Hours more passed when, finally, they crested a hill higher than the rest and they call came to a stop at its peak. They paused atop a wide plateau, on which stood a tall, wooden beam with arrows pointing in four directions. Kyra saw well-worn paths leading from the hill in all directions, and she knew they had reached a crossroads.

She studied the horizon, while Dierdre came up beside her.

"That road leads to Ur," Dierdre pointed. "My city."

Kyra followed her glance and saw on the horizon the outlines of a magnificent, sprawling city, its spires and domes and parapets shining in the sun; just beyond it was the faint outline of what appeared to be the sea, light reflecting off of it and illuminating the city. At the entrance to the city there sat a temple, following the tradition of many of Escalon's western cities, with an arch cut through its center to allow travelers to pass in and out. It was crowned by a steeple, higher than any she'd ever seen, and she studied it in awe, amazed a temple could rise that high. Ur, the city of legend, the stronghold of the west, the gate to the open sea, the sea through which all commerce flowed in and out of Escalon.

Dierdre turned and pointed to the road leading the opposite direction.

"Perhaps a day's ride north lies the peninsula of Ur," she explained. "That way lies the tower you seek."

Kyra studied the contours of the land, the long skinny peninsula jutting out into the ocean, so far that she could not see where it ended, disappearing in a cloud of mist. Kyra knew that somewhere out there, beyond the mist, lay her destination. Her uncle. Her quest. She looked down and saw one of the roads forking towards it, a road less traveled—and she felt her destiny calling her.

At her heels Leo whined, as if he sensed it, too.

Kyra turned to look at Dierdre, and for a moment, she felt a pang of sadness. Their journey together had come to an end. Kyra hadn't realized how accustomed she had grown to Dierdre's presence; she had become a true friend, like the sister she'd never had. And as she looked out at the faces of all these other girls, hope in their eyes, freedom before them, she felt reluctant to leave them, too. But she knew her calling awaited her, and it lay in the opposite direction.

"I shall miss you, my friend," Kyra said.

She saw anxiety etched across Dierdre's face, too.

"Shall we not see each other again?" Dierdre asked.

Kyra was wondering the same thing, but did not know the answer.

"When I finish my training," Kyra replied, "I vowed to my father to return and help our people."

"I shall help our people, too," Dierdre replied. "I shall rally men, perhaps, do whatever I can to help the cause. When two people's paths are meant to cross, nothing can keep them apart. I believe we shall meet again. Somewhere, somehow."

"We shall."

Dierdre reached out and they clasped arms, looking each other in the eye. Both of them had aged, both had grown stronger, since they had met.

Kyra dismounted, to everyone's look of surprise, and handed the reins to Dierdre.

"You have many girls here to take care of," Kyra said, seeing the girls tripled up on the horses. "You shall need this horse more than I."

"Then how will you reach the tower?" one of the girls asked.

Kyra turned and looked.

"It is hardly a day's hike," she said. "And I have Leo. I would like to walk. I have my staff and my bow, and I fear nothing."

Kyra saw the look of respect in all of their eyes, and the look of gratitude, as two girls, tripled up on a horse, dismounted and mounted hers.

"I never met anyone like you," Dierdre said. "I had always thought that bravery was reserved for men. But now I see it can be for us, too. You have given me a greater gift than you can ever know—and for that I can't thank you enough."

Kyra's eyes welled as she looked over these brave girls who had a second chance at life.

"Take care of these girls," Kyra adjured her. "If they want protection, give it to them—but if they want to learn to fight, give that to them, too. If you shelter a warrior, you save their body, but kill their spirit. And these girls all have great spirit."

Kyra watched as the girls all rode away, galloping down the hillside, into the setting sun and toward the shining city of Ur. She watched them go for a long time, leaving a cloud of dust in their trail. Dierdre turned back, once, and looked for her, raising a single fist high in the air—and Kyra raised her fist back.

Then, just like that, they were over the hill, gone from sight, nothing left but the distant rumble and vibrations of their travel.

Leo whined beside her, as if sad to see Dierdre go, and Kyra turned, took her staff and began to hike. She marched down the hillside in the opposite direction, heading northwest, toward the peninsula of Ur, and somewhere beyond that mist, toward the tower.

As she marched through a field, a million thoughts raced through her mind. She pondered her destination, the tower, her uncle. She thought of the training she would receive, the powers she would gain, what she would come to know about herself. She thought of all the secrets awaiting her. Her mother's identity. Her destiny. It made her nervous, but also excited.

It was overwhelming to even consider it, and her heart beat faster at the thought. More terrifying than any foe out there, more terrifying than the idea of not completing her quest, was the idea of completing it, of finding out about herself, of getting to the bottom of the riddle that had plagued her her whole life: who was she?

*

Kyra hiked for hours, excited, determined, feeling each step take her closer to the end of her quest, and the beginning of her new life. She hardly felt the burning in her legs as she ascended and descended the gently rolling hills and she did not even think of pausing until, hours later, she crested a hill and reached a broad plateau. She leaned against her staff and took in the vista, and the sight was startling: the whole peninsula of Ur was laid out before her, the ocean now visible in the distance, its waves already audible. A mist blew in and out, still obscuring the tower, but she knew that it was close.

She stood there, taking in the sight, feeling as if she were seeing her future unfold before her—when suddenly, she heard a distant noise and detected motion out of the corner of her eye. She wheeled, gripping her staff, on guard.

As Kyra saw the sight before her she blinked several times, hardly comprehending what her eyes were showing her. She suddenly felt overwhelmed with emotion as she watched the creature approach, walking slowly up the hill, his head down, covered in wounds, looking exhausted, but still marching on—all the while keeping his eyes fixed proudly on her. As he came closer, Leo did not snarl as he once had; instead, he whined in excitement. And in pride.

Kyra could hardly breathe. She stood upright, her mouth agape, hardly believing what she saw. She had never been so happily surprised in her life. There, approaching her, having crossed Escalon all by himself to find her, was her loyal friend: Andor.

Kyra's eyes welled up at the sight of him. She was overjoyed, speechless. He had survived. And he had found her.

Kyra rushed forward and hugged Andor, throwing her arms around his neck. At first, proud, wild, and determined not to show emotions, he jerked away. But then he leaned his head into her chest and she kissed his mane several times and hugged him tight, tears rolling down her face, overwhelmed at his loyalty. She had been so heartbroken to leave him behind, as if she had left a piece of herself back there, and seeing him here, alive, made her feel whole again.

Leo, too, came up and rubbed against his leg, and Andor made a snorting noise, stomping, but not pulling away. Those two finally had reached some sort of peace.

"You killed them all by yourself, didn't you?" Kyra asked in admiration, seeing his hide covered in blood.

Andor grunted as if in response, and Kyra's heart broke as she examined his wounds. She could not believe that he had single-handedly killed all of those hornhogs, that he had made it all the way here with his injuries. She knew, after this, that they would be together for life.

"We have to get you fixed up," she said.

Andor snorted, as if in defiance, and instead he lowered his body, gesturing for her to ride. She was in awe at his strength.

Kyra mounted, and vowed to never leave his side again.

"We shall be together forever now," she said. "Nothing shall ever get between us again."

He neighed and reared, as if in response.

Kyra turned and looked north and west, towards the tower, somewhere at the end of the peninsula, and with Andor beneath here, she felt her heart pounding with excitement. Now, she would be there in hours.

"Our destiny awaits us, Andor. Take us there!"

Without another word he took off at a gallop, Leo at their side, the three of them cutting through the countryside of Ur—and riding headlong into their destiny.

CHAPTER THIRTY

Alec trekked across the Plain of Thorns, Marco beside him, the gray landscape and endless rolling thorn bushes matching his somber mood. The sky was gray, the earth was gray, the thorn bushes, filling the landscape as far as he could see, were gray, scratching at him as he walked. Marco weaved his way between them, but Alec no longer cared; he let himself be scratched. In fact, he welcomed the pain. Having just come from burying his family, it was the only thing that made him feel alive.

They had hiked from Soli through these desolate plains, the most direct way, Marco had said, to Ur and avoid detection by Pandesia. Alec, though, was barely cognizant of where he was as he went. With each step there flashed through his mind images of his brother, his dying words, his plea for vengeance. *Vengeance.* That was the only thing that kept him going.

Alec put one foot before the other, feeling as if he had been walking for years. He was grateful for Marco's companionship, who had allowed him his silence, who gave him his space to grieve, and who had given him a purpose to go on living.

The wind whistled through and another thorn bush whirled by and stuck to Alec's leg; Alec felt the blood trickle down, but he didn't care. Marco, though, leaned over and kicked it with his boot, sending it rolling away, and Alec felt the thorns dislodge from his leg. He watched it roll, skidding across the hard, baked earth, and turned to see a landscape filled with rolling thorn bushes, looking like a sea of creatures coming alive. He could no longer imagine grass, trees; it was as if the world had ended.

Alec felt a sudden hand on his chest and he came to a stop, as did Marco beside him. He looked down and was surprised to see, a step before them, a drop-off, a steep decline into a valley. As he looked out, in the distance he saw an entirely new landscape. There, before them, was a valley of rolling hills, lush with green, dotted with grazing sheep. And beyond that lay something he could hardly fathom. He brushed the dust from his eyes and blinked against the rays of the setting sun, and he saw the outline of a vast and beautiful city, its spires and domes and parapets rising into the sky. Beyond this city was the outline of an ocean, and Alec knew this was someplace special. The sight yanked him from his reverie.

"My home," Marco said, standing beside him, looking out and sighing. "I hate my family," he continued, "but I love my city."

Alec saw Marco studying the city with what appeared to be a mix of emotions.

"I had planned to never return to Ur," Alec said. "But life has a way of changing our plans. At least it's a place I know. More importantly, I have friends there—friends who are like my real family. Friends who will give up their lives to fight Pandesia."

Alec nodded, feeling a new sense of resolve, reminded of his purpose.

"I should like to meet your friends," Alec said.

Marco smiled wide as he turned and nodded.

"You shall, my friend. You shall."

The two of them set off down the steep ridge, away from the Plain of Thorns and toward the city, and as they did, Alec felt himself slowly welling with a new feeling. The feeling of grief and emptiness that had taken over his spirit was now being replaced by one of anticipation. Of purpose. Of determination. Of vengeance.

Ur.

Perhaps, after all, he had reason to live again.

CHAPTER THIRTY ONE

Merk leaned against the cold silver doors of the Tower of Ur, seated on the ground as he had been for days, despite the cold, the stiffness of his limbs, the hunger, refusing to leave. He would not accept the Watchers' rejection. He felt, deep inside, more than he had ever felt anything, that this place was home, that he was *meant* to be here.

He also could not walk away in the face of the great riddle posed to him. Above all, Merk hated riddles. He loved reason and order, expected all things to follow a logical and rational pattern. He had always lived life as a rational man, even when he killed people. He did not like mysteries, and he did not like things that could not be explained—especially when they had to do with him.

And this mysterious riddle tormented him. He had entered a different realm in this place, and he was not on his own terms anymore. He realized that. Yet he was not used to being posed questions that had no simple answers. He did not like questions that could be answered in different ways for different people. He preferred to see the world as black and white, right and wrong, good and evil.

Merk grappled with their question as he sat there, his head hung in his hands, turning it over again and again. It reverberated in his mind again and again.

Are you worthy?

It was a question that made him ponder not only his reason for being here, but struck at the core of his entire life. It was a question that, he realized, had lingered at the edge of his consciousness for all his life. Why was he worthy? So many people had told him he was worthless in life, starting with his father. What made him worthy of serving Escalon? To be feared by other men? To have the skills that he had? Why was he, indeed, worthy of living?

The more he pondered it, the more he realized that, deep down, he did not feel worthy at all. He never had. Since he was a child, his parents had made it clear to him that he was not worthy of his

209

brothers and sisters, not worthy of their great family name. He had never felt worthy in his own eyes or anyone else's. So this question that the Watchers had posed to him had struck him in more ways than one. Had they known that it would? Was the question different for each person who knocked?

Merk realized, as he pondered it, that the riddles were designed to make petitioners go away. They did not want anyone here who did not truly want to be here. They wanted people so desperate to be here that they were willing to not just give up everything, but to also grapple with their own demons, to face their own worst fears.

Merk leaned back and shrieked in frustration. He stood and slammed his palms against the silver doors until he could stand it no longer.

Why was he worthy?

Merk paced back and forth, determined to get to the bottom of this answer that had tortured him his whole life. He was not worthy because of his skills. That had been the wrong answer, he realized it now. Many other skilled contenders desired to be here, too. They were turned away, too, despite their skills.

His whole life Merk had taken pride in his skills. But the Watchers wanted something more. But if not skills, then what?

The more Merk dwelled on it, the more his mind went numb and began to, finally, go blank. As it did, he began to experience a new place in his mind, a place of calm, of a quiet unlike any he'd ever known. It was a strange place, a place where he no longer tried to rationally think of the answers. It was a place of a deep stillness, where he no longer grappled for answers, but waited to allow the answers to come to him.

As he stood there, breathing deep, slowly, an answer began to come to him. The less he tried to figure it out, the more clear it became, like a flower blossoming in his mind.

Perhaps he was worthy not because of his past but because of his *present*. Because of who he was *right now*.

And the person who he was right now could not be worthy. Not yet. After all, he had never been here, had never served here.

That was the answer: he was *not* worthy. They demanded someone with the awareness to know that he was unworthy. That

210

awareness, after all, was the foundation one needed in order to learn, in order to become worthy.

Merk turned, heart pounding with excitement, and slammed the door with his palm, knowing he had the answer this time, feeling it as certain as he felt he was alive. He also knew somehow that this time, they would answer the door.

Merk was not surprised when the slot in the door slid back instantly. Whoever was behind that door seemed to sense the shift in him.

"I am *not* worthy!" Merk called out quickly, in a rush, thrilled by his realization. "And that is precisely why I am worthy to enter here—because I know I am not. Because I am willing to become worthy. None of us are born worthy. Only those who realize this have the chance to become worthy. I am worthy because I am…nothing."

Merk stared back at the fierce yellow eyes, which seemed to examine him for a long time, expressionless. He sensed something shift between them as a long, tense silence followed. He knew his whole future depended on these next few moments, on whether this man would let him through those doors.

But Merk's heart slammed like a lid on a coffin as the metal latch slammed closed again.

He was crestfallen. A long silence ensued, an echoing silence that seemed to last forever.

Merk stood there, shocked. He could not understand. He had been so sure he had been right, had felt it without a doubt. He stood there, staring. He had no idea where to go, no idea what else to do with his life.

Suddenly, to his shock, there came the sound of multiple latches opening, echoing behind the silver doors—and soon, the silver doors began to open slowly. First they opened just a crack; then the crack widened.

Merk stood outside, mouth agape, as an intense light began to flood him, to beckon him. He knew that once he passed through those doors his life would change forever, and as they widened all the way and the light flooded over him, he was breathless. As he took that first, fateful step, he could hardly believe what he saw before him.

211

CHAPTER THIRTY TWO

Duncan braced himself as the ice bats engulfed him, squealing in his ears, clawing him in every direction. His skin scratched, the bats swarmed him, pulling at his hair, slicing him anywhere they could find, and with each cut he felt himself growing weaker. On his back the wounded soldier groaned, while beside him, Seavig cried out as he swatted at them unsuccessfully. Separated up here from the rest of his men, far from the plateau, and getting weaker with each moment, Duncan knew he would not survive.

There suddenly came the sound of picks chipping away at ice, and Duncan looked over and was surprised to see his commanders, Anvin and Arthfael, appearing beside him, joined by dozens of others, all of them picking their way up the mountain despite the swarm of bats attacking them. They had all come, he realized, to save him.

The men swung wildly with their picks, dropping bats from the sky, the screeches rising up. They came close and shielded Duncan and Seavig with their bodies, slashing at the beasts to divert the ice bats' attack. Duncan found himself momentarily relieved from the swarm as some of the bats shifted to attack the others—and he was overwhelmed by their loyalty: they'd all risked their lives for him.

Yet no sooner had they made headway when the bats regrouped, more and more arriving. He joined his men in swatting at them, but it did little good. His men, Duncan was horrified to see, were now also getting clawed and bitten to death. Duncan knew there wasn't much time before they were all finished. He felt a bat bite his shoulder and he shrieked, as more and more landed on his back, the bats getting bolder as the sky turned white with their translucent bodies. His hands were shaking, and he felt himself losing his grip.

Suddenly, the bats let out a chorus of shrieks. It was not a shriek of victory—but one of agony, carrying a different pitch to it. As Duncan felt them begin to back away, he could not understand what was happening. And then, he realized: something was attacking them.

Duncan heard a whooshing noise beside him and felt a rush of wind and he looked up the mountain face, blinking into the snow, and was amazed at what he saw: high above were what dozens of soldiers, hardened warriors with long beards and fierce, square faces. They peered down over the mountaintop and tilted huge cauldrons, leaning them over the edge of the mountain face. As they did, a black liquid came gushing down the mountain like a waterfall, just far out enough so that it just missed Duncan—yet close enough to be able to douse the swarm of bats. Whatever was in that liquid must have hurt the bats, because many of them dropped limply, killed on the spot—and the ones that survived, screeched and flew off, the entire flock lifting, disappearing as quickly as it had arrived.

Duncan breathed hard as he clung to the ice, scratched and bleeding, arms shaking, yet somehow still alive. He turned and looked for his men, taking stock, and was relieved to see they were still there. A sense of quiet and calm had finally descended over them, and despite his wounds, Duncan felt, for the first time, that he was going to make it. The men of Kos were in sight. He would have another chance at life. They would reach the top.

Adrenaline pumping in his veins, Duncan reached up and with a renewed strength slammed his ice pick into the mountain face, then his feet, stepping up, climbing again. The men all around him did the same, and soon the air was, once again, filled with the sound of ice chipping, and of men climbing.

With each pick, one step at a time, his army ascended the mountain face.

Duncan pulled himself up with one last heave as he reached the top, then collapsed onto the floor of snow, beyond exhausted, breathing hard, hardly believing he had made it. Every muscle in his body burned.

Duncan rolled to the side and released the injured soldier on his back, freeing himself of the weight. The young soldier groaned beside him, and looked at him with a look of gratitude beyond any Duncan had ever seen.

"You saved my life at the risk of your own," the man said, his voice weak, "when you had every reason not to."

Duncan felt a wave of relief as he saw his men ascend all around him, all gratefully collapsing on the mountain top, and he slowly rose to his hands and knees, gasping for air, feeling all the bat wounds, his arms still shaking. Sensing a presence, Duncan looked up to see before him a broad, muscular hand reaching down for him.

Duncan let himself be pulled up, and as he stood, he was amazed by what he saw. Standing there before him were the proud warriors of Kos, men adorned with furs, with long beards sprinkled with white, thick eyebrows, broad shoulders and faces of earnest men who had lived hard lives. The broad plateau atop the mountain stretched as far as he could see, and he stared back at these men admiringly, men who did not bother to wipe away the ever-present snow accumulating on their faces, beards, eyelashes, men with wild, long hair, filled with snow. They wore all-white armor beneath their furs, clearly prepared for battle at all times, even in their home. These were the men he remembered.

The warriors of Kos.

A warrior stepped forward, a man with a scar across the bridge of his nose, shoulders twice as broad as any man, and who wielded a great war hammer as if it were a child's stick. Duncan remembered him fondly from years ago, recalling a battle they had fought in together, side by side, until the sun had set and all their enemies were dead. Bramthos. Duncan was surprised to see him still alive—he could have sworn he had seen him get killed in a battle years later.

"Last I saw you you had a sword in your gut," Duncan said, surprised to find his friend alive. "I should have known."

Bramthos beamed, turning side to side, proudly displaying the scar across his nose.

"Lovely thing about battle," Bramthos replied. "Your foe never knows if you're going to live long enough to kill him back."

Duncan shook his head, wondering at the stuff these men of Kos were made of.

"And you," Bramthos said. "Last I saw you, you were leaping off a horse into the arms of three soldiers hoping to kill you."

214

Now Duncan beamed.

"They should have hoped harder," Duncan replied.

Bramthos grinned.

"Looks like we came to save you just in time," he said, examining Duncan's wounds.

Duncan grinned back.

"We had them just where we wanted them."

After a long, shocked pause, Bramthos grinned wide, then stepped in and embraced Duncan. Duncan embraced him back, lost in this bear-of-a-man's hug.

"Duncan," the man said.

"Bramthos," Duncan replied.

"Ironic," Duncan continued, as he stepped back and examined his old friend. It felt good to see him again, to be in the company of such great warriors. "I came here to save you, and you ended up saving us."

Bramthos's grin widened.

"And who ever said we needed saving?" Bramthos replied.

Duncan grinned, seeing that his friend meant every word, and knowing it was true. These warriors of Kos needed no saving. They would fight anyone to the death and think nothing of it.

Bramthos clasped Duncan's shoulder, turned and began leading him and his men across the broad plateau. The hundreds of soldiers of Kos, gathered around, parted ways for them, all of them staring as they passed, strong, somber men, bedecked in armor and furs, wielding halberds, hammers, axes, and spears.

Duncan found himself being led through a land of stone and ice, snow-covered peaks all around them, the wind whipping with a vengeance. In the distance he could see the outline of a city amidst the fast-moving clouds, a barren city atop the world. Duncan breathed easy, realizing they had really made it, had finally reached, against all odds, the brutal and unforgiving home to the people of Kos. He sensed that Bramthos was bringing him to their leader, Bramthos, and as they neared the city, Duncan knew that the meeting he was about to have, up here, high in the sky, would change the fate of Escalon forever.

215

CHAPTER THIRTY THREE

Kyra rode on the back of Andor, charging up and down the hills of Ur, riding into the scarlet sunset, her heart slamming with anticipation. She had been riding for hours, farther out into the peninsula, the ocean crashing on both sides of her as the land became increasingly barren. Now, finally, she was so close. Now, after her journey across Escalon, after all she had been through, she could see before her the object of her dreams. A tower she only dreamed existed.

There it was, on the horizon, at the end of the lonely peninsula: what could only be the Tower of Ur. It stood so majestic, so proud, alone on the barren, windswept peninsula, its round tower rising straight into the air, hundreds of feet high, capped by a shining, golden dome. It appeared to be built of an ancient stone, an unusual shade of white, lit scarlet rays by the last rays of the sun. It was magnificent, unlike anything she had ever seen, a place of dreams. She could hardly believe that such places could exist in the world.

As the sun lit up the tower, what caught her eye most were its doors—those incredible golden doors, arched, soaring fifty feet high—looking like great works of art. They were forbidding and welcoming at the same time. Framing the tower on all sides was the majestic crashing of ocean waves, the Sea of Sorrow as its backdrop, blanketing the horizon as far as she could see.

Kyra paused on a hilltop, breathing hard as Andor did, too, taking a much needed rest as she took it all in. She could feel a magical power, an incredible energy, emanating off of this tower even from here, at once drawing her in and pushing her away. She recalled all the tales her father had read her of this place, the ancient bards who had sung of it, generation after generation, and she knew it held some of the great secrets—and most guarded treasures—of Escalon. Centuries of Watchers had inhabited it. It was a place of warriors, of creatures, of men and of honor.

Kyra felt light-headed as she pondered who awaited her. Her uncle, the man who would reveal everything, who would teach her

216

about her mother, her identity, her destiny and her powers. The man who would train her. Was it possible, Kyra dared to wonder, that her mother was alive? That she was here, too?

So many questions raced through her mind, she did not know where to begin. She could hardly stand the anticipation, and she prodded Andor and breathlessly took off, the two of them galloping across the hills, down the final stretch.

As she neared the tower, Kyra's blood was coursing through her ears, making it hard to think. She had somehow crossed Escalon all by herself, without her father's protection, or his men. She felt stronger from it already, and she had not even begun her training. She realized that her journey had been necessary preparation for her training. Now she understood why her father had sent her alone. He had wanted to make her stronger, to prepare her, to make her worthy.

Kyra rode up and down the hills and as she was perhaps a hundred yards away from the entrance, she passed a curious marker. A circular staircase, carved of stone, rose perhaps twenty feet high and ended in nothing. It was like a stairway leading to the sky, an unfinished stairway that led to nothing, and she wondered what it signified.

She continued riding, drawn to the tall golden doors, like a magnet pulling her in. As she approached the tower she looked everywhere, searching for any sign of her uncle, of anyone awaiting her.

Yet, curiously, there was none.

Finally, only fifty feet away the entrance, Kyra stopped, dismounted, and stood there, staring, breathing hard, taking it all in, wanted to approach it on foot. It was even more awe-inspiring up close. The doors were etched in strange golden carvings, filled with words, images. She walked slowly toward them, wanting to take in their beauty, and as she neared she squinted and was able to read the ancient script, once she had learned in her youth. It was a lost language of Escalon, a language dead for thousands of years. It was a script the king's tutors had taught her well. She had been the only girl allowed to learn, and she had always wondered why.

Kyra reached up and ran her fingers along the etchings, the words, reading passages which riveted her. Slowly, she pieced together their message. They were ancient sayings and parables aimed about the nature of honor, of valor.

What is battle? read one of them.

Where does your strength hail from? read another.

Do you aim for your foe or for yourself? read another.

There were secrets contained in these riddles, she felt, secrets that could take a lifetime to ponder and decipher.

Kyra looked over the arched doorway, and high above read something etched in gold over it:

Only the worthy may enter here.

Kyra wondered who had carved these. It looked as if it had been done centuries ago, yet it resonated with her as if it had been written yesterday. She stepped forward and placed her palms on the doors, feeling the energy radiating off of them, then leaned back and craned her neck so that she could look straight up the tower. From this angle, it seemed to stretch into the heavens themselves.

Kyra stepped back and slowly turned, looking around, getting her bearings for this strange place. It was utterly silent, except for the crashing of a wave, Leo's whine, or Andor's snort. The wind ripped off the ocean, whistling and howling in her ears. She looked everywhere, but to her surprise, saw no sign of her uncle—or of anyone else. It was hardly the welcome she had expected. Had this place been abandoned? Was she in the right place?

Finally, she could wait no longer.

"Uncle!" she cried out, unsure what to do.

Where could everyone be? Was it possible that her uncle did not know she was coming? That he did not want to see her? Or worse—that he was already dead?

Kyra drew her staff and knocked on the golden doors, at first quietly, then with more and more force.

No one answered.

She suspected no one would. After all, would he not have seen her approaching?

Kyra, feeling confused, defeated, did not know what else to do. Night was falling, and she could not return to Volis. Not after all she'd been through.

Kyra turned, put her back against the golden doors, and slowly slid down, until she sat on the ground. Leo came and lay down beside her, resting his head in her lap, while Andor stood close by, grazing.

She sat there, looking at the last rays of the dying sun as darkness fell all around her, and she wondered. Had her quest been for nothing?

CHAPTER THIRTY FOUR

Duncan walked beside Seavig, Anvin and Arthfael, hundreds of their following close behind, as they all entered the city of Kos. Duncan could hardly believe this place, this vast plateau on top of the world, at least a mile wide, nestled amidst snow-capped peaks. It was a perfect home for the people of Kos, a people strong and silent, separatist and unflappable, a people who lived not in fear of the elements around them. They approached massive arched gates, a hundred feet high, soaring into the clouds and carved of ice—ice, Duncan realized, that never melted. Duncan examined them in awe as they passed through them.

They walked over a bridge of ice, and Duncan looked down and saw the chasm it spanned, twenty feet wide, the fall that would kill any man. He looked ahead and saw the bridge was leading them right into the city of Kos.

They entered the city and as they did, the people of Kos emerged to watch them, hundreds of men, women and children appearing out of the wind-whipped snow, staring back expressionless, women standing over children, all watching wordlessly. They were a people who was hard to read: Duncan could not tell if they were ready to embrace them or kill them. Perhaps both.

Fires somehow managed to burn in structures carved into the ice, curved to shelter them from the wind, and the air here was filled with the welcome smell of roasting meat. Duncan looked ahead and as a gust of wind drove away the clouds, he noticed a singular structure built from the ice, around which the entire city revolved: a temple. Shaped in a triangle, ending in a point, carved of ice, it rose a hundred feet, etched in an elaborate design, its facade carved with the faces of bearded warriors. The huge structure had a small opening, an arch just tall enough for people to walk through. A door into a world of ice.

Bramthos led the way and Duncan entered, and as he did, he was in awe at this place: carved entirely of ice, this temple, with its

220

translucent walls, filtered in sunlight, seemed to be glowing, alive. A quiet, empty structure, so high in the sky, it felt solemn, sacred. It was even colder in here, if possible, than outside, yet no one seemed to mind.

A long walkway stretched before him, its floor made up of hammered swords, leading to a massive star-shaped altar at the far end of the temple, with a gleaming halberd perched at the top, like some sort of ornament to war. And kneeling before it, Duncan saw a dozen warriors, their backs to him, hands clasped. In the center of the group knelt a man larger than them all, the only one wearing red furs, with wild red hair, and a red beard. Even with his back to him, Duncan could recognize his old friend anywhere. Kavos. Their leader. A man famed to have killed more men in battle than anyone Duncan had ever met. A man whom Duncan had seen stand still when a lion pounced on his chest, knocking the creature back.

Kavos had a mystique about him, and one that was justified. Duncan had personally witnessed him receive dozens of vicious wounds, yet he had never heard him cry out once. He did not know what stuff he was made of—he was just glad that they fought for the same side.

Kavos, Duncan knew, was a difficult man to read even in the most simple of times—and these were not simple times. Unlike many leaders, whatever Kavos commanded his people followed religiously. There was no questioning, ever. And Kavos never changed his mind. Duncan knew he would only have one chance to convince him.

As Duncan slowly crossed the temple, he felt a great sense of anticipation, knowing that everything would ride on this encounter, all of his efforts and journeys up until now, the very fate of his people. If Kavos refused to join them, the war, Duncan knew, would be lost. Escalon would be lost.

He reached the end of the long aisle, and Duncan stopped and waited patiently behind Kavos and his men. He knew that Kavos was not a man to be rushed.

Duncan examined the curious altar, the candles burning around it, and he wondered about the gods of Kos. They were no gods that he prayed to. These men were different, in all that they did, from the rest of Escalon, separatist enough to make Duncan wonder if they would ever really join his cause. All the way up here, with their own climate and culture and gods and city, they were, oddly, not even a part of Escalon—and they never had been.

After a long silence, Kavos slowly rose and faced Duncan, all of his men standing with him on cue. Kavos stared back at Duncan, expressionless, his eyes dark and sunken, holding within them, surely, the memory of thousands of foes he had defeated in battle. He was as hard as these walls of ice, and he remained silent so long, Duncan did not think he would ever speak.

Duncan then recalled that it was *he* who would have to begin. Unlike the rest of Escalon, it was the etiquette for the visitor to speak first.

"What do you pray for?" Duncan asked. "Victory? Conquest? Glory?"

Kavos stared back, silent for so long, Duncan wondered if he would ever respond. He began to wonder if he even remembered him.

"If it is victory you pray for," Duncan added, after a long silence, "you shall not find it here. Victory lies below. With me—with all of us—in ridding us of the invaders. In serving Escalon."

"The men of Kos serve no one," Kavos replied, his voice deep, filled with finality, furrowing his brow. "Escalon least of all."

Duncan stared back, unsure how to respond.

"The weak king betrayed us," Kavos said, "and the men of Kos do not lend their loyalty to weak men—and we do not lend it twice."

Duncan understood his sentiment, having felt it many times himself.

"Yet still," Duncan countered, "it is Escalon in which you live—and the Pandesians block your mountains at the base. They have you surrounded."

Kavos smiled for the first time, his face bunching up with lines, a hardened smile, more like a scowl.

"Have you ever considered that it is we who have them surrounded?" Kavos replied.

Duncan frowned, frustrated, expecting that response.

"You are untouchable up here," Duncan admitted. "Yet no people are an island. Escalon is meant for all of us. You should be

222

able to roam freely about this entire land which is yours, you and your men. If the trade routes were opened again, it would help your people."

Kavos shrugged, unimpressed.

"There is no commodity we can't live without," he replied. "Honor is our most precious commodity. And we have it in abundance."

Duncan studied his old friend, having a sinking feeling he would be refused. He was as stubborn and implacable as he recalled.

"Are we not all one Escalon?" Duncan finally asked, pleading to his sense of loyalty to the other warriors.

Kavos sighed, his expression softening.

"At one time we were," he finally said. "When you and I rode forth and crushed skulls together. If you had taken the kingship, then yes, we would be. But now, we are nothing. We are each warlords scattered to the corners, each for his own stronghold, his own people. There is no king to bind us anymore, and no capital, except in name."

Kavos examined him, an intensity in his eyes, as he took a step closer.

"Do you know why the Pandesians were able to invade?" he asked. "Not because of our weak king—but because of our weak *nation*. Because we are scattered. Because we were *never* one. We never had a king strong enough to truly unite us all."

Duncan felt a rush of determination, realizing the truth in this warrior's words.

"What if we have a chance to be?" Duncan asked, his voice filled with intensity. "What if we have a chance now, for all time, to become one people? One Escalon? One people under one banner? I do not know if we can ever be—but I do know that we shall continue to be nothing if we do not, as one nation, attack the strangers amongst us."

Kavos examined him for a long time.

"One people needs one leader," he countered. "Are you prepared to be that leader?"

Duncan's heart pounded at the question, the one question he did not expect, and the one question he did not wish to ponder.

Leadership was the last thing he craved; but he needed Kavos, and he needed Kos. He did not want to risk losing him.

"Would you lend us your men? Would you join us?" Duncan countered.

Kavos turned and walked silently toward the exit of the temple, Duncan following as his men gestured for him to do so. He walked beside him, wondering where they were going, wondering what he was thinking.

Duncan was met by a cold breeze as they exited the temple from a side door, the wind howling here, atop the world. All of their men fell in together, mingling with each other, trailing behind them.

As the two made their way across the plateau, Duncan wondered what this man was thinking. They finally came to a stop at the edge of a cliff, and as his friend looked out, Duncan looked out with him. Below them there unraveled all of Escalon, the late afternoon sun lighting up the snow-capped peaks and, in the distance, the immense capital city of Andros.

A long, comfortable silence fell between the two warlords as they surveyed their homeland.

"It would be madness to attack," Duncan admitted. "After all, there are countless Pandesian garrisons below. We would be outnumbered ten men to one, at least. They have superior armor, weaponry, and have organized forces in every town in Escalon. They also still control the Southern Gate—and the seas. It would be suicide."

Kavos looked down below, nodding.

"Keep talking," he finally said. "You're convincing me."

Duncan smiled.

"I doubt we'll win," Duncan said. "But I vow to you that I shall not remain standing as long as any last Pandesian stands, as along as any Pandesian banner sits in our ground."

Kavos finally turned and studied him.

"If we ride with you into battle," Kavos said, "I will need you to vow something to me: the weak King shall not reclaim his throne. If we win, you, and you alone, shall rule Escalon."

Duncan grimaced, unsure how to respond. It was the last thing he wanted.

"I am no politician," Duncan replied. "Just a soldier. That is all I've ever wanted."

"Sometimes life demands of us more than what we want," Kavos countered. "I want our country ruled by one of us—by a man I trust and respect. Vow to me—or my army stays here."

Duncan sighed, long and hard, wishing it had not come to this. After a long silence, pondering his options, punctuated only by the wind, he knew he had no choice.

Finally, he turned to his friend and nodded.

They reached out and clasped arms, and in that clasp, Duncan felt the fate of Escalon—the new Escalon—being forged.

Kavos smiled wide.

"Long life is overrated," he said. "I'll take glory any day."

"To Andros!" Kavos shouted out, joy spreading across his face as all of their men gathered around, raised their weapons, and shouted out, as one, behind them.

"TO ANDROS!"

CHAPTER THIRTY FIVE

Ra, Supreme Leader of Pandesia, sat on his golden throne in the vast Hall of Thrones, in the center of the great capital of Pandisiana, and he gritted his teeth and looked out over the room, towering over his dozens of advisors, and was filled with fury at the scroll before him. A messenger knelt below him, trembling, knowing. His Glorious Ra did not welcome bad news, and it was at one's own peril to deliver it.

Ra, seven feet tall, olive-skinned, with long, golden braids for hair tied tightly to his head and clear, translucent eyes, felt a great anger welling up as he pondered the scroll's message. He clenched and unclenched his fists, his muscles rippling in the warm weather, visible for all to see as he wore but a golden chained vest and golden loincloth, bedecked with jewelry. Ra, supreme leader, had spies in every corner of the kingdoms, and he was never—ever—caught off guard. He was Ra, the All-Knowing, the All-Mighty, the Omniscient, the One Ruler Over All, the one that all of the empire prayed to in their morning prayers, the one deified in every statue in every town of the empire.

Yet this day was different. This message which wafted in, like a foul breeze, had caused him consternation, had disrupted his immaculately constructed peace.

Ra clenched his jaw, pierced with a golden and sapphire chain, wondering how he could have not anticipated this, wondering how any of his necromancers could not have foreseen this. The men of Escalon, those rebellious scum, had begun a revolution. His soldiers had been killed. Lord Governors had been killed. And the rebellion was spreading across Escalon like a cancer.

His authority was being threatened. And that could not be: to erode his authority would be to erode the entire authority of the empire. After all, if the great and supreme Ra showed weakness in one corner of Escalon, then no one, anywhere would respect him.

Ra looked about the Hall of Thrones, a vast chamber with a dome-shaped ceiling a hundred feet high, his throne perched atop a

226

dais twenty feet high, with a long series of narrow ivory steps leading up to it. The floors, the walls, everything was covered in shining gold, gold he had personally captured in conquests from around the world. And yet he fumed. He took no joy in all the splendor about him, as he usually did, no joy in gazing down upon the dozens of men all patiently awaiting his command. He saw only in his mind's eye the rebellious men of Escalon—and he wondered how *anyone*, in any corner of the world, would dare defy him.

Clearly, he had underestimated these men of Escalon. Clearly, he had not been brutal enough.

"Most Honorable and Supreme One," one of his advisors finally called out. "Shall we raze Escalon to the ground?"

Ra was pondering the same thing. In most territories he conquered he simply killed everyone, not wanting to waste the effort to beat them into submission. Often it was easier to just wipe out a single country, a single race, and just take all that was theirs. But he had seen an advantage to keeping the people of Escalon alive. The men were famed warriors, having never lost a battle before his invasion, and he admired their skills; he had already drafted many of them into his armies and he could use their skill. More importantly, their weak king had submitted without a fight, which sent a positive message to those around the world. And most importantly, he needed the men of Escalon to patrol The Flames. Only they knew how to keep the trolls back, how to contain Marta. Ra, despite all his might, did not want war with Marta. One day, perhaps—but now was not the time. It was a primitive, savage place, besides, with nothing to offer but useless hills and rocks. Escalon was the prize.

By instituting his new law of *puellae nuptias*, by taking their women, by letting them know they were all Pandesian property, Ra had assumed it would send Escalon into final submission. He had been wrong.

Ra blinked down at the messenger and he realized that all of his concerns were nothing, still, next to the final words of the message. A dragon had appeared in Escalon. And a young girl had been able to command it to destroy his men. He could hardly fathom it.

"You are certain this message is correct?" Ra asked.

The messenger nodded back, fear in his eyes.

For the first time in as long as he could remember, Ra felt a pang of fear. He could not help but think of the prophecy that had haunted his reign: *There would come a rise of the dragons, followed by a rise of the valiant.* A single girl would rise up, with powers never before seen, and control the north. She would command them to destroy Pandesia—and she could only be stopped before her powers were complete.

Ra sat there, feeling his heart slamming his chest, and he knew now that the day had come.

"Where is she?" Ra asked the messenger.

The messenger swallowed.

"Our spies have been told she heads to the ancient Tower of Ur."

Ur. The Tower. The Watchers. That only cemented Ra's fears. He knew the power that lurked behind those walls. If she reached that tower, she could become more powerful than he could control. He had to use all the force at his disposal to stop her before it was too late.

There came a shout outside the hall, and Ra caught a glimpse, through the open-air arch, fifty-feet-high, of the companies of soldiers patrolling the courtyard. They were an army grown idle. An army that needed to be fed. An army ready for war.

Ra stood to his full height, his muscles bulging, his golden armor jingling. He casually swung around his golden dagger and sliced the throat of the messenger before him, as if scratching his arm. He saw fresh fear in the faces of all those stationed in his chamber. They should be afraid, he realized. For Ra was not only a great leader, not only a god, but also a great warrior. He could feel his blood boiling, itching for bloodlust, for complete domination, for the urge to have all peoples in every corner of the world bend their knee to him.

Ra looked out and surveyed his commanders, all afraid to meet his gaze.

"Assemble all my armies," he commanded. "We shall stop at nothing until we find this girl."

CHAPTER THIRTY SIX

It made no sense. Vidar stood atop the parapets of Volis and looked north, for the horizon, towards The Flames, and he wondered. So far off, their dim glow was slowly becoming visible as afternoon gave way to dusk, and as he stood there, a dozen of his brothers-in-arms around him, all Duncan's men, he was perplexed. For hours, he'd been feeling the tremor, a slight vibration that rang through the ground, through his feet, like a mild earthquake. His whole life in Volis he had never felt anything like it.

Vidar reached out and laid his hands on the stone, and as he did, he felt it again: a tremor. It came every minute or so, then disappeared just as suddenly. It seemed to be getting stronger.

Vidar could not fathom what it could be. Had the dragon returned? Was it stomping through the countryside? No, it could not be a dragon. If it were, would he not see it, or hear it?

There were no earthquakes in Volis, either, no fault lines as far as he knew.

Perhaps, he thought, it was an approaching army. Was Pandesia heading this way with all its might? That wouldn't make any sense, either, because the shaking stopped every minute before starting again. An army would not pause.

What, then, could it be?

The whole day he had shrugged it off as nothing, expecting it to go away. But now he could ignore it no longer.

Vidar felt a great responsibility; after all, this was the first time that Duncan had left him in charge of a fort—much less Volis—and he was determined to make him proud. With the bulk of their force headed south with Duncan, someone had to stay behind, to man this fort against an unexpected attack. He clutched his sword, not wanting to let Duncan down, and wondering why this would happen on his shift.

Another tremor came, this stronger than the last, and as Vidar watched, the stone a small pebble jumped off, falling off the parapet. He felt a pit in his stomach. Whatever it was, it was real.

Vidar turned and faced the others, who all looked back at him, pale. He detected something in their faces he had never quite seen before: fear. Vidar himself was unafraid to meet any enemy. At the first sign of any foe, he would rally his men and rush to defend, and would challenge any man—or army—sword to sword. It was what he did not know that concerned him.

Vidar looked north, toward The Flames, and a sinking feeling washed over him. He did not know why, but he felt that, whatever it was, it was coming from that direction—and that it was coming for them all.

*

Vesuvius stood deep underground, below Escalon, watching with ecstasy as, up ahead in the tunnel, the giant creature he had captured smashed and pounded its way through the stone. With each blow the earth shook, strong enough to make Vesuvius sway. His army of trolls, all around him, stumbled and fell, but Vesuvius managed to keep his footing, hands on his hips, as he stood there and watched with glee. He could remember few moments of greater satisfaction in his life. His plan, after all these years, was hatching perfectly.

The clouds of dust had not settled when the creature charged forward in a burst of rage, butting the stone wall with his head, reaching up and clawing, tearing at rock and stone, trying to break free and too stupid to know he was only digging deeper. It turned and turned, frustrated, unable to find its way out. And it smashed the stone some more.

Every once in a while the giant turned, as if second guessing itself, and ran away from the wall, back toward Vesuvius. In these instances, Vesuvius had hundreds of his soldiers rush forward and goad it with long pikes, making it turn back around—but not before it swiped and killed dozens of his men. Indeed, Vesuvius' ranks were quickly thinning—a small price to pay for the conquest to come, the victory nearly in his grasp. After all, when this tunnel was finished, when the pathway connecting Marta to Escalon was done, then his entire nation of trolls could invade and destroy Escalon once and for all.

Vesuvius followed the giant at a safe distance, his heart pounding with excitement as the beast burrowed deeper and deeper underground, smashing its way south. As he stepped forward, Vesuvius suddenly felt himself sweating, and sensing something, he reached up and laid his palms on the ceiling. He was giddy with excitement. The rock was warm. That could only mean one thing: they were now directly beneath The Flames.

With a thrill unlike any he had ever felt, Vesuvius marched forward, following the beast, feeling his destiny in his grasp. As the beast smashed through rock again and again, sending small boulders rolling back his way, Vesuvius felt a bigger thrill than he knew was possible. Victory, total subjugation of Escalon, was finally in reach. With each step he took, he was now in enemy territory.

Yet they were still hundreds of feet below ground, and Vesuvius knew he had to get the creature to burrow upwards. When they had passed a good distance past The Flames, Vesuvius summoned his soldiers.

"Prod the beast!" he called out. "Drive it upwards!"

His soldiers paused, unsure, knowing it would mean their deaths to march forward. Seeing his men's hesitation, Vesuvius knew he had to take decisive action.

"Torches!" he called out.

Men rushed forward with torches, and Vesuvius took one himself, let out a great battle cry, and led his men forward in a charge.

They all followed, hundreds of trolls racing forward, lighting the blackened tunnel as they headed for the beast. Vesuvius was the first to reach it and as he did, he touched it to the beast's foot, prodding it to smash upwards.

The beast shrieked, turned, and swiped for him. Vesuvius, anticipating it, stepped out of the way just in time, and the beast swiped several of his men, killing them instead, then smashed a huge chunk out of the wall.

Another one of his men rushed forward, then another, all setting their torches to its feet, following Vesuvius command—until finally, the giant, enraged, its feet burning, began to jump straight up. It smashed its head on rock, then shrieked and reached up and clawed at the ceiling—exactly as Vesuvius hoped it would.

Vesuvius squinted at the clouds of dust and watched, heart pounding, as the creature made its way upwards, burrowing the tunnel on an angle. This was the moment he had been waiting for, had dreamed of for as long as he could remember.

As Vesuvius watched, waiting, breathless, peering into the darkness, there came a tremendous crash—and he suddenly found himself flooded with light. Sunlight. Glorious sunlight.

Sunlight from Escalon.

Dust swirled in it as the sunshine flooded the tunnel, lighting it up. The beast smashed through again, widening the hole above ground, sending rock and dirt and grass everywhere, like a great geyser emerging from hell.

Vesuvius stood there, too frozen in shock to move, hardly able to process what had just happened. With that final blow, the creature had finished the tunnel, had opened the gateway for the invasion of Escalon. The Flames were now useless.

Vesuvius smiled wide, it slowly dawning on him that his plan had worked. That he had outsmarted them all.

It was time for the great invasion to begin.

CHAPTER THIRTY SEVEN

Aidan, still groaning in pain, braced himself as the man lowered his boot for his face, knowing his skull was about to be crushed. He would give anything to have his father by his side now, to have his brothers here—or most of all, to have Kyra here. He knew she would protect him. Now, he would have to meet his fate alone. If only he was older, bigger, stronger.

As the boot came lower and Aidan raised his hands, cringing, bracing himself, a sudden snarling noise cut through the air—one that made his hairs rise on end. Aidan looked over and was shocked to see White rushing forward. The huge, wild dog, somehow finding a reserve of strength, lunged and jumped onto the man's chest, sinking his fangs into him before he could stomp Aidan.

The man shrieked as White snarled viciously and shook his head every which way, biting the man on his hands and arms and chest and face.

Finally, the man, bloodied, rolled to his side, groaning.

White, still snarling, mouth dripping with blood, was not done. He stepped forward, clearly aiming for the man's jugular, preparing to kill him for good. But White then stumbled and keeled over, and Aidan realized that he was still too injured to finish the man off.

The man, sensing an opportunity, did not wait. He quickly crawled to his hands and knees, then stumbled to his feet and ran all the way back to the front of his cart, woozy on his feet. He pulled himself back up, and sitting unsteadily, lashed his horses.

They took off, Aidan was dismayed to see, at a gallop. In but moments the wagon disappeared into the night, leaving Aidan and White utterly alone in the black woods, days away from civilization.

Aidan lay there, his body still wracked with pain, too exhausted to stand, and he was surprised to feel a tongue on his face. He looked over to see White leaning over, lying down, too, and licking him.

Aidan reached out and hugged the dog, and the dog, he was surprised to see, leaned his head into his chest.

"I owe you my life," Aidan said.

White looked back at him with eyes that seemed to respond: *And you saved me, too.*

Aidan knew that by doing what he had done, he had probably just forfeited his only chance at survival. Now here he lay, alone, on this cold night, hungry, beat up, a wounded wild dog beside him, the two of them without anyone to help them. Yet Aidan didn't care. He had done the right thing, and nothing mattered more than that.

Aidan couldn't give up. He couldn't just lie there and die—and he couldn't let White die, either. And if they didn't start moving, he could feel, they would both soon stiffen up and freeze to death.

Aidan mustered a supreme effort and got himself unsteadily to his feet, clutching his ribs where the man had kicked him. He then helped White up, dragging him to his feet, too. The two of them stood there, facing the long, open road ahead of them. Aidan knew they would most likely die out here—but no matter what happened, he had saved this animal.

Aidan put one foot before the next, White limping beside them, and the two of them set off together—one small boy and one wounded dog, alone beneath the stars in the vast, black forest— taking their first steps on the impossibly long walk to Andros.

CHAPTER THIRTY EIGHT

Theos circled high over Escalon, above the clouds, out of sight of the humans, soaring from one end to the other, taking in, with his magnificent vision and focus, the vista below. He flew into the sunset, flapping his great wings, moving across hills with each flap, covering more ground than these humans could in days, as he searched. Until he found what he was looking for, he would not rest.

This land of Escalon was so different than his home on the far side of the world, so much smaller, and devoid of the lava and ash, of the endless stretches of black rock that made up his homeland. It was also devoid of the omnipresent screeches of his fellow dragons. It was almost too quiet here—and it unnerved him. It reminded him of how alone he was, how far from home he was. But for this mission, he would venture to the ends of the earth.

Theos narrowed his eyes and far below, through the clouds, he spotted Kyra, before the tower. He watched her with a mix of curiosity and respect, more protective of her than she would ever know. He kept an eye on her when he could, as the role she had to play in the coming war was too important, their connection too strong, and her life too fragile. She was not a dragon, after all.

Theos flapped, kept flying, past Kyra, past the tower, and back across Escalon—still searching. He lowered his head and increased his speed and in moments was able to cross half the land. He spotted Kyra's father in the mountains, atop Kos, preparing, no doubt, for the great war. He turned and flew north, and saw Volis, unguarded. He flew further and, not far from The Flames, he saw the great hole in the earth, the giant emerging from the tunnel and the great army of trolls following on its heels.

He criss-crossed Escalon, and in the far corners he saw some legions of Pandesia beginning to rally, they, too, preparing for war.

Theos, though, did not have much interest in these human dealings. He could destroy them all in a second if he wanted to. All of their movements, their machinations, were ultimately inconsequential to him. It was Kyra he cared about—for a very special reason.

And one other. The only thing more important to him even than her, the only thing that made him stay, the only thing that had made him come here to begin with. He searched again and again, screeching in frustration, for the one thing he had to find. The one thing that had made him vulnerable.

His child.

Theo screeched again and again in frustration, shaking the very air as he flew once again over the Wood of Thorns, near the place where he was wounded, searching, scouring the land. He scanned the forest below, through the trees, over the hills—everywhere. But it was nowhere to be found. It was as if his child had vanished, as if the very egg he had come here to protect had disappeared.

Who could have taken it? And why?

Theos screeched again, a screech of urgency, of despair, as he soared up into the heavens, ready to tear apart the fabric of the world, to rain fire on all of mankind if he did not, soon, find what he was looking for. He could feel the rage burning, mounting within him, and as his eyes glowed yellow he knew that he could no longer control it. He had to let it out on someone. And those cities below, milling with humans, would have to be as good a target as any.

He tucked into a dive, sped for the city below, and opened his mouth to breathe fire. It was time for the great war to begin.

CHAPTER THIRTY NINE

Lying all alone, just north of the Wood of Thorns, in an empty plain beneath an ancient tree, its branches concealing it well, sat a single egg.

A dragon's egg.

Large and purple and hard, covered with scales, it sat there alone, as if waiting for its father to arrive. It was so out of place here in Escalon, not surrounded by molten fire, by lava and ash, by circling dragons, hovering, protecting, waiting for it to hatch. It could already feel it was different than all the others.

It sat there, waiting to die—or to hatch. It could feel how vulnerable it was.

Despite all odds, it had survived. Animals had come, sniffing out of curiosity, yet so far they had left. But now, he sensed, another one came. More than one—a pack of wolves. They were fast approaching his egg, and they were hungry. This time, they would kill him.

He knew he was not meant to hatch anytime soon, but this dragon summoned all his willpower, forced himself to move within the egg, to defy the natural waiting period. With all his might, he moved one arm, then one shoulder, then his knee. He did what no dragon was supposed to do, what no other dragon was able to do. For he was different. He was, he sensed, more powerful than them all.

As the final rays of the sun began to set, far out of earshot of all humans, in this barren countryside, there came a single crack.

Then another.

A small claw emerged, its fingernails reaching for the sky as if to claw it. This was followed by another.

Soon, the egg began to shatter, and finally, the arm, then the head of a baby dragon emerged. The son of Theos.

The wolves stopped in their tracks, for the first time in their lives experiencing fear of another creature.

The dragon leaned back and took his first glance at the world, the sky, and he blinked. It was not the world he had expected to see.

237

He screeched. It was a young sound still—yet even so, terrifying enough to scare away anyone close.

For this dragon already wanted to breathe, to live, to kill.

He arched back his neck and breathed, his first breath, and out came a stream of fire. The fire of life. And the fire of the death to come.

The pack of wolves turned and ran, never looking back.

They were smart to run. For the first time in a millennium, in the land of Escalon, a dragon was born.

CHAPTER FORTY

Kyra blinked and looked up to see her mother gazing down at her, her face a silhouette, masked in a silver light, as light shined down from behind her. She had long golden hair, Kyra could see, and she could feel the kindness, the compassion, emanating from her, though her features were obscured. Her mother smiled down as she reached out a hand, her fingers long and smooth and slender.

"Kyra," her mother whispered to her.

It was a whisper that reverberated throughout Kyra's soul, the sound of a voice she had not realized she had been longing to hear her entire life. Kyra basked in the warmth of her mother's love for the first time in her life, and it felt good. She felt as if a part of her, long missing, had been returned.

Kyra took her mother's hand, shocked by her touch, like a bolt of lightning racing through her. She could feel the warmth spreading through her hand, then up her arm and her entire body. She slowly sat up as her mother pulled her gently, as if to embrace her.

"Kyra," her mother said. "It is time. Time for you to know who I am. Time for you to know who you are."

"Mother," Kyra tried to respond.

But the words stuck in her throat. No sooner had she uttered them when suddenly, when she leaned forward to embrace her mother and reached out to feel nothing in her arms. As quickly as she had appeared, her mother had vanished.

Kyra blinked and saw a strange and exotic landscape before her, one she could not decipher, with twisted trees, burned branches—and yet no matter where she looked, her mother was nowhere to be found. She looked down and saw herself sitting at the edge of a cliff, about to fall off, the ocean waves crashing like mad beneath her.

"MOTHER!" she cried out.

Kyra sat up breathing hard as she woke, disoriented. Leo nudged his head on her lap, and it took her several moments to collect herself, to realize it had been a dream. It had been the most vivid dream of her life—more like a mystical encounter.

There came a gust of wind, followed by another, foreign sound. It sounded like footsteps approaching, crunching on the grass. Kyra instinctively tightened her grip on her staff and sat up, on alert.

Kyra blinked into the morning sun, realizing she'd slept here the entire night, shivering from the cold, from the ocean spray, and she tried to see. Dawn was breaking, spreading across the horizon, it still more dark than light, and as she blinked, struggling to see in the fading darkness, there slowly came into view the silhouette of a man. He was dressed in long robes, wore long hair, she could see that much, and he wielded a staff as he walked. He approached, and Kyra felt her heart slamming in her chest as she wondered.

Could this be him? Her uncle?

As the sun slowly rose behind him, making him a silhouette, Kyra struggled to make out his features, but she could not. He stopped before her and Leo, oddly, did not growl, but rather watched him, as if he, too, were transfixed. The man stood there, looking down at her in a silence that never seemed to end, and Kyra was too breathless to speak. This was the moment, she knew, the moment that would change her entire life.

"Kyra," he said finally, his voice resonating, rolling off the wind, the hills, as ancient as the tower behind her. "I have been awaiting you."

Finally, he pulled back his hood and looked right at her, and her heart stopped in her chest.

She could not believe who it was.

COMING SOON!

Book #3 in Kings and Sorcerers

Books by Morgan Rice

KINGS AND SORCERERS
RISE OF THE DRAGONS

THE SORCERER'S RING
A QUEST OF HEROES
A MARCH OF KINGS
A FATE OF DRAGONS
A CRY OF HONOR
A VOW OF GLORY
A CHARGE OF VALOR
A RITE OF SWORDS
A GRANT OF ARMS
A SKY OF SPELLS
A SEA OF SHIELDS
A REIGN OF STEEL
A LAND OF FIRE
A RULE OF QUEENS
AN OATH OF BROTHERS
A DREAM OF MORTALS

THE SURVIVAL TRILOGY
ARENA ONE (Book #1)
ARENA TWO (Book #2)

the Vampire Journals
turned (book #1)
loved (book #2)
betrayed (book #3)
destined (book #4)
desired (book #5)
betrothed (book #6)
vowed (book #7)
found (book #8)
resurrected (book #9)
craved (book #10)
fated (book #11)

About Morgan Rice

Morgan Rice is the #1 bestselling and USA Today bestselling author of the epic fantasy series THE SORCERER'S RING, comprising seventeen books; of the #1 bestselling series THE VAMPIRE JOURNALS, comprising eleven books (and counting); of the #1 bestselling series THE SURVIVAL TRILOGY, a post-apocalyptic thriller comprising two books (and counting); and of the new epic fantasy series KINGS AND SORCERERS. Morgan's books are available in audio and print editions, and translations are available in over 25 languages.

Morgan loves to hear from you, so please feel free to visit www.morganricebooks.com to join the email list, receive a free book, receive free giveaways, download the free app, get the latest exclusive news, connect on Facebook and Twitter, and stay in touch!

Made in the USA
Middletown, DE
28 January 2019